# THIEVING HEARTS

*Driven Hearts Book 2*

## NIKITA SLATER

*Part One*

# LOST TREASURE

# CHAPTER ONE

*How dare he show up on their door step?*

Katie flew out the door, a raging inferno of gangly limbs and teenage emotion. She was tall for thirteen. Her shiny blond hair was pulled back in a messy ponytail so it wasn't in her face while she studied her biology textbook. Her bedroom window faced the street. She'd heard the roar of his car first. She pushed herself off of her stomach and peeked through the window as it pulled up to the curb. A tall, dark brute of a man got out of a black, older model vehicle and strode up *their* lawn toward *their* house as though he owned the place. He looked more evil than anyone she'd ever seen and she lived in a bad neighbourhood filled with gangs. She'd known right away who he was, which is why, stupid or not, she'd gone in for the intercept.

She shivered under the malevolent look he gave her. His relentless eyes held nothing. They didn't even gleam with life the way normal people's did. What had she been thinking, deciding to confront the guy who'd been hanging around her 18-year-old brother? But she had to do something! Ever since Dexter decided he was big shot gang, he'd been disappearing more and more from his family and falling in with people like

Roman Valdez. She couldn't stand it. She was determined to say her piece, even if his body language promised she wouldn't survive the experience.

God, he was big! He was several inches taller than her with thick muscles roping his bare, brown arms. His skin was covered in tattoos. Some she recognized as local gang while others were foreign. All were terrifying to her, signifying blood and death. She hated them on sight. He wore a black sleeveless shirt over what she suspected were more tattoos and rippling chest muscles and a pair of old, torn up blue jeans. Though his clothes looked old and carelessly chosen, they were clean and fit him well. He reeked of death and danger.

She suspected he was Latino, most likely Mexican, given his beautiful skin and eyes, and his last name. Plus, they were only a few hours from the border. She wondered if he was legal. Maybe she could have him deported. They stood facing each other for long minutes, the tension ratcheting up. So far, neither had moved a muscle, but under her fearful blue gaze, his lip quirked a tiny bit.

"I can see your thoughts, little girl."

His deep, accented voice struck at her like a snake. She suppressed the need to shake under his scrutiny. He took a sudden step toward her. She jumped back, hitting the door-frame with a gasp. His hand landed above her head with a thud. He stared down at her with such loathing that she was certain she was about to die. She understood this intimidation tactic though. She wasn't new to the neighbourhood. She did wish she was wearing more than a pair of ratty old sweat shorts with paw prints on the butt and a powder blue tank top. Thankfully, he didn't seem to notice her lack of attire. His entire focus was on her eyes.

She glared right back at him and then poked him in the chest. The dead cast to his eyes flared to life for just a second.

"Back. Off. Our. Porch!" she snapped, shoving herself into

him with the intent of off-balancing him and making him stumble backwards so she could leap back inside, slam the door and lock it. All she did was press herself up against the big man.

They both stood frozen like that for several seconds, Katie seriously regretting her actions and wishing she'd let Dexter answer the door after all. She waited breathlessly for Roman to make a move. She didn't have long to wait. His hands landed on her arms like steel vices as he shoved her backwards. Her head bounced off the doorframe. Luckily, her ponytail cushioned the impact.

He bent so his lips were inches from hers. "Never touch me unless you mean it, little girl," he hissed.

She glared up at him, refusing to back down. "You're just a bully!" she snapped.

He shrugged, hands still bruisingly tight on her arms. "Maybe. Be a good kid and get your brother."

Lifting her chin, she stubbornly persisted. "No. I want you to go away and leave him alone. You're bad for him."

His lips tightened for a brief moment and he looked torn between amusement and annoyance. She suspected she didn't want him to fall on the side of annoyance. Oh god, why was she goading this man? She wanted to protect her brother, but what about her? Everything about this brutal human screamed violence. The very air surrounding him was a chaotic mist of death and she'd willingly flung herself into it for family loyalty.

Finally, he let out a tiny huff and said from between gritted teeth, "I will say this once only, *chica*, then you will back the fuck out of my space before I hurt you. I am the only thing keeping your brother safe on these streets. He is in over his head and… he is good people… a good friend to me…"

He trailed off, making a frustrated sound as though he didn't know how to finish. Katie tilted her head, trying to look past the tattoos and brutality. After a moment of silence, she asked quietly, "You don't normally like people, do you?"

He nodded, his gaze flickering down to her. He studied her as though seeing her for the first time. Her breath caught in her throat. She didn't want someone like him to see her. He was far too predatory. Even at such a young age, she could feel something shifting between them. She tried to edge sideways, but he held her tight against the doorframe as he looked her over. After what felt like ages, he released her. She didn't waste a single second. She turned and hurried inside, leaving him to find Dexter in the comfortable recesses of her family home.

His deep voice followed her back to her room. "Run away, little rabbit, we'll play another time."

# CHAPTER TWO



## One Year Later

"You said you would keep him safe," Katie choked, glaring at the tall shadow standing in the door of her bedroom. "You lied to me!"

She didn't know how he got into her house in the middle of the night. She didn't care. She wanted to hurt him as badly as she was hurting inside. And she knew each tear that dripped down her face was like a punch in the gut to him. She could see it written on his normally emotionless face. His hands were fisted at his side. Clenched as though he'd gladly enjoy every second of the agony he would cause the ones that dared to give her pain.

They had barely spoken since that day on her family doorstep, but she saw the 21-year-old gangbanger her brother drove around with more and more often. Hanging out in the shadows, watching. For her part, Katie ignored the big, frightening man. Not always an easy task when her mom, a bleeding heart, seemed determined to coddle her oldest son's best friend. Luckily, Roman wanted none of Mrs. Pullman's affection and rarely accepted the many invitations she extended to the 'poor' orphan boy. Not unless Katie was going to be home as well. And she did her best to stay out of Roman's way, disturbed by the way his eyes followed her every move, whether there were others in the room or not.

Katie's dad seemed indifferent toward Dexter's friendship with Roman. Not that he had a choice. Mr. Pullman was a bookie who'd worked for the mob for more years than Katie even knew. It was how Dexter got involved in gang. They did dirty work for the guys her dad worked for. She resented the hell out of the connection, but what could she do? She was terribly afraid that Wendell, her next brother in line, would get sucked into the abyss of gang or mob life next. She just wished the entire family could move away and start fresh somewhere else. Some place safer.

Now Dexter was dead and Roman had somehow known to come to Katie in her darkest moment. She wanted to cling to his strength, but she also wanted to scream at him and beat him. Her brother was dead and he couldn't make it better.

Her anguished eyes never left his face as his long legs ate up the steps between them. Her body was collapsed in on itself on the bed, where she spent most of her time these past weeks since the funeral. There was no one to stop her. Dexter's death had devastated the entire family. Her mom rarely left her own bed, lost in a world of prescription sleeping medication. Her dad almost never came home from work. Wendell was hanging out more and more with Alan Bancroft, finding comfort in the cars Dexter had loved. She was glad for him.

Roman reached out and touched the top of her head, stroking her blond hair. He tugged several wet strands away from where they stuck to her flushed cheeks and tucked them behind her ear. She knew she must look awful, yet he looked at her as though she were beautiful. He always did, she realized. She didn't know when he started looking at her that way, just that he did.

"You need to eat, *chica.* And to sleep," he murmured huskily.

"I…" her voice cracked on a sob. She licked her lips and tried again. She whispered into the dim light of her bedroom, "I can't… Dexter can't do any of those things anymore. I just don't want to, Roman."

His hand clenched over her head for a second and then he opened it to cup the back of her skull. His fingers were so long they slid into her hair and enveloped her completely. She closed her eyes and leaned into the comfort with a sigh. He stood so close to her that she could feel his chest moving as he breathed. She thought of how this man had protected Dexter, of how they had talked together, laughed together, driven around the city together. She was certain that Dexter was the only person that could draw out this side of Roman. The human over the killer. Just as she was sure Roman would have traded his life for Dexter's.

"I'm sorry," she cried, fresh tears springing to her eyes. "I know you couldn't have done anything. You wer… weren't there when they got him."

He stiffened next to her. "I wish I was."

She shook her head, her hair pulling sharply in his fingers. She savoured the pain. It was the first thing she felt after weeks of numbness. "No, Roman, if you were there, you might have been killed to."

"Fuck," he growled, his fingers tightening in her scalp to a painful degree. She knew that he didn't realize. "I wanted to die with him. He was my best friend."

She reached out and touched him. Putting her hands on him for the first time since that day on her doorstep, winding her fingers in his T-shirt as though she would never let him go. She looked up at him, her eyes pools of blue sadness. "I don't want to lose you too," she whispered, the tears flowing freely once more.

"Katie," he groaned, dropping his heavy frame onto the small bed next to her. He pulled her onto his lap and held her while she sobbed for her dead brother, soaking his T-shirt through.

# CHAPTER THREE

## Four Years Later

He'd waited five long years for her to grow up. He wasn't going to wait a minute longer. He'd watched and waited as she'd flitted gracefully through her teenage years. He'd stepped in when it looked like a boy might be getting too close. As far as he knew, she never suspected a thing. His beautiful, innocent Katerina. He would do anything for her. Except let her go.

He expected her to do the normal 'girl' thing on her eighteenth birthday and throw a party, or go out with friends. Not his Katie. She was busy packing her stuff in boxes and driving it over to the small, dingy apartment she'd rented a few blocks away from her family home. He was the muscle behind the move, so he was around to hear the worried arguments her mother subjected her to. She counter-argued every one. His girl was independent.

Again, he underestimated her if he thought she would throw a party her first night in her new apartment. Instead, she shooed her *mamacita* out the door with a lingering hug and promise to call. Then she stepped back, locked the door and twirled on the spot, her lithe body twisting beautifully in the sunlight filtering through the grimy living room window.

Her long, blond hair swung around her shoulders. Hunger beat a fierce tattoo in his chest. He was certain she forgot he was there. After he set down the last box he'd melted into the shadows and watched as she'd gently soothed her mama's anxieties.

*I have a good job, mom, I can afford the rent. I'm about to start college and I need the space. I promise I'll come home for Sunday dinners every week. You can use my bedroom for that extra office you always wanted. I'll be fine, you'll see!*

She would *not* be fine. The big, bad wolf was about to eat her up. Take the sweet virginity he'd been protecting for so many years and then never let her go. He'd wanted her from the moment he set eyes on her. Only, back then, when he was a stupid 20-year-old with no money, a black heart and a lot to prove, he had no idea what that 'want' would turn into. The kind of twisted, painful heart-wrenching love that would rip his soul apart. Katie was his salvation and she was about to find out.

As he stepped out of the shadows, she proved to him that she knew he was always there by looking right at him and giving him one of her cock-hardening smiles that never ceased to make his chest swell with love.

"Should we order in? I know it's not the best birthday dinner in the world, but I really want to order from that diner down the street my first time ever in my new apartment. Will you stay and share it with me?"

How the fuck could he say no to that? He'd introduce her to the new realities of their changed relationship after she ate her birthday dinner. He wanted her to take him seriously, he didn't want to terrorize the delicate blond. He was a big, scary, tatted up motherfucker. He was seven years older than her. Not as wide a gap as it used to be now that she was getting older, but still a lot to an inexperienced 18-year-old. Not that he'd been able to touch anyone else since her intoxicating presence had taken over any thoughts of another woman. He'd been loose with himself in his youth, but not since coming to realize exactly what Katie meant to him a few years back.

They sat on the cracked linoleum floor of her new kitchen, leaning against her cupboards, eating Chinese food straight out of the containers with plastic forks. She didn't have plates yet. Or a table and chairs. Roman yearned to provide her with everything she would need, but it wouldn't be necessary. She would be moving in with him in a matter of days. She just needed to get used to the idea. Get used to being with him.

He watched her mouth as she chewed her food and slurped at the Szechwan noodles. She savoured each bite and licked the fork to make sure she got each and every flavour morsel. He loved that there was no pretence with this girl. She ate with gusto and talked with her hands, describing the courses she was enrolled in at the local college. She didn't seem to care that he made no effort to contribute to the conversation, only grunting his responses as he ate, never taking his eyes off her. She was used to Roman's silent ways. They didn't see each other often, but when they did he never deviated. He couldn't tear his eyes from her.

Finally, she dropped her fork into the empty container, set it on the floor beside her and leaned back with a sigh, rubbing her full stomach. A satisfied smile stretched her beautiful lips and she shifted her blue eyes toward him. "What do you think?"

He dropped his half-finished container beside hers and leaned forward, his long legs stretched beside her bare ones. He lifted her hands in his and tried to think of what she'd been talking about. He could tell from the stiffening of her body that she was nervous. She wasn't used to him touching her. Hell, she wasn't used to him spending any time alone with her. Except for the time he sought her out after Dexter's shooting, he usually avoided situations where they might be together. He didn't trust himself around such temptation.

"Food was good, you should order from there again," he guessed at what she'd been talking about.

She laughed out loud and gave his leg a light nudge with her knee. He almost groaned out loud when her short skirt shifted just enough that he should see a shadow between her legs. "I was asking about work, Roman. I wanted your opinion about the restaurant. Do you think I should take an extra hostessing shift?" she asked softly.

Her pretty sky-blue eyes held his like he had all the answers. And fuck he wanted to have them for her. He was nothing compared to this angel, yet she saw something in him nobody else saw. Except maybe her mama. Even her mother had never been able to kick his gangster ass to the curb. He wanted to deserve their regard, he really did. But he just wasn't any better than he was born to be. No matter how hard he tried, he kept getting sucked back into the life. After avenging his friend, he went to work for some of the scariest fuckers on this side of the United States in a bid to wipe the rest of the opposing gang off the map. He'd been obsessed with the Red Brotherhood until there wasn't a single one left. Hell, he'd even gotten himself arrested so he could take one out in prison.

Now, Soloman Hart was sniffing around his business. And the offer was good. Almost too good to turn down. But looking at Katie now, touching her soft hands, he didn't know if it was worth his soul to keep killing for money. She wouldn't like that. So he decided to answer her question instead.

"Don't want you to take any more shifts, baby," he answered gruffly.

She blinked at him, startled. He'd never used an endearment with her before. Her tongue peeked nervously out from between her lips and she whispered, "Why, Roman?"

He sighed heavily and rubbed his thumb over the back of her hand, marvelling at how delicate it looked with the pale skin and blue veins just beneath the surface. He wanted to suck each finger into his mouth and introduce her to the intense pleasure of eroticism. Soon, very soon.

"Why don't you want me to take any extra shifts, Roman?" she asked again, frowning now.

He realized he was somehow fucking this up. Not that he was surprised. There wasn't a romantic bone in his body. He was the son of a drug baron and a sex slave. He'd spent half his life in a cartel and half his life surviving in the shadows of these city streets. He didn't deserve this girl, but fucked if he wasn't going to take her anyway. His hand tightened around hers when she threatened to pull back. Her gorgeous blue eyes flared wide. Time to tell her the truth.

"Because no girl of mine is going to be working in that shit restaurant," he growled.

Her mouth fell open and he actually did groan out loud this time, picturing his dick sliding right into that moist, unbroken recess. Using it until he'd had his fill while mussing up the perfection of her beautiful blond hair.

"I-I'm not your girl!" she gasped, her back shooting straight against the cupboard behind her.

He growled and reached out to take both of her wrists in his hands. Gently but firmly, so as not to bruise his precious madonna, he pulled her forward until she was forced to slide across the cheap tiles of the kitchen toward him. She was too shocked to put up a real fight, but she did twist her hips a little, unknowingly causing her jean skirt to move up her smooth thighs a few precious inches.

"Roman, what are you doing?" she cried out, trying to pull back. She was tall for a girl, but not even close to him in height and weight. He pulled her right into his lap and held her tight against him, enjoying the rapid flutter of her heart against his chest.

He used his finger to tilt her chin so she was forced to look up into his eyes. He searched her face and saw in there everything he'd ever hoped and ached for. Fear, yes... but also curiosity, hope and arousal. She was turned on by him. Maybe she didn't want to admit it. Fuck, maybe she didn't even recognize it for what it was, but he did. And he would be more than happy to introduce her to the sensation. She gasped and wiggled in his lap, clearly able to feel the evidence of his own arousal branding itself against her bottom.

"If you don't fucking sit still, little girl, I'm going to toss you back on this floor and bury myself in you," he snarled down at you. "Was hoping our first time might be more romantic than that."

"Oh god!" she gasped and froze in his arms.

When he was certain he had her full attention, he began speaking, his gaze boring into hers. "From that first moment you spoke to me and touched me, you belonged to me, Katie girl. I made a vow to your brother, God rest his soul, that I would wait for my girl to grow up before I took her. You're done growing up now, baby."

A whimper of pain escaped her lips at the memory of her dead brother. It was something they shared. While it seemed that the rest of the world had somehow moved on from the murder of Dexter, the two people closest to him never really did. Roman continued to shadow the underworld with his presence, stalking and killing while Katie closed in on herself, never quite able to pull herself out of the numbness of death.

"Hush, love," he murmured rocking her. "I'm here for you."

He slid his hand into her hair and pulled her head up, his possessive eyes intent on her lips. Before they could touch for the first time, her voice stopped him cold.

"Please don't, Roman," she whispered.

She lay helpless in his arms. Not even resisting him. He could have easily forced her to submit to his kiss. He knew she wanted him. Had almost from the beginning. He probably could have taken her at thirteen without much of a struggle and taught her to submit. They could have had years together while he moulded her into the perfect mafia girlfriend and, later, wife. But, as always, Katie Pullman held his heart in her tiny hand. And she was asking him to stop.

"Why?" he demanded, attempting to hide the pain and fury he was feeling from that single word.

She brought a fist up between their bodies and pushed a little against his chest, trying to put some distance between them. It felt like a stab in the heart. He allowed her a few inches, but that was all. He could see her eyes glowing with fear and determination. He hated it. He knew what that look meant. It meant she wouldn't go with him. She wouldn't fucking be his. He wanted to throw her over his shoulder, take her into the bedroom and show her exactly how his life taught him to deal with women like her.

"I can't let you, Roman," she whispered fiercely, never taking her eyes from his. "You'll take me away from the things I want. If I stay with you I won't keep my job, I won't finish school and… and I'll hardly ever see my friends and family. Just try and deny it."

She was right. She was absolutely fucking right. He was just surprised she saw through his obsession to the point that she understood exactly what being with him meant. He *would* isolate her from her family and friends, because he was jealous. She would see her mom and her brother once in a while, because they deserved her love. Her father was a degenerate fuck that did not deserve this angel. She would quit her job immediately and never go back. Roman had more than enough money for both of them. She could go to school for a while if she wanted, but he didn't see it working out in the long term, because it would eat up too much of her time.

Her too sharp eyes watched his face like she was some kind of living, breathing lie detector. "Fuck, Katie, what do you want me to say? I don't know, okay? We'll work it out."

His hands tightened around her, but she squirmed in his grip.

"It's not okay, Roman. That's my family you're thinking about taking away. My hopes and dreams for the future you'd just carelessly crush under your fist. I'm too smart to waste away as the kind of woman you'd want me to be," she said accusingly, her blue eyes now bright with tears. "This is why we can't be together."

"Enough!" he snarled viciously. He pushed her off his lap so she was on her knees on the floor facing him. He slammed her into the cupboards, hard enough to make the fronts clatter, but he was careful to place a hand behind her shoulder blades to absorb the impact. Even angry, he protected her. "I've waited years for you. I made a vow to a dead guy to wait for you. I'm done fucking waiting!"

Katie surprised them both when she slapped him. Just hard enough to get his attention. Then she gripped his unshaven chin in her small hand and forced him to look at her furious expression. "Don't you dare speak about Dexter that way, asshole. He would never have said something like that about you!"

She wrapped her arms around her middle and leaned forward, pressing her head into his shoulder. Huge wrenching sobs escaped her lips as tears rolled down her cheeks. The anger left Roman as quick as it came, leaving him with horror at what he'd done to his beautiful Katie. Just as he'd done years earlier, he pulled her heaving body into his arms and held her while she cried.

"I'm sorry, baby girl. I'm so sorry," he murmured against the top of her head.

When she finally calmed down, he lifted her in his arms and carried her through to her bedroom, which he had set up earlier. He laid her gently on the bed and crouched next to her, sweeping the soft strands of blond hair off her forehead while she watched him warily. He smiled sadly at her expression. She was afraid of him. No more curiosity or arousal.

"We belong together, Katie," he told her quietly.

Panic flared bright in her eyes. "Please, Roman," she whispered, bringing her hand up to clutch his where it touched her face. "Please, just give me more time. I-I'm not ready for this kind of relationship. I think what happened to Dexter… it broke something inside of me. I just need to be alone for a while. I need to go to school and work… I need time to figure out who I am. Alone."

He studied her face in the dim light from the hallway and finally nodded. He stood and stepped away from her. She pushed herself to lean back on her hands and watched as he made his way to the door. He stopped and turned for one last long look, as if memorizing every part of her. He pointed that finger at her, the one with her brother's name tattooed on it, 'For Dexter.'

"I'll come back for you, Katerina."

# CHAPTER FOUR

## Katie's Wedding Day

*This is my redemption.*

Her happiness was in his hands. She wanted a normal life with a normal man. And though Katerina Pullman was anything but normal, Roman would give her the fucking Pope's head on a platter if that's what she demanded. A task that would've been easier than knowing his woman was being claimed by another. Allowing the woman he loved to marry another man would be his redemption for all the blood on his hands.

But if this was his redemption, then why did is hurt so fucking bad? More than watching his entire family slaughtered. More than bullet or knife wounds. Knowing Katie was willingly tying herself irrevocably to another man ripped his guts out like nothing else could. He felt cold from sitting alone in the dark warehouse, wearing only a pair of unzipped jeans, but his insides were being eaten up by fire. He was surrounded by the busted shards of his life. Rather than fly up to Seattle and kill her groom, Roman had taken out his rage on the few items he'd collected over the years.

The only thing he hadn't been able to tear apart were the books. Her books. He picked up the one he liked best, her favourite, and flipped to Woman with Folded Arms. He loved and hated the replica of Picasso's famous blue period painting. He loved it because Katie loved it. But he despised it because he knew it called to her, sucked her deep into an abyss where he wasn't able to follow.

That was why he had to let her go. Be normal. Maybe Colin Schell, a laid-back West Coast painter, could pull her out of the hellish depression she kept getting sucked into. It was impossible to imagine a killer like Roman, Mexican cartel royalty, exiled from his homeland, would be the man to help her. He wasn't good. He wasn't light. He would be more darkness to her dark. He would suck her further into the abyss until she could never hope to claw her way out. Katie was too fucking amazing for that. She was a goddess. She was everything.

He would let her be free, without the spectre of him. Her freedom would be his redemption, even as he sunk further into the darkness without the hope of her. He would not be free of her though. He didn't want to be. She had wrapped herself steadily around his heart, her nails piercing right through what was left of the fucker since the moment they met. He hadn't touched a woman since she was sixteen and he'd decided to just wait her out. Now he was doomed to a lifetime of celibacy. No woman could replace his Katerina. If she didn't eventually come to him, then he would live the life of a murderous monk. Sleeping, eating and killing until he died.

Redemption was going to be a bleak and blue balls kind of place to live.

Roman glared at the textbook and set it aside before he did something unforgivable. Fuck, he needed something to kill before he went back on his hours old vow to himself and took the next flight to Seattle. Katie wouldn't forgive him if he sank a blade into her brand-new husband. Maybe Roman could just stab him a little? Make it look like a tragic accident. No one would even have to know.

Fuck, she would know. She was razor sharp and had a sixth sense for when her long-time stalker was near. Dammit. He would just have to wait. Bide his time and watch from a distance. Hide in the shadows until the fucker slipped up. One wrong move, one bad decision with *his* woman and Roman would be right there, ready to take him down.

Yes, that was the new plan. Fuck redemption. He was killing her *culero* husband the second he did something to make Katie cry. Knowing there was no way anyone could love Katerina the way Roman did, he didn't think he'd have long to wait. She could have her "normal" and her "happy" for now. As soon as she was tired of it, Roman would be right there, ready to swoop in and save her from her own folly.

He reached for his phone and hit the contact for his boss, Soloman Hart. The man picked up right away.

"Roman," he acknowledged coldly.

Roman didn't speak for a minute, then he stood and reached for his leather vest, letting the coldness seep into his soul. "Give me a job," he demanded.

*Give me something to kill.*

Katie grinned.

It was like taking candy from a baby. Not that she would ever do something that heartless. She wasn't a mean bitch. She opened the door to the safe with a small flourish and did a little dance. She *almost* wished she had an audience. So few people knew what she was actually capable of. Everyone back home thought she was this good little girl with her Master's degree in art history. They thought she travelled the world in style, buying and selling paintings for wealthy clients.

Well, technically she did *sell* paintings. It was the buying part that was a little less crystal clear. She walked into the safe room and looked around, impressed with the sizeable cache of goods. It wasn't the best she'd ever seen, but it certainly wasn't the worst either. Paintings, jewels, high-end liquor, and one-of-a-kind brand label clothing lined the beautifully lit room.

"Concentrate, Pullman," she reminded herself, when a big, sparkly tiara caught her eye. Such a shame. That beauty would look amazing perched atop her stylish, blond coiffure. Lise Rousseau had no idea how to truly appreciate such a piece. Clearly, since it was sitting in a safe room instead of on the woman's head while she drank chocolate martinis with her lover on some beach in Portugal. If Katie owned an honest to goodness tiara it would be on her head all the freaking time.

Katie turned away with a sigh and forced herself to move toward the item she had come for. She eyed the painting for a moment, her azure eyes sweeping over the landscape critically. Each line screamed fruit bowl romantic era. She didn't get it. But then, she was more of a modern Warhol kind of girl herself. Whatever. It would pay the bills. Lifting it, she retraced her steps, leaving the tiara sadly untouched on her way out. She slipped the painting into the leather folio case she'd brought for that purpose, then closed and relocked the walk-in safe.

She swung the leather case onto her back and strapped it carefully on before making her way out of the master suite of the Rousseau's penthouse bedroom. She glanced out the window and pursed her lips in disappointment. Shouldn't people this rich have a spectacular view of the Eiffel Tower? There seemed to be a building, or several, in the way. If she were them, she'd want her money back.

Katie climbed out the fourth-floor window she had come in and carefully made her way back along the ledge until she was once more clear of all the building's security measures. She pulled herself up into a crawl space that had probably been storage once upon a time but was now a pigeon coop. Lucky for her, the building manager hadn't thought to put a camera on that particular spot. She crawled through the tunnel until she was in the ventilation system and once more back in the building where she quickly exchanged her black leggings and turtleneck for a revealing dress. She mussed up her hair and smeared the make-up she'd carefully applied earlier. She added a pair of sky high heels and tossed a cashmere wrap over her leather bag.

She took the elevator down to the lobby and stumbled into

the marble entranceway with a half ashamed giggle. She shot the concierge and security guard a sexy look from under her long, fake lashes and stumbled against the marble desk, dropping her wrap on the floor. She swung the leather bag into the folds of her skirt so it would go unnoticed. The guard was the first to react when she bent over to adjust her heel as though she hadn't put it on properly while leaving one of the apartments doing the walk of shame. She knew he would get a superb view directly down the front of her dress, nearly to her naval.

"*Laisse moi aider*," the guard said reaching for the wrap, his eyes never leaving her pale chest. He handed the buttery soft material to her, his fingers caressing her wrist for just a moment.

"*Merci, vous etes trop gentil!*" she rattled breathlessly, a grateful smile lighting up her face. She included the concierge in her look, drawing him into her orbit so he wouldn't wonder where she had come from, as she most certainly hadn't entered the building with anyone.

She accepted the expensive wrap from the guard, squeezed his arm, slid her shoe back on and breezed out the front door of the building with a wave. She would be memorable, but not for the stolen painting that would be discovered in several days when Mrs. Rousseau opened the safe to choose jewelry for the upcoming Paris fashion shows. If she was remembered, there would be no record of her face. Katie was very careful to keep her profile away from the cameras. And just in case she was unable to keep track of all angles, she had a hacker in the system erasing her footprints as she made them. It helped to have an ace in her pocket at all times.

Katie hailed a cab and headed immediately for the airport. Now that she had what she came for, her benefactor would have a plane waiting for her. He would want the painting stateside and available for auction as soon as possible. She didn't mind. She could sleep on his private jet. He never seemed to care when she used his things.

Besides, she had fourteen hours before she needed to make her next instalment to Colin, and Paris was a long way from Seattle. She wasn't looking forward to this meeting. Not that she ever looked forward to seeing Colin. Maybe after the divorce she'd been pathetic enough to hope he might take it all back and welcome her home again. Now, she wished she never had to see him again.

She knew it made her a horrible person, but a small part of her wished he would just up and die. Like, she had actual fantasies of police officers coming to her apartment and telling her that Colin was killed in a car accident. Then she would collapse in a sobbing heap and the big, strong officer would hold her while she calculated the insurance payment in her head, because she was pretty sure Colin never took her off his insurance plan. He was kind of an idiot that way.

Not so stupid that he couldn't figure out how to blackmail and extort his ex-wife though. Her stomach twisted in protest at the thought of what exactly she would have to do with him in less than a day. She sighed and stared longingly up at the Eiffel Tower as the taxi made its way through the city of love. She closed her eyes, settled back in the car and switched to her favourite fantasy of climbing to the very top and leaping off. Not of ending her life. Never that. She wasn't brave enough for suicide. No. She would stretch her arms wide and fly into the inky darkness, rushing over the beautiful buildings with all of their incredible history. Eventually, she would float softly down. In this fantasy, landing didn't hurt.

---

The razor-sharp knife penetrated the artery with the smoothness of silk. It was a beautiful blade. The only vanity he allowed in his simple existence. It had belonged to his *culero* father. One of the few things he'd managed to grab, after the fall of his family, before his race for the border in the middle of the night. The handle was bone with a wolf carved into it and a metal grip welded around the edge. There was a matching dagger that had been lost that night.

He eased the victim away from his body and held him against the floor as life quickly ebbed away. He'd played for long enough. Taped the man's mouth and landed his fists in different parts of his body until the little bitch squealed and begged beneath his gag. If he'd been allowed to live, he would've peed blood for a week. Roman would have enjoyed making the man suffer for longer, but he had work to do. He would need to get rid of the body and then come back to collect the girl.

Katerina.

Everything he did was for her. This was for her. Even if it wasn't exactly what she would've chosen for herself. Retribution and death for her extortionist was essential. He lived by only one code. She'd belonged to him from the moment he set eyes on her all those years ago. She had been too young to claim. She had been thirteen and he had been twenty. She'd gone toe to toe with him when she found out he was in the same gang as her big brother. This tiny little, yellow-haired thing, yelling at a big, tattooed gang animal, fresh out of jail. She'd been lucky he hadn't raped and killed her on the spot.

Back then he had no moral code, he had no sense of honour or family. Just black rage and his best friend, who was behind the door she was standing in front of. Instead, he'd fallen in love with the first syllable she spoke, the first poke of her little finger against his leather-clad chest as she told him to get the fuck off their family lawn and never come back. She'd been way too good for the likes of him, even once she grew up. He had been a dirty street rat. Piece of gang shit. So, he had watched from the shadows as she bloomed in the sun.

But then something happened. She had wilted under the touch of the scum currently dying in a pool of his own blood. *Her husband*. His lip curled in disgust as he watched the other man coldly. There was no understanding her choice. He was small in Roman's eyes; weak. Had barely put up a fight when he understood what Roman had come for. He'd begged like a cunt and offered money. *Her fucking money*.

Roman didn't know why or what had happened to go so wrong in her life. He'd done as she'd asked. He'd kept to the shadows and allowed her to live her life separate from him, despite the out of control chemistry that flared up between them every time they set eyes on each other. He would force her to tell him, once he got his hands on her. And he *would* put hands on her. He was done keeping his distance. She'd begged him to leave her alone, to let her live her own life. She hadn't lived it well. She'd allowed this limp-dicked, now dead, piece of shit to fuck with her head and to damage her perfect self.

Now he was coming back to pick up the pieces of her life. He was coming for Katie and he was coming with a vengeance. He was going to put her back together and then he was going to keep what was left for himself.

# CHAPTER SIX

Revulsion hit Katie like a punch in the stomach. It was everything she could do to search for the key to her old apartment in her Coach bag, fit it in the lock and open the door. She wasn't sure who she hated more, her ex-husband or herself. She didn't understand how he could feel such disgust for her and her profession, yet summon her here month after month. Oh, she understood the money. Blackmail for money was an easy concept to comprehend. It was the sex she didn't get.

She shifted uneasily in her knee-length button up tan coat. Reaching for the belt, she knotted it tighter around her too-slender waist. She knew she'd lost too much weight recently. Constant fear and agitation had taken its toll on her figure. She spent every waking moment terrified that the FBI were going to break down her door at any moment. All because of the man whose apartment she was about to enter.

Something didn't feel right. Usually she heard the sound of music or the TV blaring. Colin liked to surround himself by noise. The smell of food would hit her as she cracked open the door and stood nervously waiting for his summons. Colin liked to keep her waiting. Like a dog or a slave. Today she heard and smelled nothing.

She pushed the door open further and saw that the interior of his apartment was flooded in darkness. Had he forgotten about their appointment? Impossible. It was the same time every month. Since the day of their divorce a year ago. She would come to him on the 25th of the month at 8pm, like clockwork. If she didn't, he would make the call that would end her life.

Something definitely wasn't right. Her legs began to shake. She wished desperately that she wasn't wearing four-inch heels. Not that it was her choice. Colin chose her apparel for these visits. It rarely deviated. He liked the easy access of the coat, heels and nothing else.

She stepped further into the apartment, allowing the door to close behind her. The sound of the muffled slam made her jump. Her heart pounded in fear and her palms dampened. She smelled something metallic.

Blood.

She bit her lip to hold back a whimper. "C-Colin?" she whispered. Then realized he wouldn't possibly be able to hear her unless he was standing right next to her.

"Colin!" she called in a stronger voice.

When he didn't answer, she took a few more steps closer to what used to be her kitchen before the divorce. Before Colin had taken everything from her and then demanded more every month after. A $25,000 payment and her on her back with her legs spread, a willing vessel for him to use as many times as he wanted before kicking her out like some dirty whore. Something he liked to call her during their hours together. She shuddered.

With shaking fingers, she reached for the light and pushed. The bright overhead light blinded her for a moment. She blinked and then turned her head toward the metallic smell, forcing herself to brave the possibility that something might have happened to Colin. She gasped in horror as she took in a pool of blood far too big for someone to simply walk away from.

She whimpered and backed away from the kitchen, intent on reaching the door, her eyes glued to the blood. It was almost perfect in its shiny depth, the way it was spread across the floor. No smears, or prints to mar its glassy surface. She forced herself to blink and continue moving toward the door. She would call the police as soon as she got down to the lobby.

Her heels were the only sound in the apartment as she shuffled slowly backward toward the door, keeping her eyes on the blood, as though it would attack her. Before she reached the door, her back hit a solid wall of muscle. She opened her mouth to scream and would have jumped away, but a hand clamped over her lips and another around her waist, pinning her arms to her side. She was dragged backward into the heat of a very hard, very male body.

She knew instantly the man holding her wasn't Colin. Her ex-husband was the same height as her when she wore heels. And he wasn't near as hard as whoever was pressed against her back. This man was rock solid. The man no doubt responsible for the massive pool of blood on the floor. Her eyes fell to the crimson lake of their own volition. She tried to struggle, but the man held her so tight all she could do was wiggle helplessly against him.

He groaned and pushed his face into the back of her neck, nudging his nose into her blond hair and breathing deeply. W-was he actually smelling her? He tilted her head to the side and forward a little so she was forced to look down. He ran his nose down the exposed arch of her throat from her ear all the way down to her shoulder. He was definitely inhaling her scent. His lips teased her shoulder and he tugged the sleeve of her coat a little until it moved toward the edge of her shoulder exposing more skin.

Oh god, what was he doing? Was this man going to rape her in her ex-husband's apartment? Had Colin's depraved mind come up with some new kind of punishment? But how did that explain the blood? Somehow she *knew* deep inside that the blood belonged to Colin. Just as she knew no one could survive the loss of that much. She whimpered against the hand.

Her fear seemed to penetrate his fascination with her skin. He straightened to his full height, which was still several inches taller than her, even in heels. Though his broad palm remained firmly over her mouth, he used his thumb to rub her cheek soothingly as though to calm her. She blinked rapidly as his thumb brushed too close to her eye, her eyelashes sweeping over the rough pad. He groaned again from behind her and tightened his arm in response, pulling her further into the cradle of his thighs. She gasped into his hand, feeling the rigid length of his cock through the back of her coat.

Then she caught sight of the tattoo that ran along the edge of his forefinger. His trigger finger. "For Dexter."

She stiffened in his arms, anger suffusing her as she realized exactly who held her. She didn't bother struggling. There was no point. He was too tall and outweighed her by a lot. The bastard also had a ton more street fighting experience than she did and wasn't afraid to fight dirty.

He chuckled darkly from behind her. He knew the exact moment she realized who he was. He dropped his hand from her lips, no longer worried that she would scream bloody murder, and slid it down the front of her body. He wrapped both arms around her waist, still keeping her arms pinned to her sides, and dragged her tightly back against him. He thrust his erection into her ass.

"What are you doing here?" she hissed angrily.

"Think that's obvious," he growled, bending his head to speak in her ear. "Come for you, pretty lady."

She shivered against him, her eyes falling on the blood. "Wh-what did you do to Colin?" she asked, her voice both a plea and a hope.

His body became rigid, his arms so like steel bands around her that they hurt. He didn't speak for a moment. She got the feeling he was controlling himself so he didn't say or do something he might regret. She frowned, her breath catching in her throat. Roman would never hurt her. Would he?

"You don't have to worry about him anymore."

Katie opened her mouth to argue with him, but he brought his hand up to cut her off, pressing his palm against her lips once more. "You don't want to talk to me about your husband right now, Katie. Nod if you understand?"

She shivered and nodded quickly. She wanted to know what he did to Colin, but Roman was like a wild animal. He'd always been dangerous and unpredictable. There was no telling what he was going to do next. Until she was in a better position (like on the other side of a locked door), her questions could wait. He moved his hand again.

"What happens now?" she whispered, hoping that one question would be okay. Was he going to let her run back to her life now that he'd done whatever he'd come to do?

"You come with me, like you should have years ago when I asked you to."

She gasped and jerked in his arms. "Impossible!" she told him. She had a job in Milan in just a few days. She absolutely couldn't go with Roman. She knew the odds of his letting her out of his sight. The man had an eerie way of tracking people. The only way she'd managed to escape him all those years ago was because she'd begged him to let her go. And for some reason her opinion had always mattered to the street-hardened criminal.

"Not impossible, Katie," he growled. "In fact, it's a fucking promise. You're coming with me this time. I'm done living without you. We belong together and I'm going to do what it takes to prove it to you."

"No!" she gasped, lunging in his arms. "You can't do that, Roman. I have a life. I won't go with you!"

"I've been watching you, Katie, my love," he growled at her, lowering her struggling body to the floor as she twisted in his arms. He took her elbows and locked them behind her in one strong grip. He pulled something from his pocket with his other hand. "You live a half-life. I'm done watching from the shadows while you slowly kill yourself. It's time to start living again."

"With you?" she spat out, glaring at him over her shoulder.

"With me," he confirmed.

When she realized what he held, she begged him to stop. She threatened him and tried to kick him with her sharp heels. He ignored her threats and her pleas. He pinned her to the floor, lifted her coat to her thigh, baring the smooth naked skin. He froze when he realized she was completely bare underneath. Then he shoved his hand roughly into her coat to confirm his suspicion, cupping her bare breast.

She gasped and surged up into his hands. He slammed her back into the floor, treating her with a lack of care she'd never felt from him before. He leaned over her, his breathing finally as heavy as hers and growled in her ear, "Knew the fucker was blackmailing you. Had no idea you liked it enough to spread your legs. Maybe I should've let him live and just walked away from your mess."

She screamed and fought to get away from him. He cut her screams off with a heavy hand over her lips and plunged the syringe viciously into her thigh while she beat at his chest. After a few seconds she stopped fighting, her body gradually going limp beneath him. He pulled her across his lap, cradling her head against his arm and smoothed the coat over her nakedness.

She watched his dark, sinister face as she drifted into unconsciousness. The only man she ever truly loved. The man she feared above all others. He'd finally come for her.

## CHAPTER SEVEN

*"Mujer hermosa, mi corazón."*

Katie woke gradually, her muddled brain grasping onto the bits and pieces of consciousness that floated by her. She tilted her face slightly and rubbed her cheek against what felt like the roughness of denim. She imagined Roman's deep, accented voice calling her his beautiful woman and his heart in his native language. Another fantasy to keep her warm and whole during the cruel nights that taunted her with loneliness.

Fingers caressed her cheek and smoothed the strands of hair off her head. She frowned. It didn't usually take her so long to wake up. In fact, she was an incredibly light sleeper out of necessity in case she needed to make a super fast exit. She forced a moan past stiff lips and urged her body to move. Her fingers twitched and she nearly cried out in distress when her body refused to obey the dictates of her brain.

"Easy, baby." Roman's voice came to her in the darkness, frightening and soothing at the same time.

She felt the fingers brush across her lips and down her throat, touching her while she was helpless to resist. Memory began to return. Colin's apartment. The blood. She whimpered in fear and shivered. This was no fantasy. She was actually here, drugged and laying in Roman's arms. He meant what he said. He'd killed her ex-husband and he was keeping her for himself.

Finally, after a great internal struggle, Katie was able to force her eyes open and stare up at the man holding her. Accusation shone through clear azure eyes, stabbing him with their sweeping intensity. He stared back, his dark gaze just as intense. They battled in silence, the air around them sizzling with the heat of their attraction. The enthralment that had captured Roman from the first moment this goddess had spoken to him. The same allure that now captured her.

She lay sprawled across a huge bed, her upper body cradled in Roman's lap, her head on his muscular thigh. He sat hunched over her, watching and waiting, like a big, dark wolf protecting its mate. She knew he wouldn't let her go now that he finally had her. It was a miracle he'd allowed her the years of separation they'd had. The years that she had run free, away from her stalking predator. He had spent those years honing his ability to track, while she'd practiced her ability to escape. Sadly, she knew she was going to need every skill she possessed, because as much as her body cried out for his, she had things to do and places to be. She couldn't stay with Roman Valdez here in… wait… where was she?

Katie broke eye contact first to roll her head to the side and glance around the room. She raised an eyebrow in surprise. This place was not Roman's usual style. He lived in the dark and the shadows. She'd never been invited to his place before, but she followed him once. About five years ago. A sort of curious kitty, revenge thing, for the amount of times she knew he'd stalked her in the shadows, frightening her without saying a word. Just that one time she'd invaded his privacy without his knowing. Because she was good at breaking into places uninvited.

He lived in an abandoned warehouse. Not a scummy

place, filled with rats or anything like that. No, he just really liked his privacy. She'd waited until he left and climbed up the fire escape, then slipped down the elevator shaft and into his giant warehouse. It was heartbreakingly empty. He only occupied a small section of it. Very much a bachelor. She was pretty sure he owned the whole building and just chose to live alone there in that small, lonely section. In one of the worst areas of the city with a huge gang problem. His old stomping grounds. Not that it would have mattered. No one would fuck with Roman Valdez or his property. That would be asking for instant death.

She had stared in wide-eyed surprise at his empty existence and wondered what drove the big, dark man. Then she wondered what drove *her* to finally seek answers from him. Why had she come? She couldn't have him. He was too frightening. Too much for her. She was too fragile on a good day. On a bad day? She was a kaleidoscope of crazy, out of control, ready to fly off the planet on the wings of depression. Roman was not for her.

She might have stayed in his space all day, or until she heard the clatter of the old elevator labouring its way up. She might have laid on his bed and taken his scent deep into her lungs and stored the fantasies away for later. But she found the books beside his bed. Worn from his big hands flipping repeatedly through the pages. Some of the pages were dog-eared. With shaking hands, she picked one up. It opened automatically, as though it had been opened so many times the page was cracked from use. Her eyes widened as she realized the significance of the books littering his bedside.

Each book was an exact copy of her university text books. The ones that were worn and marked from his hands were art history books with the paintings she liked best. Katie's eyes lovingly traced the lines of her absolute favourite painting, Picasso's Woman with Folded Arms. How could Roman possibly know? Katie never told anyone about her affinity with Picasso's Blue Period. God, why would she? They would think she was crazy. Instead, she buried it like she buried everything else. But somehow her shadowy stalker knew about the depression that hugged her close and never let her truly surface.

She had dropped the book and backed away, unable to handle the meaning of her discovery. It was one thing to believe Roman wanted her for her body. She was tall, thin, blond. Sure, she could see the appeal. She even used her sex appeal to her advantage when she had to. She sold her soul years ago, it didn't really matter anymore. But this. This was something different. It was like the man saw into the heart of her and loved her for herself.

But that was impossible. Because there was nothing to love. She was a shell. A thing to be used for her body and her skills. Not a person to be loved. Roman deserved so much more than Katie. Roman had avenged Dexter. He was the angel of death. He was perfect. He didn't want the head case mess that was Katie Pullman.

Yet, now, he was looking at her like he wanted to devour every inch of her. And she was starting to suspect that he had kidnapped her and brought her to some kind of fancy hotel or something. Which he would have done just for her, because she knew he wasn't into this sort of thing. There was a chandelier over the bed and a gorgeous ensuite peeking around the corner for goodness sake. No, just nope. She was putting a stop to whatever this was. Roman had finally gone too far. She moistened her lips, forced herself to roll away from his thigh and push herself up onto her hands and knees.

She swayed precariously and nearly collapsed back onto the very soft, very inviting bed. She frowned in confusion as the entire room swayed around her. Was that the effects of the drug or... wait... was that a porthole?

"Easy, baby," Roman said again, his amused eyes

devouring her as she swayed on her hands and knees attempting to process what was happening to her.

She swung her face toward him and glared. "Stop saying that," she snapped, her voice cracking. She moistened her lips again and backed slowly toward the edge of the bed, watching him warily. When he made no move to stop her, she tentatively moved one long leg over the side, careful to keep her coat draped over her thigh so she wouldn't accidentally flash him. "I'm not your baby. Roman... are... are we on a boat?"

He straightened and pushed himself off the bed, his sharp eyes never leaving her. "It's a yacht. Friend gave it to me."

Her mouth fell open as she glanced around, taking in the luxury. She had some good friends. None had given her a yacht. Maybe she needed new friends. "Must be a good friend."

He shrugged. "Thought you'd like it."

Her sharp mind read between the lines. Yeah, he thought she might like it, but he also knew she wasn't going anywhere fast while out on the ocean. "You knew I wouldn't be able to escape this thing easily," she said accusingly.

He ignored her and reached for her arm when she slid off the bed and stood up on wobbling legs. She swayed with the gentle rocking of the boat, but tried to jerk away from him when Roman wrapped long, hard fingers around her upper arm. He held her steady, refusing to let her step away from him. She knew she should be grateful. Knew she would fall without his assistance. But right now she didn't want his touch. It was too confusing. The chemistry that sizzled between their every exchange hung thick in the air. She couldn't forget that the strong hand holding her up was the hand that had most likely murdered her ex-husband.

She looked down the length of her body and cringed a little. She still wore the knee length double-breasted trench coat. To her relief, it was still tied tightly at the waist. She was barefoot though. A quick glance around didn't reveal the heels anywhere. Not that she ever wanted to see those symbols of her subjugation again. But a little added height wouldn't hurt. At 5'8", Katie wasn't a short woman. Roman was still eight inches taller than her and outweighed her by a good hundred and thirty or so pounds of solid muscle. Unless she got her hands on a gun, she wasn't going to be fighting her way off the boat.

"Is there anything else for me to wear?" she asked quietly.

Roman made sure she was steady before removing his hand and walking toward a closet. Opening it, he showed her a walk-in wardrobe with blue LED lighting. It was filled with women's clothes. Katie walked slowly toward him, careful not to actually touch the big man as she approached. She gasped in appreciation as she neared the closet. All of the clothes were gorgeous and brand label. Roman pulled out drawers filled with make-up and jewelry before stepping away to give her room to inspect her new possessions. She turned awe-filled eyes toward him. Who was this street thug turned big time criminal?

"Meet me topside when you're dressed," he said gruffly. "We'll talk."

She nodded mutely and watched her captor stride away, terribly afraid she'd been underestimating Roman all along.

# CHAPTER EIGHT

Katie chose her outfit carefully. She needed something sexy in case she wanted to distract Roman, but she also didn't want to find herself on her back any time soon, so she needed to balance the skin to cloth ratio. She settled on a bikini (it was unlikely she was close enough to land to swim, but hey, a girl could hope), layered with a sky blue wraparound skirt and a white sleeveless top.

Katie always chose her clothes carefully. She had 'heist' clothes and 'playing with the ex-douche-bag' clothes. She had 'visiting the fam' clothes and 'entertaining clients' clothes. Katie had become such a clothing chameleon that she wasn't actually certain what her natural style was. When she hung out by herself in her apartment she tended to wear leggings and T-shirts with funny cat memes. She'd always wanted to get a cat, but her jet-setting lifestyle wouldn't allow for it.

Katie decided to use the gorgeously furnished ensuite while she had free run of the master suite. She washed her face and brushed her teeth with a brand-new toothbrush that she suspected was there for her. She ran her fingers over the glass surrounding a huge shower and looked around in appreciation. There were even fresh lilies in a small crystal vase on top of the vanity.

She emerged out onto the main deck, bare feet brushing against the warmth cast by the morning sun. From the look in his eyes as she approached, it probably wouldn't have mattered what she wore. She was always going to capture and hold Roman's attention. She had from the first moment she'd spoken to the dead-eyed gangbanger seventeen years earlier. She blushed and looked away from the heated stare he was giving her and awkwardly tucked a lock of blond hair behind her ear.

He stood and took her arm, maneuvering her into the cushioned seat next to him. It was a long, padded bench over-looking the Pacific Ocean. Katie was dismayed to realize that she saw no land in any direction. She was well and truly trapped.

"Where are we?" she asked, shading her eyes and looking all around.

Roman watched the flickering emotions for a moment before saying, "You're here with me."

She shook her head and frowned at him pleadingly. "I can't stay with you, Roman. I have a job. Please, you can't keep me here, I have to be at work in a few days!"

He didn't respond for a moment, just continued to watch her face as though she weren't begging him to let her go. When he did speak, it was on another topic entirely. "Why were you naked, Katie?"

"Wh-what?" she asked, confused at the switch in topics. Then her brain caught up and she realized what he meant. She dropped her eyes, shame suffusing her features in colour.

"You there to fuck him?" Roman snapped, his fingers biting into the edge of the cushion next to his thigh so he wouldn't reach out and grab her. She shivered, eyes locked on his long, blunt fingers, tracing over the old gang tattoos, knowing what those hands could do to her.

She'd never been on the receiving end of Roman's violence before, but she'd witnessed enough and heard things. She'd been fourteen when Dexter died at the hands of the Red Brotherhood. The entire family had been a wreck. Much later, she had finally been cognizant enough to catch the rumours of a brutal gang war that lasted less than a week. Of an entire gang faction taken out by a single man in bloody retribution for death of his best friend. She knew it was Roman, because he had come to her in the night, months after the killings, and promised her that she and her family were safe. He had held her tight against his body while she cried for her brother, then he'd walked away and let her grow up.

"Asked you a fucking question, Katie," he snarled, turning dark, aggressive eyes toward her. "Answer."

She shivered and cringed back against her seat. What could she tell him? He would know a lie if it fell from her lips. So, she nodded and flinched back when he swung his fist as though he would hit her. Instead, he brought it crashing into the seat behind her while she cowered away from him. She tried to remind herself that Roman had never hurt her before. That he had done everything to protect her.

He leaned forward, his entire body seething with rage, and said one word. "Explain."

Katie understood that he was giving her an opportunity. She also knew that Roman was unpredictable at the best of times. A dark beast lurked within her lone wolf. The man that dedicated his life to working with a lethal mobster, hunting and killing. Stalking the shadows. Stalking Katie. He was good at the things he did. She needed to be very careful what she said to him. He brought her here, out into the ocean, for a reason. He wanted her isolated and alone so he could keep her to himself. So, she would have nowhere to run.

She leaned back against the cushions, putting precious inches between herself and the man whose entire focus was on her. She swept her long lashes down, over her eyes, concealing the expression. Licking her lips, she spoke softly, "You know about the money?"

He grunted in affirmative, but didn't speak.

She looked at him through her lashes. His broad shoulders blocked out the rising sun behind him. Was it morning already? He'd given her enough drugs to knock her out overnight. She looked him over in the light of the early morning sun, trying to calm herself enough to figure out what to tell him. He wore a black button-up shirt with the sleeves rolled up his tanned forearms and a pair of light blue jeans that moulded to his muscular thighs. Though they were good quality, there was a hole in the knee from wear. He had old, faded tattoos from his gang days littering his arms and neck where she could see his skin. His dark brown hair was short, but not too short, as though he buzzed it with an electronic razor and it was overdue for a cut. His square jaw and sharp cheeks were covered in at least a week's growth of beard. Somehow, she didn't think it was on purpose. It was just Roman. He would find grooming to be an annoyance that he indulged in only when he had to.

"He started blackmailing me after the divorce," she whispered, dropping her eyes to where his hand was clenched in the cushion next to her thigh.

"I guessed as much," Roman gritted out. "Not what I asked."

Katie took a breath and tried not to roll her eyes. He wasn't going to make this easy on her. "Okay," she said as calmly as she could, "well, he decided he also wanted sex with the monthly payments."

"Fuck, Katie," he snapped. "I already guessed that shit. Start telling me something I don't know. Like why you agreed to spread your legs? Thought you hated the guy. Or is that what turns you on? You into twisted shit like that?"

The breath caught in her throat and Katie clenched her fists so she wouldn't slap him. She had to remind herself that she wasn't violent. And that to react violently with someone like Roman would absolutely set the big guy off. That likely he was trying to bait her so he would have an excuse to put his hands on her. To treat her the way he wanted to treat her in that moment. He was at war with himself. He'd spent years putting her on a pedestal only to discover she wasn't worthy. Well, he could join the club. She was a disappointment to everyone else, including herself.

"He found something out about me," she said in a rush, knowing she didn't have a choice. "If I didn't give him what he wanted he would go to the FBI and get me arrested. I... I couldn't risk it. So I gave him what he wanted."

Surprise flickered across Roman's features before he masked them with his usual indifferent expression. "Why didn't you come to me?" he demanded.

It was a valid question. When Colin had first approached her with his ludicrous demands, Roman's face was the first to enter her thoughts. Even then, she knew her dark protector would swoop in and save her from her own mess, she also knew she didn't deserve saving. She deserved every second of the year's penance she'd been made to suffer at Colin's hands. It hadn't been so bad. The money was nothing, a drop in the bucket. The sex had been disgusting only in that she'd had to endure his hands on her body, his breath in her face and his tiny dick working away at her for as long as he could keep it up while she fantasized about something else. *Anything else*. Thankfully, though a disgusting little worm of a man, her ex-husband had not been sadistic. He didn't have the imagination.

"I couldn't tell you, I knew you would kill him," she whispered.

Now, looking up into the eyes of a man that truly wanted her, every part of her, a man that truly understood the meaning of the word *hell*, she knew she was in the power of someone that had the imagination to make her suffer if he wanted to. A shiver of both fear and anticipation slithered down her spine. She deserved whatever Roman decided to dish out to her. She *wanted* whatever he decided to hand out to her. She would have no choice but to take it until she found a way off this boat and back into her bleak existence.

He moved over her until she was forced to lean back against the cushions. His powerful arms flexed around her slender body, showing her how breakable she was. When he spoke, his voice was soft, like deep velvet, though his words were terrifying. "Should've told me, Katerina. Would have taken care of the problem a year ago. Could've been fucking me in payment, instead of him."

She gasped and tried to roll away from him off the side of the bench. He caged her against the seat and dropped the weight of his lower body against her, pinning her in place. She shoved against his chest, but his arms tightened in response until she was only bruising herself against his muscular body. Finally, she subsided, relaxing in his hold, breathing heavily. She balled her hands into fists in her lap and refused to look at him.

"Is he dead?" she whispered, not looking at him.

Roman hauled her up against his body, refusing to allow her the room that she craved. He took her jaw in his big hand, caressing her chin with his long fingers and held her face up to his. He pierced her with his dark, almost black eyes and forced her to read the truth within. He tilted her face just a little and touched the edge of her mouth with his hard lips before tracing a line up her cheek toward her ear. She shivered as his tongue darted into the delicate shell of her ear before tracing the lobe.

He pulled back slightly and spoke in a hard voice, "Yes."

Katie's stomach plunged and she went limp in Roman's arms as she remembered the pool of blood in Colin's apartment. The blood that had belonged to her ex-husband. The blood that had been spilled by the hands that were now holding her. She blinked as tears pricked the corners of her eyes and blackness started to edge in on her vision. Her chest rose and fell in rapid succession as she gasped for breath.

"Don't you fucking dare grieve for him," Roman snarled, shaking her hard.

Katie's head snapped like a rag doll's causing the yacht and the ocean to spin around her. Roman lifted her as though she weighed nothing, turned her so she was facing him and forced her to straddle his lap. He snaked an arm up her back and held her by the back of the neck, forcing her head up to his. He used his other arm to wrap around her waist and anchor her against his incredibly hard body. She whimpered and squirmed against him.

"You will not mourn for the man that blackmailed you. Turned you into a ghost. I did the world a fucking favour, Katie. Do you hear me?" he snarled in her face.

She knew what he was doing. In his own way, he was begging her to tell him he hadn't fucked up and killed someone she loved. Roman couldn't handle all the twisted emotions that came with love. Because he hadn't ever been loved. Katie's family had always been close.

When Dexter was still alive he'd told them about his best friend. Roman had spent the first twelve years of his life in Juarez, Mexico. The son of a sex slave and a big-time drug cartel guy. Though his upbringing was anything but loving, it had been filled with wealth and privilege, with the expectation that he'd take over the family business. A competing faction had taken out Roman's entire family. Roman had escaped with a few low-level drug dealers to the States and joined the gang where he'd met Dexter.

She nodded her head against his, fighting the tears. "I hear you," she whispered. She felt some of the tension leave him.

She wasn't going to cry for Colin. He was a weasel. A disgusting bastard that deserved whatever he got. She cried for Roman. For the beautiful, fucked up, lost soul of a man that deserved so much better than her. He'd taken her penance. He'd blackened his soul just a little bit more for a woman that didn't deserve his adoration.

She felt his body tense up once more, felt his chest expand as he prepared to ask her the question she knew she wouldn't be able to answer. He took her by the neck and pulled her head away from his so he could see her blue eyes when he spoke.

"What did he have on you that kept you going back every month? Why would the fucking FBI get involved, Katie?"

Her knees tightened involuntarily on either side of his legs. Heat flared in his eyes. She held onto that look. Knowing it was about to turn ice cold. She clenched her fingers against his arms, preparing for his reaction.

"I can't tell you," she whispered.

As she predicted, any warmth in his eyes turned immediately to ice. His hands dug into her soft skin until she knew there would be bruises. She didn't think he even realized what he was doing. He yanked her forward on his lap, slamming her chest against his. She brought her hands up to put some distance between them, but he pulled her arms around her back and held them in one hand. He gripped her jaw with the other.

"Won't," he growled.

Her breasts lifted and fell quickly with her gasping breaths. She was completely trapped against him, her legs spread across his on the bench. Though she was terrified, she knew her pussy was wetting the bikini bottom she'd pulled on earlier. She desperately hoped he couldn't feel the wetness soaking through the denim of his jeans.

She licked her lips and forced herself to focus on the man who was threatening her well-being in a very elemental way. She needed to put sexy thoughts away for the moment. "Either way, I'm not telling you, Roman."

She cried out in actual terror at the look that crossed his

face. It was a look she'd never seen before on Roman's face. It looked like instant death. She imagined it was similar to what Colin, and many others, had experienced right before lights out. Katie began struggling in earnest, trying to pull her arms away from Roman's grip and twisting frantically on his lap. She knew right away that she'd done the wrong thing. That she was inflaming the big man past the point of reason.

He stood abruptly, his hand circling her neck. He shook her and then pulled her into the heat of his body. She felt his cock hard against her stomach. His voice was harsh as he spoke, his accent much thicker than usual. "Refuse to give me anything, Katie, then I am forced to make assumptions. I will treat you like the *puta* you act. Since I took care of your problem, you can make payments to me instead. Go downstairs and spread those legs, I'll show you what a real cock looks like."

# CHAPTER NINE

Katie smashed her fist into the side of his face. She didn't have a lot of leverage, he was holding her too close, but her closed fist probably hurt enough to get the point across. He didn't even flinch. He just grabbed her small fist, wrenched her arm down, flung her around and forced her forward down the passageway toward the main cabin.

"You bastard!" she cried out as she stumbled forward into a wall. He checked her fall so she wouldn't hurt herself. She was so angry and hurt by his words she could barely walk. She collapsed onto the shiny floor, panting and struggling, trying to get her arm back. Roman was much too strong, she didn't stand a chance. He went down onto one knee behind her, crouching over her body, owning her. He sunk his teeth into the skin over her collarbone. She cried out, arching back against his chest. Moisture flooded her core and her eyes flew open in surprise as she stared up into his evil expressionless face.

"Get up," he snapped, yanking her to her feet with a hard hand on her bicep.

Katie stumbled to her feet. He shoved her forward, forcing her the rest of the way down the hall, back into the master stateroom. He rounded the corner and flung her onto the bed. Katie collapsed against the beautiful bedspread and rolled over to look up at his hulking form. His face was unreadable, but his eyes told a different story. His eyes were glowing with fury and possession. It was the same war she'd seen earlier. He finally had his love where he wanted her, but he was seeing her through new eyes. God, he was going to hurt her if he didn't slow down!

Katie put a hand up and said softly, "Please, Roman, can we just talk about this? You don't want to do this."

He raised his eyebrows, his eyes never leaving her body. His hands went to the buttons on his shirt where he began slowly undoing them one at a time.

"I've wanted to do this since before you were legal, Katie. Let's don't pretend I'm the good guy here," he sneered down at her. "Never forget where I come from."

Tears pricked her eyes. His words, his actions were so cruel. But the Roman she'd known over the years, the one that had held her after her brother's death, the one that bought and read every one of her school textbooks, was not the man who was threatening her now. How was she going to get through to him? She pushed herself up as he wrenched the collared shirt off his broad shoulders and let it fall to the floor. The breadth of sinew and muscle held her bound for a moment. She didn't stand a chance physically against this man. He dropped his hands to the button on his jeans. Her eyes flared in panic and she began backing up on the bed.

"Roman… please," she begged desperately. "I… I've never been with anyone but Colin…"

He frowned, staring down at her, then shook his head. "You're lying."

"Why would I lie?" she cried throwing up her hands.

"To stop me from taking the payment you owe a dead man."

She gasped and flung herself off the other side of the bed.

"Stop saying that! I don't owe you anything," she snapped at him.

He shrugged, muscles rippling down his shoulders and torso. Her panicked eyes followed the movement, tracing the tattoos that flowed across his chest and arms. A simple, stark cross stood out directly in the middle of his chest. Apprehension and need built within her, creating pulses deep within her stomach.

"Don't matter how you come to my bed, Katie, so long as you get there. Done waiting for you, woman," he said, his eyes glowing at her from across the distance of the bed.

It was a big bed, but in that moment, it felt tiny. Roman was such a large man; his broad frame could eat up any room. She'd always found him so solid and comforting. Yes, a little scary, but that scariness had never really been turned her way. A small part of her knew that one day his focus would land completely on her. It had always been inevitable. And truth be told, she'd been waiting in breathless anticipation. But not like this. Not with the death of her husband and independence all in one stroke. Not with the terrifying spectre of her career hanging over their heads. He had no idea what he'd done.

His hands landed on his belt. His eyes never left hers as he unbuckled the metal and pulled the thick leather through the loops. She lunged sideways toward the ensuite. Of course, she trapped herself in the washroom and his much longer strides ate up the distance between them. She ran up against the wall and whirled around to face him. His expression didn't change as he reached for her.

"Don't do this, Roman!" she begged as he hooked an arm around her waist and whirled her out of the corner as though she weighed nothing. She flung her arm out to grab hold of something, but only managed to sweep the tiny vase of flowers off the counter and onto the floor, shattering the crystal.

Roman ignored the glass crunching beneath his shoes, only lifting her off her feet so she wouldn't be cut as he strode out of the washroom. He flung her down on the bed and fell on top of her before she could roll away from him, pinning her arms over her head with one hand. He took her jaw in the other hand and forced her to look at him. His familiar, dark face hovered over hers, so close his breath shivered over her cheek. He ducked his face and pressed his lips to hers, pressing them hard against her soft mouth until she was gasping.

He lifted his head and stared down at her, frustration and lust etching his hard, stoic features. "Kiss me, Katie. This is going to happen, make it good for yourself."

She glared up at him and pressed her lips together. She'd loved and hated Roman for seventeen years. The big, dark man fucked with her head in a way no one else could. Maybe she wanted him, but she wasn't going to give it up to him because he demanded it. He could either take what he wanted from her by force, like everyone else, or he could treat her properly. She jerked her chin in his grasp. His fingers tightened.

When he didn't let go, she did something she'd never in her life contemplated doing to another human being, let alone one as terrifying as Roman Valdez. Perhaps it was her driving need for pain and punishment, or the same thing that made her climb high buildings and break into impossible-to-break-into spaces. With her heart pounding crazily in her chest, she spat in his face.

"Kiss my ass," she snapped at him defiantly, trembling under the force of her emotions.

His eyes widened in surprise before narrowing. His entire body tensed over top of hers. She knew any other person in the world would die for such an insult. Her heart thumped in anticipation as she waited for his reaction, she'd just spat on the son of a cartel boss. He brought his leg up the bed, scraping it along her thigh. She felt the wrap sliding up her leg as his jean clad leg landed heavily across her body, trapping her. He let go of her jaw and slowly wiped the spit from his cheek with two long fingers. His dark eyes never left hers as he licked the spit from his own fingers.

"I'll get to your ass later, baby. Right now, I have other things I want to kiss first." His dark voice washed over her like honey, sticky and smooth.

Katie's mouth opened in a tiny gasp. An unexpected punch of pleasure went zinging through her and her hips lifted ever so slightly in response. Her eyes flared in reaction. God, she hoped he didn't notice. But of course he did. His own eyes flickered down her prone body. This intense chemistry was exactly what he was playing on with her. This is why he was driving her, pushing her for answers. Because he knew she would fight back and it would give him an excuse to put his hands on her.

Without warning, he shoved his fingers into her mouth, forcing her to taste his own saliva combined with hers. She tried to snap her teeth closed, but he released her hands and gripped her jaw in one hand, shoving the fingers of his other hand deep into the recesses of her mouth. She gurgled and choked on his fingers, arching in his grip, trying to buck him off. She brought her hands down and gripped his biceps, trying to push him away, but it was like trying to move a boulder. Using his grip on her jaw, he twisted her head to the side.

"Never forget who I am," he growled in her ear, licking the skin of her neck before sinking his teeth into the tender skin beneath her ear. "I am not the good guy, here to save you, baby."

He breathed heavily against her, thrusting his jean-clad erection into the cradle of her thighs, forcing her to feel every inch of him against the thin fabric of her wrap and bathing suit. She moaned in both fear and arousal as he shoved his fingers in and out of her mouth, showing her exactly how he would love to use her face.

"You need to be more careful, because I'll hurt you. I'm going to fuck you and maybe fuck you up if you keep fighting me. You understand, *mujer*?" he breathed against her, biting his way down her neck.

"Why, Roman?" she asked when he took his fingers out of her mouth and dropped his hand down her body. Her voice was a thin cry of desperation. "I th… thought you cared. All these years… you don't care at all."

"You were always mine," he growled against her. "I just waited. You're the one that fucked it up. Went and got married. Fucked up what we could've had."

Her body moved with him in supplication, desperately wanting the man on a primitive level, while her mind fragmented at the harsh treatment. His harsh words. She couldn't believe the man that had treated her so tenderly over the years could be this way. None of her thousands of fantasies of Roman had ever played out this way. Fantasy Roman had always been so tender. Had healed her many wounds. She was such a fool.

A scream escaped her lips as he dug his fingers into the knotted wrap at her waist and tore it from her body. The fabric tore easily, parting like tissue under his brutal hands. She felt a slight sting where the strands whipped her bare skin before falling away to the floor. She felt him moving down her body and knew that he would soon see her legs. Shame flooded her. Desperately she wrapped her arms around his shoulders pressing him against her body, her trembling lips against the thick cords of his neck, she tasted the slightly salty tang of him. The breath hitched in her throat as arousal crashed through her.

"Fuck, Katie," he growled, stiffening against her. He thrust his erection against her, shoving himself into her so hard he pushed her up the bed. "Fucking cocktease. You shove me away with one hand and pull me closer with the other. I'm done waiting. I want what's mine."

She moaned, a combination of distress and capitulation to his words leaving her lips. He captured the sound with his mouth, taking her lips with his for the first time, stealing her breath with a growl. He wasn't gentle. There were too many years of waiting between them. Too many long, agonizing years. Too many spoken and unspoken words. He took her mouth with a violence that shocked her to the core, yet told her unequivocally whose woman she was. There would be no escape for the escape artist.

He thrust his tongue deep into her mouth until she thought she would choke on it. He forced himself into every part of her mouth, memorizing every facet and imprinting himself on her. Taking from her without asking. His teeth clashed against hers until she was sure he would cut her. She whimpered, desperate for the assault to end, but still he continued. She could do nothing but curl her fingers against his bare shoulders and hold on for dear life while he took and took from her what she had denied him for so many years.

Finally, after what felt like ages, he pulled back. He dropped his forehead onto hers. She could feel him practically vibrating with restraint. Holding himself back from just tearing into her the way he'd torn into her mouth seconds before. Her lips felt swollen and sore from his ravishment.

"Jesus fuck, Katie. So fucking good. I don't know how I can be gentle enough with you," he gritted against her cheek. His body caged hers on the bed. She felt every inch of his much bigger frame against hers.

He clenched his fingers in her hair, controlling her, while his lips explored her face and ear, returning to her lips again and again. She moaned as pleasure and pain merged each time he pressed himself against her swollen mouth. His other hand roamed her body, sweeping down her ribcage, touching her body intimately for the first time. She felt the tremors going through his big frame and knew it wasn't from nervousness. No, it was the savagely leashed aggression threatening to break loose at any moment and light the bed on fire with them in it. He wanted her with an intensity that could wreck her, but he didn't want to hurt her beyond repair.

She trembled underneath him, afraid of what he could do to her. She felt his big palm caress her breast. Her back arched of its own volition, pushing her chest into his hand. He groaned and closed rough fingers over the perfect globe, squeezing her. His hand snaked behind her neck and made short work of the halter on her bikini top. With a tug he pulled it down, revealing both of her round breasts.

Katie's hands jerked up automatically to cover them, but he smacked them away with a growl. She blushed and refused to look at him. "Too small," she whispered.

He frowned and took her chin in his hand, jerking her face back to him. His dark eyes glowed with anger and frustration. He always hated when her insecurities showed. "Perfect," he growled. "You will never insult what's mine again."

His hand dropped from her face to touch the B-cup breast, tipped with a large pink areola and now stiff coral nipple. He pinched the nipple between thumb and forefinger and steadily applied pressure until she cried out and reached for his tattooed wrist. Her hips bucked underneath him in perfect response to the bite of pain. His eyes flared in acknowledgment.

"Understand?" he growled.

She gasped as her pussy flooded with heat and moisture. "Yes," she moaned, rubbing herself wantonly against him, uncaring that she looked like a desperate slut, eager to get off because he was giving her the bite of pain she needed with her pleasure. It felt so incredibly good. Her head tipped back and she forgot to tug his face up to hers as he licked a path down her body, between her breasts toward her flat stomach.

Her eyes flew open in remembrance only when she felt

him approach her naval, felt the tug of the bikini bottom loosening against her hips as he pulled the ties and muttered against her waist, "Have to taste you."

"No!" she cried out reaching for him just as he lowered his head to her thighs. He might not have even noticed the faint scars if she hadn't made the colossal mistake of jerking her thighs out of his hands and attempting to roll off the bed.

"Yes, Katie!" he roared, his fingers biting deep into her hips as he flung her back onto the bed. She could tell from the tone of his voice and the brutal bite of his hands that he thought she was teasing him once more and withholding the ultimate prize.

She cried out and began struggling as he dragged her under him. He reared back, reaching to shove the jeans down his muscular thighs, a savage look on his face. He was done waiting for her. If she wasn't going to come easy then he was going to take what she wouldn't give willingly and they would sort the rest out later. They had a lifetime to figure things out.

Katie held her breath, her arms lay stiff at her side. She waited for him to crawl over top of her and take by force what she would have willingly given him if he'd just given her more time. Been a little sweeter. She waited, expecting to feel his bruising touch as he fell on her and ravaged her flesh. Instead, she felt something far worse, something she dreaded from the first moment she realized that Roman loved her and would one day come for her. Because she knew he would see her damage and discover she was as fucked on the outside as she was on the inside.

He caressed her. His fingers lightly running down the inside of her thigh. She flinched away from him, knowing he'd discovered her shame. Of course, he wouldn't allow her retreat. He took her thighs in two huge hands and wrenched them open. Her eyes flew wide and she cried out. Not wanting to see him staring down at the scars that covered the inside of her soft flesh, she stared at the ceiling over the bed, unseeing while he examined her.

Roman instantly recognized knife wounds for what they were. God knows, he'd inflicted enough of them on others to know exactly what they looked like. These were delicate, almost beautiful, like poetry or art. Crisscrossing her legs from mid thighs right up to her tender pussy and further. He leaned closer, his warm breath caressing her labia. All arousal had fled though. He wasn't pleasuring her, he was examining her. He was looking at the tiny white raised scars across her labia and further inward on her inner lips and even on the hood of her tiny clit.

She felt the fury rising within him like the tide of an ocean as he took her pain into himself. He thought he knew everything about her. What a joke. Roman knew nothing except what she gave. Tiny little breadcrumbs. Until somehow, he'd discovered the blackmail and ended Colin Schell for her.

"He did this to you?" Roman demanded.

Katie sighed, the sound of her lungs deflating was loud to her ears. He knew better. He just wanted to believe that someone else had done this to her so he wouldn't have to deal with her fucked up head. Poor Roman. He'd kidnapped the wrong woman. The Katie he thought he loved didn't exist.

"Of course not," she said softly.

His fingers tightened on her thighs, bruisingly. She was going to be a canvas of bruises by tomorrow. Oddly the thought turned her on, despite the intensity of their current situation. Roman released her thighs and moved back, his dark eyes never leaving her. Katie immediately clamped her thighs together but didn't move otherwise. She was afraid he might grab her again.

"You did this to yourself," he growled accusingly, disbelief echoing in his voice.

She just stared at him, neither confirming nor denying his words. She didn't need to, he already knew. He got off the bed, pulled his pants back on and paced the room. Katie sat up on the bed and pulled a fake furry blanket over herself to cover her nakedness. She watched him warily. His face had fallen back into its familiar lines of unreadability.

Finally, he turned to her and snarled, "Why?"

The single word felt like a bullet. Katie almost wished it was. She'd been waiting for this moment for years, knowing eventually Roman would see her shame. His reaction was so different from what Colin's had been that it was almost laughable. Colin hadn't even noticed for months after they'd started making love and when he had, he'd simply given her the name of a psychologist friend of his and rarely mentioned them after that. For an artist, true pain and passion had always made him uncomfortable.

Katie shrugged, her bright blue eyes never leaving Roman. She didn't trust him not to grab her again or decide to just fuck her anyway and get it over with. He was being extremely unpredictable. Which was saying something for a cat burglar!

"What can I say, I'm a head case," she replied with a shrug.

His head swung toward her and, though his expression didn't change, his eyes blazed with fury. His fist crashed onto the mattress beside her drawing a shriek of fear from her. He wrenched the blanket from her hands away and tossed it onto the floor. When she brought her hands up to fight him he clamped his hand around her wrists so hard she cried out, afraid he might break them. He shoved her backwards onto the bed with her hands against her stomach. He shoved his knee between her legs and shoved them apart once more.

He reached down with his other hand and cupped her pussy, pressing his thumb hard against her clit, drawing a scream from her. He continued to hold her slippery nub as he leaned forward and got in her face. She panted as sensations overwhelmed her.

"You have damaged my woman. *Mi mujer!*" he snarled, his accent thickening as he spoke. "So many things you have done wrong, Katie. But this? This is unforgivable."

He released her, shoving her into the bedding before standing up. He ignored the tears that shone brightly in her beautiful eyes and strode away as they spilled down her cheeks and soaked into the bed.

# CHAPTER TEN

He would kill anything that hurt his Katie. *Anything.* But he could not kill her.

So how the fuck did he deal with a woman intent on doing herself harm? Hell. The extent of the harm she had done herself was incredible. It nauseated him to picture her sitting on her bed, or a toilet seat somewhere with a little mirror, her pale legs stretched wide and a razor blade clutched between her slim fingers. Why the fuck had she done it? It must have been agonizing to feel the blade tearing through such tender skin. He should know, he'd been stabbed enough times in his youth before he became top of the food chain.

Her poor, tiny clitoris. Why had she gone there? Wasn't it enough that she'd scarred up her thighs so bad she could never wear a bathing suit in public again? Did she also want to damage the nerves in her sweet little cunt as well? He wanted to storm down to the lower deck, into the master stateroom and demand answers, but he knew he could not be gentle enough.

He was a thug. The son of a dead cartel legend turned gangbanger turned professional enforcer and right hand to the city's highest standing mafia kingpin. He had no experience in this psychological bullshit. Too fucking bad Katie hadn't taken any of those classes in university. He could use one now to deal with her shit.

Shoving tattooed fingers through his short hair, he paced the deck in frustration. Besides her family, she only socialized with one person that he knew of. And there was no way his boss, Soloman Hart, was going to allow Roman anywhere near his woman to get the answers he needed. Despite their odd friendship, Soloman would tear his heart out if Roman so much as caused Riley to frown in concern over her little friend. If Katie's best friend was off limits, then who the fuck did he talk to?

Then the image of a small, dusky skinned woman flashed through his mind. Allison Le Croix, wife to one of the biggest players up on Canada's West Coast. Jay and Soloman were business partners and wary friends. After Riley's drug-fuelled ordeal, locked up in the trunk of her kidnapper's car, Soloman had sent Roman up to Vancouver to engage Allison's counselling services. Jay had, of course, disapproved, disliking the thought of his wife crossing the border into another man's territory. Her tender heart and soft eyes had won his approval. She'd been escorted stateside by her husband, a dozen of his men and her grouchy, over-protective stepfather.

But she had fixed the haunted look in Riley's eyes. With each of the half dozen visits that she made, Allison managed to get Riley to talk about, not only her horrific experience, but growing up in the home of an autistic mother. Though she was specialized in addictions counselling, Allison Le Croix's gentle presence had a way of drawing people into talking.

*Maybe she should've been a cop,* Roman thought sardonically.

Roman pulled out his phone and connected it to satellite. Checking the time, he decided to call her office at the shelter where she worked on the off chance she'd have a few minutes. She answered on the first ring.

"Roman Valdez here," he grunted.

After a moment of surprise when she realized who was calling her, she answered back, concern lacing her soft tones, "Roman! Hi, how are you doing? Is everything okay with Riley?"

"She's fine. Not calling about her."

She didn't say anything right away while her sharp brain processed what little he was telling her. Roman wasn't exactly a man of many words. He didn't share. He especially didn't like the idea of sharing Katie. It made him want to kill. But he understood that he was out of his element with whatever was happening in her beautiful head. He needed help and this woman could give it to him.

"What can I do for you, Roman?" Allison asked quietly. He could hear a chair creak and then a door close. She probably closed the door to her office, giving their conversation more privacy. He knew from his brief meeting with her at the shelter that, unless she was with a client, she preferred to have her door open so the shelter residents felt free to wander in whenever they wanted. He wondered how Jay Le Croix handled the constant stream of junkies spending time with his wife. Even with several guards, Roman would still hate the thought of having his woman exposed to such an unpredictable environment.

Roman closed his eyes, his big body stiff where he sat on the deck bench, his shoulders hunched over his knees. He forced himself to speak, though it was like dragging nails from his throat. "My friend hurt herself," he grunted.

"Does she need a hospital?" Allison asked immediately, her voice alert to a possible emergency situation.

"Nothing like that," Roman said, trying to keep the irritation out of his voice. How the fuck did he make this woman understand what he needed from her without giving more than he wanted? He gritted his teeth and started speaking. "The wounds are old. On her thighs. She cut the shit out of herself with a razor blade. Judging from the scars, she's done it different times over the years. Probably a lot. She even... she even cut her... fuck..."

He couldn't say it. Couldn't tell the counsellor that Katie had cut her pussy too. It was too private. He fisted his hand and pressed it into the side of his head, wanting to beat the image of her pain out of his head. He dropped his face into his open hand and waited for her to speak, to tell him how to fix Katie.

Allison sighed. "Self-harm," she said softly.

"Obviously she fucking hurt herself. I figured that much out. I need to know how to fix it," he snarled into the phone.

"I mean," she said patiently, as though she weren't talking to an extremely dangerous man that could go off at any moment, "that the phenomenon you are describing is called self-harm. It's a unique and heartbreaking disorder, Roman. I'm very sorry that your friend has gone through this."

His chest ached, both in pain and in hope. He *knew* he was talking to the right person. Maybe she could do something, tell him how to fix Katerina so they could get on with their lives. He was desperate. He'd never imagined this. He thought he would get rid of Katie's problem, bring her on the boat he got for her, a yacht he knew she would like and then they could finally be together. He wasn't naive or stupid. He knew there would be issues. That she would probably fight him. But he'd been counting on their insane chemistry to help overcome her resistance. He hadn't counted on her fucked up head being the problem to their happily ever after.

"I specialize in drug addictions. Although I've worked with people in this area, I'm not an expert by any means. I'm not a psychologist, Roman, I don't know if I'm the right person to advise you..." Allison was saying, her voice hesitant.

He could feel frustration welling up inside. He wanted to punch a wall and set about intimidating the small First Nations woman, but he knew better. First of all, he needed her help, and secondly, it wouldn't be good for his health to bully a woman as connected as this one. He took a breath and reminded himself that he would do anything for Katie, including cultivating the same patience he had learned over his years of watching her and waiting for her to grow up.

"I trust you, Allison," Roman said as calmly as he could. "You helped Riley. I know you can help my girl too. I just need to understand why she'd do this to herself."

She didn't say anything so he continued. "Known Katie since she was thirteen. It kills me that she's been doing this to her own flesh and I never fucking knew, was never around to stop her. Please, Allison, help us."

It must have been the plea that softened her. Roman didn't ask for anything. He took what he wanted and if he couldn't get it the first time, he killed whatever stood in his way and took it anyway.

"Alright," she said softly. "I'll tell you what I know."

"Thank you," he said gruffly.

He could hear her settle back in her chair as though getting comfortable. "I've worked with a few people that have had concurrent addictions and self-harm issues. The two do often go hand-in-hand. I'm not sure if your friend has any addictions, but it's something to consider. The most common types of self-harm are cutting, burning and scratching and it often starts in the early teens. It can begin with something as awful as a rotten childhood or home, or perhaps a traumatic event. The common myth is that it's a cry for help or an atten-tion-grabbing stunt, but of course, that's definitely not the case. Many youths that self-harm are desperate to hide their activities and will harm in places on their bodies where other people can't see."

Roman's head spun with every word she spoke. He felt

nauseous, like he was being punched in the stomach over and over. Words never had this effect on him because he didn't care about people. Except for Katie, he stopped caring the day Dexter Pullman had died in his arms. Now, he was forced to feel the pain of words and sentences as the little counsellor forced him to see life through Katie's reality.

"Some self-harmers need the release, while others do it as a way of feeling something other than numbness. Those are the ones that are often connected to a traumatic event or were harmed as children and have trouble accepting physical contact. They crave the adrenaline associated with the pain. Sometimes, as they grow into adulthood and mature, the physical self-harm can mature and morph into other forms of self-harm, such as placing themselves in extreme or dangerous situations, becoming addicted to psychoactive substances..."

"Accepting blackmail as a form of penance," Roman growled, beginning to understand what was going through Katie's mind as she forced herself to go back to her ex-husband's apartment month after month.

"I suppose so, yes," Allison said, slightly taken aback.

"What else?" Roman demanded.

Allison sighed softly. "People who self-harm are extremely vulnerable, Roman. They usually have very poor self-esteem. They don't think they're worthy of any kind of love or affection. They blame themselves for everything. You have to be careful with your friend. Treat her gently."

Roman nearly snarled into the phone for her to mind her own damn business how he treated Katie, but he still needed her to answer one more question. "What do I do?"

Allison had clearly been preparing herself for that question, because she answered quickly. "She needs treatment, Roman. Self-harmers aren't usually suicidal, but they can accidentally take things too far and hurt themselves lethally.

Someone should assess her situation. Will you bring her to me so I can talk to her?"

"No," he snarled. No fucking way was he letting Katie off the boat. She was incredibly talented at disappearing. He could track her, of course, but it would take time and, after Allison's words, he wasn't taking the risk that Katie might hurt herself while out of his sight.

She sighed, clearly expecting his answer. "The underlying issue that's triggering her to self-harm needs to be identified. Then she needs to learn how to manage her triggers and find new ways to cope with the stresses. If she thinks she feels numb, then she needs to learn how to feel emotions in a healthier way. Then she'll need to learn how to regulate her emotions and boost her self-image to a healthy level. Depending on her age, she may have already dealt with some of these issues. How much have the two of you talked about this, Roman? Once someone that self-harms reaches adulthood, they usually become pretty good at understanding their own condition."

Roman grunted in response, absorbing her words. It was probably a good thing he'd read all of Katie's textbooks and done so much reading on the internet while stalking her or he wouldn't't've understood half of what the woman was saying to him. He began to form a few ideas on how to handle Katie, lost in her own head. He was pretty certain Allison Le Croix would be horrified if she knew what he was thinking, but then, he wasn't a typical guy and Katie wasn't a typical girl.

"I hope your friend will be okay, Roman," Allison said, sincerity strong in her soft voice. This was why he called her even though he hated the idea of anyone getting in his business. He knew he could trust her. Knew she wouldn't even mention the conversation to her mobbed up, over-protective husband.

"Thanks, Allison. I'll call if she needs anything."

"Please do that," she replied sincerely. "And if you change

your mind about bringing her to see me, I'll make room in my schedule any time you want."

He hung up.

Roman sat on the bench holding the phone between his legs, staring unseeingly. The sun blazed down on his bronze back, heating up the old, faded skull and crossbones tattoo emblazoned there. He knew what he had to do. It wasn't what he imagined was going to happen when he killed Katie's husband and brought her on board the yacht, rescuing her from a year of slavery.

Allison's words played in his head. He understood.

Katie needed pain, *craved* pain, to feel.

Roman could make her feel.

He would break her apart until she felt nothing but him. Then he would put her back together, binding her to him so tight she would never think of hurting herself again. He stood and crossed the deck toward the stairs. Starting now she would feel only the pain he chose to give her.

# CHAPTER ELEVEN

"What the fuck are you doing?"

Katie jumped and dropped the shard of broken glass she was holding. It fell to the washroom floor and broke apart into several more pieces. She stared up at the towering mass of boiling anger and rolled her eyes. Did he have other modes besides brooding and angry? Because she had yet to see them. She was just about to open her mouth and tell him she was in the process of cleaning up the vase he had so inconsiderately broken when he reached down and hauled her ungently away from the mess. She squeaked and clutched his biceps as he swung her out of the washroom and back into the bedroom. The skirt of the long white summer dress she'd put on to cover herself swished around them.

As soon as his hands fell away from her, she jumped back, putting some distance between them. Unfortunately, she chose the side of the bed with the closet instead of the door leading topside, meaning her only escape from him was into a walk-in closet. Not that the top deck was much better, unless she intended to swim out into open sea to get away from him. She wasn't that desperate yet. She watched him warily. He watched her… broodingly.

"Stay the fuck away from sharps," he snarled, his eyes hard on her face, arms crossed over his big chest.

She sighed and tried hard to control the eye roll she felt coming on. She *really* didn't want to have to talk about this, but apparently Roman didn't intend to give her a knife to butter her bread with until she explained a few things to him. So, gritting her teeth, she said, "Can we talk about… what you saw on my legs? I think I need to clear a few things up with you."

He raised an eyebrow and arrogantly gestured for her to proceed.

She pressed her lips together and suppressed a glare, telling herself she needed to work with him instead of against him if she were to negotiate her way off the yacht. She closed her eyes for a moment and forced herself to speak of something she hadn't allowed herself to dwell on in years. "As you saw, I used to cut myself, Roman. I haven't done it in years though. After Dex… it was a release… a… a way to make myself feel again. Back then, I was so numb. I started cutting because it made me feel alive when nothing else could."

She lifted her eyes to Roman's, begging him to understand. His gaze remained unmoving. She couldn't divine his thoughts. But that was Roman. No one ever knew what was going on in his head. It was a violent cauldron of death, except for her. It always came back to her. Now here she was, finally within his grasp. And god what a disappointment she must be to him!

"You should have come to me, I would have given you what you needed," he finally said.

She gave him a tiny smile and shook her head. "No one could give me what I needed, Roman. The only thing that helped was blood on my hands and the bite of the knife as it sank into flesh. The feel of adrenaline rushing through my body." Her eyes held his as she whispered, "Same as you."

His sudden roar startled her so much that she jumped

back toward the closet and actually contemplated locking herself inside. He paced the end of the bed, his body tense. "Not like me," he snarled. "I didn't cut on myself, baby. I killed the people that hurt Dexter, and others yeah, but I didn't need to slice up my own skin to feel good."

Tears sparked in her eyes. He knew the truth about her and it clearly disgusted him. She lifted her chin and said softly, "Yeah, well, right or wrong, that's what I did and I can't take it back. And I *told* you, I haven't done it in years. I don't cut myself anymore. You can trust me not to hurt myself now, okay? I was just cleaning up the vase we broke earlier."

His head swung toward her, his dark eyes pinning her to the spot, the heat of accusation slicing through in a way the blades she had used on herself never had. She gasped, pressing her fingers against her sides. He had a way of standing eerily still, like a snake about to strike its prey that made her feel small and vulnerable whenever she was in his presence.

"Maybe you don't cut on yourself anymore, Katie, but you sure as fuck aren't done hurting yourself, are you, little girl?" he asked softly, his words cutting through her.

Her face drained of any colour it had before their conversation started. "I-I don't know what you mean," she whispered, tilting her chin up as though daring him to keep talking. Of course, he didn't stop.

Stalking a few feet closer, he continued. "No?" He growled, his thick, dark brows drawing down. "I think you take any chance you get to punish yourself," he growled, anger seething just below the surface of his calm. She didn't understand how others saw Roman as some ice-cold killer when she got the boiling volcano of heated man. "You left the comfort of your home when you barely turned eighteen. You left the city of your birth shortly after and went to a university away from the people you love. You travel the world alone. You married a man you hated and let him treat you like dirt, even after the divorce. Your life is nothing but suffering and pain and you keep it that way because it's the only way you can feel."

She wanted to scream at him and deny his words. She wanted to hit him until he went away and left her to her misery. She didn't understand how he saw her, but somehow, he did. She opened her mouth to tell him to go away and leave her alone, but the only thing to emerge was a broken sob. Her knees buckled and she sank to the floor. He didn't catch her, allowing her to collapse. She wondered if she was too disgusting now for him to bother with.

He crouched next to her, still towering over her. She slid her arms around her middle, hugging herself, suddenly feeling cold and alone in a way she hadn't felt since her divorce. She longed for her family and her best friend, Riley. He slid his large pointer finger, the one with Dexter's name, across her forehead, sweeping her hair to the side and tucking it behind her ear.

He leaned over her and said, "I'm here now. I will be your penance and your pain, Katerina. Until you can feel only me."

She shivered violently at his words, her shoulder brushing against his chest. She turned to look at him, to beg him once more to let her go, blue eyes clashing with obsidian. Instead of the usual blank hardness, she saw… *salvation*.

# CHAPTER TWELVE

Forty-five minutes later, a pale and still shaken Katie made her way topside. After delivering his frightening statement, Roman had lifted her onto the bed, told her he was going to make them something to eat for lunch and left her alone in the cabin to pull herself together as best she could. It had taken a while. Katie had alternated between uncontrollable shaking, angry tears, pacing and, of course, breaking into the safe in the closet. Breaking into places was both a habit and a pleasurable pastime.

Of her hometown connections, only Riley knew what Katie was capable of and even her gorgeous car thief, chop shop owning bestie had no idea the extent of Katie's proclivities. As Katie had stared into the contents of the safe, a plan beginning to form, she was quite glad Roman had no idea of the extent of her abilities or he might have hidden these a little better. Of course, she couldn't use them until she got her hands on his phone and figured out his passcode. She relocked the safe and pushed the stack of clothes back in front of it, knowing he'd purposely tried hiding it from her. Like she didn't know all high-end yachts had safes in the closet.

Her darling benefactor had a yacht even bigger than this one and it had a safe in *every* closet.

Katie approached the breakfast table on the lower deck with caution, her eyes widening at the massive spread of bagels, smoked salmon, cream cheese, fruit, vegetables, and assorted breads and cheeses. She couldn't hold back a laugh of surprise and delight when her eyes fell on a bowl of freshly made popcorn, her absolute favourite treat. How well Roman knew her one weakness. She eagerly popped a handful of popcorn into her mouth, then reached for a fresh strawberry. Maybe a weird combination, but she loved them both and she was starved. She closed her eyes as she sank her teeth into the perfectly ripe berry. She hadn't realized how hungry she was until that exact moment. When her eyes slid back open, they encountered the dark, hungry gaze of her captor.

"Was wondering if you were going to show." His deep voice wrapped all around her as he rounded the table and held a chair out for her.

She sat and allowed him to push the chair in. She waited for him to take his own seat, putting distance between them before giving him a snarky reply. "I don't intend to starve myself, Roman. I told you, I'm not into self-harm anymore."

He stiffened, his cold, dark eyes on her face, taking in every part of her like a man that had been starved for years. And, as far as he was concerned, he had been forced to go without his main sustenance for almost two decades.

"You know about self-harm?" he asked.

She sighed, reached across the table and filled her plate with all of the delicious offerings he had painstakingly prepared for her. Her heart weakened a little more. It was all her favourite foods. She happened to know for a fact that he *hated* lox and capers, two items she piled on her plate with abandon. He really must be some kind of talented stalker, because her parents didn't eat this kind of stuff either. She only ever ate it alone in restaurants when she went out.

She spoke almost absently, more intent on the food in front of her, when she replied to his question. "Just because I mutilated myself doesn't make me stupid," she said, taking a huge bite of bagel with salmon, cream cheese and capers. "Of course, I googled my compulsive need to cut the shit out of myself."

She nearly choked on her food when his fist hit the table so hard the platters jumped. She stared at him, hardly daring to move. She realized right away that it was the way she spoke about herself he took exception to. Apparently, words like 'mutilation' and 'cut the shit out of' didn't sit well with her stalker/wannabe boyfriend.

Before he could fly off the handle, she quickly changed the subject. "So… umm… was that a hot tub I saw over there? So amazing that they can put hot tubs on yachts these days, you know? Something about being able to watch the cool waters of the Pacific Ocean from the comfort of a hot tub."

*Really nice, Katie. Now it sounds like you're inviting the angry, kidnapping mobster to take a dip in the hot tub with you.*

His penetrating gaze never left hers, though the anger cooled into a more speculative look. She wondered if he was picturing them in the hot tub together. The coil of tension in her chest began to ease until he spoke.

"Why did you marry him, Katie? Fuck, almost anyone would have been better. How the fuck did you choose such a spineless piece of shit…," he trailed off as if the memory of Colin wasn't even worthy of further words.

She gasped, her fork clattering to the plate. Why couldn't he just have a normal conversation, like normal people? Like about the weather, or food, or the freaking hot tub. She knew he wasn't going to let her get away without answering his question. She studied her plate for a few seconds and decided to answer him as honestly as she could.

"He wasn't always a horrible jerk, you know," she said a little defensively. She'd had this conversation before. Her mom had never liked Colin or the way Katie had rushed into the marriage without a proper wedding. As always, Katie's dad had been largely absent and without an opinion. Not that her dad didn't care, because he did. He just didn't often engage and was usually busy running errands for the mob.

Roman leaned back in his chair and crossed his arms over his chest. She tried not to notice the way his arms strained against the fabric of his shirt. She didn't need those kinds of thoughts right now. She needed to be working on how to get the phone she knew was tucked in his back pocket.

"Tell me," he demanded.

She sighed. What could it hurt. He already knew one of her darkest secrets.

"I met Colin at a gallery show in Seattle four years ago. I was shopping for a client." She had been casing the gallery for a specific painting for a client with an eye for eclectic works as well as the higher end stuff. It turned out to be one of the few times she'd just outright purchased a painting and turned it over to the client for a profit. A novelty, what with her ability to get hard-to-find items. "It turned out Colin was one of the artists showing his work in the show. He was impressed by my artistic knowledge and asked me out for a drink after the show. We had a lot to talk about, having art in common. After our drink, he invited me to see his studio the next day."

Roman's knuckles tightened against his biceps. She didn't really want to keep talking, afraid he was going to explode again, but he said, "Continue."

"Th-there's not really much to tell," Katie said, eyeing Roman nervously. She didn't understand why he wanted to rehash her history with another man. He clearly didn't enjoy hearing it, and her relationship was over now. So very, very over. He'd made sure of that.

"You were obviously impressed enough to keep seeing him," Roman gritted out. "What kept you going back?"

Okay, apparently they really were going to talk about her deceased ex-husband. Katie pushed her plate aside, her appetite now completely gone. She clasped her hands in her lap and shrugged. "He was a decent artist and he... he seemed to genuinely like me. He asked me to come see him, so I tried to make it into Seattle when I could, in between jobs for my clients."

It had been a hard several months. Colin had demanded so much of her time that she hadn't been able to see much of her family or friends further down the coast. When she tried to explain to him that she needed more time to herself, he would threaten to break it off with her. As soon as she backed off, he would apologize and beg her to come see him, blaming his artist's temperament for his outburst. She would reluctantly go back to him only to find an apartment filled with flowers and romantic declarations. In hindsight, she now saw his abusive manipulation for what it was. Before the year was up, she found herself maneuvered into a marriage she wasn't sure she wanted.

"We got married in a county clerk's office, just the two of us and a witness," Katie said in a rush, as though making a confession. "My mom was so disappointed, but Colin didn't want a big wedding. He didn't really believe in marriage before me."

"So what happened to convince him otherwise?" Roman asked, an edge of sarcasm to his rough voice.

Katie pleated her fingers nervously in her skirt and then let it go, watching the way the white cotton fabric wrinkled under her relentless grip. So like her. Pure and pretty one moment, damaged and ugly the next. She smoothed the skirt with her hand, pressing the silly thought away. She was always letting her dark thoughts in. She lifted her eyes and caught Roman's shadowed gaze in her own as though he could read what was in her head.

She started speaking before he could demand to know

what else she had been thinking. "C-Colin said he wanted to be tied to me as closely as possible, as close as man and wife. He could be romantic that way… when he wanted."

"Manipulative," Roman grunted.

Katie nodded. She wasn't going to deny it. Her ex-husband had been emotionally abusive. "Yes, he knew exactly what to say to a young woman who had already isolated herself from the people that cared," Katie said, deciding to be completely honest with Roman. "If Colin hadn't been manipulative, I never would have stayed with him, or married him. I may be into self-inflicted pain, but I wasn't that masochistic. Two years married to him was enough to try even the sweetest of saints. If he hadn't instigated our divorce, I would not have been far behind with the papers, no matter how many romantic gestures he tried to pull. Believe me, there's a reason I took so many overseas jobs."

Roman's eyes flashed and then he chuckled. Katie's lips quirked and she stuffed a piece of melon into her mouth.

She nearly choked when his eyes became razor sharp and his words hit her like bullets. "This man, your husband, the only way he would have let you go is if he found something out about you that could have fallen on his head as well. He divorced you and kicked you out to put distance between him and your activities, but he couldn't retract his claws completely. Maybe, like the little bitch he was, he wished to let you go. Maybe he even did for a few months."

Katie knew from her gasp and the flare of her eyes that she was confirming his words, but she was helpless against his verbal investigation. God! He may speak like an uneducated thug, but his brain was razor sharp and currently directed at her. She knew it wouldn't take him long to figure out what she'd been up to over the years. She was almost surprised he hadn't figured it out already. It all boiled down to that conversation on the floor of her tiny kitchen, when she had been eighteen and he twenty-five. When she had begged him for more time. More time to live her life and explore the world out from under his terrifying shadow. He had let her fly.

Yes, he had watched her, but never too close. If he had, then he would have known about the cutting, known about her ex, known about her illegal activities and he would have snatched her up long ago. He would have swooped in and saved her, like the avenging angel she knew him to be.

"He couldn't let you go, could he, Katie?" Roman's deep voice washed over her like a midnight blanket. She shook her head, helpless to look away from him. "He had to keep you close, so he blackmailed you each month. He got the best of both worlds, the *culero* fuck. He got your money. Cash, which he kept hidden so the feds couldn't link him to you if you got yourself in trouble. And he got your gorgeous body, which he couldn't give up. His greed fucked him in the end, Katerina. If he'd actually walked away from *mi mujer* a year ago, as he intended, then maybe I would not have hunted him."

Her breathing went from fast and frightened to nonexistent as his eyes slashed right through her. His lips formed terrifying words that she forced herself to listen to, despite her need to hide in denial. His finger came up to tap his lip and then point at her in promise. "I lie. He was dead from the first moment he touched you. I could have made it quicker though, if he'd been a better man."

A whimper made its way up her throat and passed through her lips as they stared at each other. She suddenly felt everything sharply. That happened to her sometimes. She usually walked through life in a numb haze, looking for her next adrenaline fix. Except occasionally the numbness would lift and the bright, shiny world would suddenly rush at her. She could feel the boat rocking gently underneath her body, hear the waves slapping against the sides and feel the heat of the sun beating on her head and skin. She focused hard on these things rather than think about how hard her heart beat for the man sitting across from her.

"Are you afraid of me?" he asked, moving his large frame to lean forward in his seat.

"I should be," Katie whispered. "You kill people. You k-killed Colin."

His eyes sharpened and she knew he was pleased with her answer. "But you aren't."

She shook her head.

He stood abruptly, pushing his chair away from the table. He stalked toward her, each step felt like a step closer to her doom. She knew what he wanted. It was a miracle he'd waited this long. And he only waited because he'd been shocked by the scars on her legs. Apparently, he was over that shock now.

He stopped next to her and, taking her chair, pulled it away from the table with her still in it. "Stand up."

She looked helplessly up at him and whispered, "What are you going to do to me?"

He held out his hand and said, "I'm going to hurt you, Katie. And you're going to thank me for the pain I inflict on your body and soul. You belong to me, you always have and I take care of what is mine."

With trembling fingers, she placed her hand in his and allowed him to pull her out of the chair.

# CHAPTER THIRTEEN

*I can't do this*, Katie thought wildly as Roman tugged her forward while he walked backward, their feet whispering against the deck. His dark eyes held her captive. As if sensing her mood, his long fingers slipped from her hands to encircle her delicate wrists, holding her more firmly.

"Roman, I don't need the pain anymore," she tried pleading with him, fearful of his intentions. "I haven't for a long time."

His lips twisted in a grim smile. She shuddered under the shadow of that look. It didn't promise good things for her. They continued to move across the deck together, then down a set of short steps. She followed him, helpless against his extremely dominant personality and sheer strength. They moved as though in some kind of twisted dance. He led while she followed, their eyes locked, their bodies in fluid motion.

He stopped. She stepped into him before she realized he was done moving. She would have moved away from him, but he brought his arms up, trapping her loosely against him. "You need the rush like you need to breath, *hermosa*."

"Okay, yes," she admitted breathlessly, "but I get my rush

in other ways now. I don't hurt myself any longer. I got over that."

He pulled her against his chest, his eyes locked on hers, drawing her in like the big, bad wolf. "Maybe I didn't, baby. Maybe I need to punish you for all those years of putting *mi mujer* at risk, of marking her up like you had any kind of fucking right to scar such perfection."

His voice rose with each word until he was nearly shouting toward the end. Katie flinched in his arms, but she raised her chin and glared up at the tall man that held her. She crossed her arms and rubbed at the sudden chill in her bare arms where her sleeveless sun dress didn't cover.

"That makes no sense at all, Roman," she snapped up at him. "You intend to… what? Punish me and make me feel pain for hurting myself? Isn't that a little ass backwards?"

He froze, his eyes flickering in remembrance for just a second. "Dexter used to say that."

"I know," she murmured. "All of us Pullmans say it."

He heaved a sigh and tightened his arms around her, drawing her against his broad chest. He hugged her tightly for a long time. She relaxed into the feeling, savouring the sensation of Roman just holding her. She drew his warmth and strength into her body and breathed deeply, taking in his scent. He smelled like hard male. A little like masculine deodorant, sweat and something indefinable but utterly mouth-watering.

"You still need the pain I can give you, Katie," he murmured against the top of her head. "Can see the numbness in your eyes. The need for an adrenaline spike. You get it from somewhere else these days. And unless you want to tell me where you're getting it and let me judge the safety of it, you'll be getting what you need from me."

Katie stiffened in his arms. How *dare* he ruin her perfectly wonderful hug with such arrogance! She wasn't going to be able to tell him where she was getting her fix from because that would lead to a whole barrage of questions that she wasn't ready to answer. And he most certainly wasn't going to deem her time spent leaping around the tops of tall buildings safe.

So, she did something she didn't usually do. She got mad and swore, struggling in his arms in a futile attempt to dislodge his iron hold. "You know what, Roman? Fuck you, you don't get to tell me what to do!"

He chuckled and continued to hold her tight. "Actually, sweetheart, that's exactly that I am doing. Right now, I'm your judge, jury and executioner."

She froze in his arms, her eyes wide with apprehension. She hadn't considered that possibility. Her voice cracked as she forced herself to ask, "Are you going to kill me too, Roman?"

He took her by to shoulders and forced her back so quickly she stumbled, he looked her in the eyes, his filled with so much anger and disgust she knew right away that she'd said the wrong thing.

"Why the fuck would you say that, Katerina?" he thundered down into her face.

She flinched, blinking at his vehemence. She'd seen more emotion from him in less than a day together than she'd seen in seventeen years of knowing him. "Be-because you said about being my ex… executioner," she stammered. "And you kill people. Roman, you killed Colin. God, I know I'm a huge pain in your ass, why wouldn't you just get rid of me once and for all."

"Fuck," he growled, taking a hand off her arm to shove it over his head in frustration. "She said you'd have low self esteem, but this is *loca, mujer*."

"Who said that?" Katie snapped. "Who have you been talking to about me?!"

"Never mind," he growled, dropping his other hand from

her arm. "Take your dress off, Katie. Time to get some things straight between us. Only one way to do that."

Katie took a quick step away, eyeing him warily. She clutched at the front of her dress, not wanting to take it off while he was in this mood, but not really knowing how to get out of doing what he wanted. Roman was more than twice her size, leagues more vicious and street smart than she was and adept at pretty much any weapon he could get his hands on. Even if she managed to get hold of something to hit him over the head with, which she was seriously considering at the moment, she was pretty certain all she would do is piss him off and accomplish exactly nothing.

"Sh-shouldn't we put the food away before we do anything else?" she asked in a hopeful voice. "I mean, that's a lot of food you have sitting up there in the sun. What a terrible waste if it was to spoil while we… while we…"

Her face flared bright red and she cursed her fair complexion as her words ground to an embarrassed halt. She studied the deck with renewed interest, noting the pretty grey texture underneath the even prettier sandals she chose to go with the sun dress. They were slip-ons with blue and gold hearts stitched into the strappy material.

"Take the fucking dress off. Now," Roman growled, making Katie nearly jump out of her skin.

*Holy crap! Could he be a little more impatient?*

Her hands flew to the buttons between her breasts and, with a deep breath, she began unbuttoning the white material with agonizing slowness. She could feel his eyes holding her in place, urging her on, but also caressing every inch she revealed. Somehow, he gave her the strength to continue, even though it was him forcing her to get naked. Something she'd never done in front of anyone except Colin. She didn't count what had happened earlier, below deck, because Roman had torn the clothes from her body. This time he was forcing her to bare her own body. This was different, and infinitely harder.

When she'd unbuttoned the dress to her navel, she shrugged the straps off her shoulders and allowed the material to fall down her arms until the top of the dress pooled at her hips. He exhaled sharply. She shivered, partly under the onslaught of his relentless perusal and partly from the shadows where he had pulled her. They were standing in a covered section of the lower deck next to a wide lounge couch with a shaded canopy. This is where the hot tub was located along with a bar and an even lower veranda. The view would have been spectacular except Katie was preoccupied with not choking on her heart, which was currently clawing its way up her throat.

Her hands fell to her hips and she glanced up to finally look at her tormentor. His arms were crossed over his incredible chest, his dark, watchful eyes taking in every move she made like a hunting predator after a frightened rabbit. A tremor trickled down her spine, loosening the dress even more. The breath caught in her chest was becoming so painful she was forced to release it. At the same time, she pushed the material off of her hips and allowed it to fall at her feet.

She watched helplessly as his fists clenched against his biceps. He nodded toward her, indicating that she should remove the bikini she had put back on from their earlier encounter. She bit down hard on her lip to distract herself and reached behind her neck to untie the top before reaching behind her narrow ribcage and releasing the clip that held the top together. It fell away from her pale body to land on top of the abandoned dress. Without bothering to look up, she pulled the bikini bottoms down her thighs quickly and stepped out of both them and the sandals. Like ripping a band-aid off. Maybe not ultra-sexy, but at least she was finished.

She kept her eyes averted and waited for Roman to say or

do something. She waited. And waited. Nothing happened. She started to cover herself with her hands but his voice reached out to lash her harshly from the shadows. "Don't!"

Her eyes jerked up in surprise. She thought maybe he was keeping her in suspense on purpose. Another game or something, but she could tell from the way he held himself that he was practically vibrating with tension. His big body was a mass of seething energy. He was holding himself back and she didn't understand why. The innocent question must have leapt into her eyes, because suddenly he uncoiled his long limbs and stalked toward her. Frozen to the spot, Katie was helpless as his legs ate up the space between them.

He circled around her, his low voice an intense growl as he answered her unspoken question. "Because I will truly hurt you if I touch you the way I want to right now, Katerina. I will take you and I will break you. We both need to see if what I have in mind of you will work, and for that I will have to control myself."

The breath hitched in and out of her lungs as she processed his words. "You... you will?" she whispered. She didn't understand what he meant, but she wasn't brave enough to ask.

"Don't get me wrong, baby." He stood right behind her. She felt every move he made, the whisper of his hands and the sudden heat of his chest against her back as he reached for the hem of his shirt and peeled it off his body. He leaned into her until the front of his jeans barely grazed the curve of her bare ass. He whispered in her ear, "Want to fuck you like I want to take my next breath."

He trailed the blunt tips of his fingers over her waist as he stepped around her body to stand in front of her. He lifted her chin so she was forced to look up at him, showing him every vulnerable flicker that passed through her eyes.

"So, why don't you?" she asked, her words still a whisper on the breeze.

His dark eyes bore into hers as he confessed. "Haven't touched a woman in thirteen years. Not since before you asked me to walk away. Knew I would be back for you eventually. Knew no one else would be good enough to take the place of *mi mujer*, so I didn't bother looking."

Her lips parted in surprise. His thumb moved from her chin to gently rub against her lip. A tear trickled from the corner of her eye, but before it could make its way across her cheek, he captured it, as though telling her he was there now to intercept all of her tears. He lifted the wetness to his lips and licked away the evidence.

"I don't deserve you," she whispered, bringing her hand up in between them to touch his chest. She traced her fingers over the cross and then further, brushing her fingers over the large scrolling outline of her name across his left pectoral for the first time, as if finally admitting it was there. She'd known he had it, but touching it made it real.

He captured her fingers and brought them to his lips before murmuring, "You deserve everything and more, that's why I'll do anything to help you."

They stood that way, locked together in a bubble of their past and present. Finally, Roman asked, "Can you be brave for me?"

She thought about all he had done for her and all he had risked to finally be with her. She knew she couldn't stay with him long, but she could give him this.

She nodded, "Yes, Roman. I'll do whatever you want."

# CHAPTER FOURTEEN

He led her toward the lounge couch and turned her so she was facing the luxurious, olive and black furniture. She was naked and exposed. It was everything she could do not to wrap her arms around herself for a little bit of coverage, but she knew he wouldn't allow it. His mercurial moods since arriving on the yacht might have taken a turn for the better, but she wasn't banking on him allowing her any concessions at this point. She could still feel the anger seething just below the surface.

Her feeling of exposure intensified when he placed a large palm against the middle of her back and and urged her forward against the seat. She glanced over at him with a frown as she bent at the waist. He took her wrist in his other hand and pulled it down, forcing her to lean. With a gasp, she fell forward until her palms were planted on the cushions with her backside facing outward. Facing him.

Being the smart, educated woman she was, Katie picked up on Roman's intentions pretty quickly. She jerked upright, coming into contact with a hard chest. His arms came around her from behind, anchoring her to the spot.

"Roman!" she cried out.

He dropped his head and growled in her ear, "You said you were going to be brave for me, little girl."

"But you're going to spank me, aren't you?" she asked, struggling pathetically in his strong grip.

"Worse," he admitted, his voice hard. "Now be the brave girl you said you would be. Shut up, bend over and take it, Katie. I can promise, after the shit you done to yourself, this'll be a walk in the park. Hopefully you'll even love it."

She shuddered against him, but settled down. After a moment of breathing heavily, she finally nodded and allowed him to bend her back over the sofa couch. He kept his broad hand on the small of her back in case she got any ideas about taking off again. He was leaning against her so she felt his every move when he unbuckled the leather belt and slid it from his hips. She tensed with fear and expectation as she watched him fold it in half from the corner of her eye. Terror set in when he finally stepped away from her, trailing his fingers tenderly down her spine as he left.

"Roman…," she pleaded one last time, hoping maybe he would relent. Give up on this silly idea of his that she somehow needed pain to truly live.

His name barely left her lips when she heard the whistle of leather slicing through air. The crack of the belt hitting her skin met her ears a split second before the pain set in. She barely had time to think, *he was right!*, before the belt landed again, and again… and again. He beat her ass relentlessly, using more strength than she thought Roman would ever be willing to use with his beloved, but far, far less than she knew those huge arms were capable of. As the old feeling of euphoria took hold, flooding her veins with familiar sensations, Katie tipped her head back and revelled in it.

Her screams of pain and ecstasy filled the air around them, getting lost in the emptiness of the open ocean around them. A tiny fraction of her mind reserved enough energy to note how careful Roman was to keep his strokes to her ass and thighs, careful never to hit her above her waist where he could do actual damage. His sexy grunts filled her head, telling her that he was not unaffected by her reddening ass. She had no idea how many times he hit her, she only knew her knees gave out before she was ready.

He stopped beating her, drawing a whimper of protest from her. He bent over her naked, bowed and quivering body. "Done?" he grunted in her ear. A drop of sweat splashed from his brow onto her lip. She eagerly licked the saltiness up.

"More!" she panted turning dilated eyes up to him.

He stared down at her for an undecided moment as if trying to work out what to do. Finally, he reached down and lifted her up by the armpits. He pushed her backwards until she toppled onto the couch behind her. She hissed and cried out, rolling onto her side when her abused ass touched the cushion. He brought a hand down onto her stomach, stopping her and pushed her further back until she was laying with her back against the cushions. He pushed her legs up until her knees were bent up against her shoulders. She tried to close them, but he forced them open, exposing her completely to both his touch and gaze.

A shudder of expectation, fear and arousal rippled through her. Her ass was on fire where it touched the couch cushion. Roman stood leaning forward between her legs, watching her. Slowly, his eyes dropped to the flesh between her legs. For the first time in her life she didn't feel self-conscious about the scars. She knew from the crazed, hungry look in his eyes that he was looking at *her*, not the marks.

He brushed his knuckle gently across her folds. Katie moaned and lifted her hips slightly to meet his touch. "You're soaked," he groaned, awe lacing his voice as if he couldn't believe it.

"Only for you," she whispered.

His body tightened over hers. She saw him warring with himself as need shuddered through his big body. She realized now why he was so fierce around her, so unpredictable and combustible. He had over a decade of pent up sexual frustration and it was all for her.

"Please, Roman," she begged him breathlessly, "hurt me again!"

He nodded, his lips pressing into a grim line. She knew he was fighting with himself. He hated the idea of hurting her. Didn't understand her need for the pain. He was probably now struggling with his reaction to her pain. He loved it and it was killing him. He wanted to revel in the euphoria she was experiencing, but he couldn't reconcile himself with how she was getting there. She didn't care. She wanted to seize this newfound high with both hands and ride it out while she could.

"Eyes on me and don't fucking move them, baby," he growled.

She nodded helplessly, her eyes glued to him as he backed up and towered over her. Without his belt, his jeans hung a little lower on his hips. She swallowed in trepidation. She hadn't been able to see him before as he stood behind her. Now she could see every part of the terrifying spectre of an incredibly ripped, tattooed, intensely angry man standing over her, his huge arm raised with a belt. A hoarse whimper of fear escaped her throat just as he brought the belt down on the fleshy part of her thigh.

A scream ripped from her lips and she almost jerked her eyes away from him before she remembered his order. Panting and biting down on her lip she submitted to the first glorious wave of rapture as it swept through her. He alternated between her thighs, striking up and down the flesh, raising painful welts in his wake while she watched his bicep bunch and release with glowing eyes. Eventually, when she couldn't possibly get any wetter, when there wasn't a single inch of skin left on her thighs to strike, he dropped the belt.

As the echo of her last scream died away on the warm

breeze, he dropped to his knees in front of her as though in prayer. His eyes met hers. She gasped, some of her happy euphoria dying away. He was livid. She had made him do something, find something out about her and, in the process, find out something about himself he didn't want to know. She loved pain. And he loved giving it to her. She started to close her legs and move back up the couch, a little afraid of this unpredictable man's intentions. She was correct to fear.

"Do not move away from me," he growled, slapping his hands down on her reddened thighs and tearing a scream of true agony from her throat.

He pulled her forward to the edge of the couch until her pussy was flush with his chest. He shoved her legs wide, moving his hands up to her knees so he wasn't hurting her anymore. She stared up at him, fear and arousal shining bright as she clutched at the couch cushions.

"You belong to me, Katerina," he growled. "I will always give you the things that you need. Even if I hate them. Now we do what I want."

"Roman…," she moaned, reaching out a hand in supplication.

He gripped her wrist and pushed his face into her dripping pussy, shoving his nose into her and inhaling, taking her scent into his body and memorizing her. He did this for a long moment, ignoring the tensing of her body underneath him. He began licking her from bottom to top in long strokes, lapping up as much of her as he could. She felt the desperation in him to just take from her everything he could get. There was no particular method to what he was doing. He just took and took from her, quickly driving her insane as he refused to find a rhythm and give her what she needed to come. One moment he would shove his tongue deep into her vaginal passage, fucking her with it, and next he would explore the folds of her labia before swirling it up to her clitoris and then back again.

Her back bowed against the couch as she keened and wiggled against him. He brought a hand down on her stomach, refusing to let her up or even move to a more comfortable position. He finally had her where he wanted her and he wasn't letting her go anywhere.

"Fuck, Katie," he moaned against her, shoving his nose against her again and breathing deep. "You taste like fucking heaven."

"Roman!" she yelled. "Need to come!"

His head came up sharply and he stared at her, his eyes sharp and possessive on her face. They glowed obsidian as they pierced through to the heart of her. "Want you to come, baby. Tell me what you need, beautiful girl," he growled.

She squirmed in his fierce grip, revelling in the way his hands nearly engulfed her narrow hips and moaned. "Finger inside. Put your tongue on my clit," she panted and slid a finger down her belly pressing it against her slippery nub. She flicked it against the bundle of nerves and watched his eyes follow the movement, memorizing the way she liked it best.

He slid one big hand under her ass, dragging his thumb across her tiny puckered hole as he brought it up, making her jump and moan with need. He sank one long, thick finger into her soaked pussy while she watched and moaned low in her throat. His finger felt like heaven and hell all at once. It was already a tight fit, telling her they were going to have a hell of a time getting more inside her. She bit her lip and wiggled her hips, drawing groans from both of them.

He leaned forward and, using his other hand to gently move her fingers from her clit, replaced them with his tongue.

She bucked against his mouth as he gave her *exactly* what she needed. *Oh, my fucking god, this man is a quick learner!* she mentally screamed, lifting her hips into his seeking mouth and bringing her fingers down on his head to scratch frantically as he drove her rapidly and relentlessly toward the most intense orgasm she'd ever experienced. The first orgasm she'd ever had that she hadn't given to herself. He twisted and pumped his finger inside her while flicking his tongue against her clit as she arched into his mouth. When he added a second finger, shoving them deep inside her until they hurt so good, she screamed and came in a rush of fluid.

Just as she collapsed back against the cushions of the couch, he surged up against her, shoving her knees back once more until they were wide open and nearly back to her shoulders. Her arms fell open and clutched at the cushions. She watched helplessly as he unbuttoned and unzipped his jeans, shoved them down his hips and kicked them away. He turned back to her, his face a canvas of intense energy such as she'd never seen before. So much lust, possession and violent love resided there that it nearly healed the things inside her that she thought were broken forever.

He crouched over top of her, reaching for her naked body and pulling her up into the cradle of his chest. His hips shoved her thighs ever further apart, forcing her to feel every inch of his massive body against her much narrower frame. She whimpered in fear and anticipation, shivering against him. He dipped his head, taking her lips in a surprisingly tender kiss.

"I got you, Katerina. Will always catch you, baby," he mumbled against her before finally released her.

Tears trickled from the corners of her eyes and she held him tightly against her. She pressed her lips against the muscle of his shoulder, savouring his scent and flicking her tongue to take his taste into her. She wanted to remember every part of him. She would disappear from his life. If this is all she could take with her, she was going to be selfish and take whatever she could.

He shifted against her, reaching down between their bodies to position himself against her. Though she knew it would hurt, she opened up to him. Roman showed her that he would only hurt her in a good way. He took her in one stroke. Though she was tight, her body was ready to accept him. She cried out and sank her nails into his shoulders, arching her neck and squeezing her eyes shut. He was wide and he was long, he bottomed out deep inside her.

He cupped the back of her head, held her close and whispered to her in Spanish until the tension in her body gradually uncoiled and she smoothed her hands down his back.

"So fucking good, Katie. I could live here forever," he groaned against her, pressing her head to his throat.

She smiled and licked his Adam's apple, laughing throatily when she felt his cock pulse inside of her. "But I can't come again unless you start moving," she whispered innocently.

Her naughty words unleashed the beast. He lifted his massive shoulders over top of her and looked down at her, his eyes fiercely possessive, devouring every inch of her face as he began moving within her. The delicious hurt began to build immediately and she knew, deep down he had somehow found the key to her lock. He found the way to make her feel alive again without making her feel like a burned-out shell. She flexed her fingers against him as though she would never let him go, even though she had no choice. She lifted her legs and wrapped them around him as much as she could, holding him tight.

"Not going to last long," he grunted apologetically.

She smiled gently. Of course not. He hadn't been with a woman in a decade. She reached down between their bodies, still savouring the delicious ache of his giant cock plowing through her, and pinched her sensitive clit, giving herself that tiny bite of pain she needed.

"*Mierda, mi mujer,*" he mumbled, watching her movements with awe.

"Now!" she said breathlessly, eyes glazing over with

passion. She could feel his cock growing within her and knew he was close to coming.

They orgasmed together, flying over the edge in each other's arms, eyes locked together. Hot semen exploded deep within her, bathing her soaked pussy and reminding her that they hadn't used a condom. She thought about saying something, but didn't want to ruin the moment. She wasn't sure if it had been purposeful or not. Roman was about as possessive as they came. She was on birth control and she believed that he hadn't been with anyone in a long time. And though she'd only ever been with Colin, that didn't mean that her ex-douche bag had been faithful. She would talk to Roman about it later. She didn't want him putting himself at risk again. Until she found a way off the boat, they would have to use condoms.

For now, she was just going to enjoy the moment. She could feel the rush of love envelope them like a cocoon. Try as she might, though, instead of hope, Katie felt despair. She closed her eyes and held him tighter.

# CHAPTER FIFTEEN

"When did you find out that Dexter was gay?" Katie asked Roman softly.

She was laying on the bed, curled in his arms, perfectly at ease with Roman Valdez for the first time in her life. After their explosively passionate encounter up on the deck, he carried her down to their stateroom. He tenderly examined the belt wounds he had inflicted, though she assured him they didn't hurt, and then rinsed them both off in the shower. After drying, he tucked her into the large bed, brought her a glass of ice water, then crawled naked into the bed and pulled her against his chest where he held her willingly captive.

His arms tightened around her. She was half afraid the big tough guy would refuse to answer her question. The only other person that had acknowledged Dexter's sexuality was her other brother, Wendell, and they'd only ever discussed it after Dexter's death. Dexter never came out. He wasn't given the chance.

"Guess I always knew." Roman's voice rumbled against her head.

His answer surprised her. Dexter had been a sweet guy,

but was not particularly open and trusting except with the people he was closest to. How had Roman figured out that Dexter was gay when they inhabited such brutal circles where he would have been murdered by their own people if someone had found out? Gangs were not forgiving about such things.

"Is that why you went out of your way to protect him?" she whispered.

He laughed harshly. "I'm not that guy, Katie. Never was," Roman said linking his fingers with hers on the quilt and lifting their hands together. He traced his thumb over the blue veins on the back of her hand. "Liked your brother. Didn't care where he got his rocks off. He didn't care about me either... so long as I didn't touch little sister until she grew up."

Katie smiled a little and tried to picture that conversation. All three Pullman children had taken after their pale blond mother. While Wendell was short and stocky like their father, both Katie and Dexter were tall and willowy. The combination looked good on Katie. On Dexter... it had looked a little ungainly, but also endearing. When he was annoyed, happy, embarrassed or anything really, his face tended to turn tomato red and the entire room would know what he was thinking. She could just picture him telling Roman, who was twice his size, to stay away from his little sister until she was mature enough to handle a relationship. The thought sparked tears in her eyes.

"Well... no matter what your motives were," she said huskily, "thank you for watching out for my brother. He deserved a friend like you."

He rolled her until she was laying underneath him. He cupped her face, sliding his fingers into her hair and holding her still. Her chest ached at the look he gave her. She tried hard to stay in the moment, but her mind kept drifting to the contents of the safe. She wished desperately they could live in their own world, just the two of them, wrapped up in themselves with no interference and no other commitments.

"I don't deserve nothing, *hermosa,* but I'll take everything from you," he growled, deliberately sounding street. He tapped his fingers against the side of her head. "I know you think of running. I can see your brain thinking, thinking. You make plans to…" he made a sound of air escaping with his teeth and lips, "go from me. I won't allow this, Katerina. You are out here on this yacht, on the open ocean. You can't go anywhere. We stay here until I am convinced that you will never leave me."

Her heart skipped a beat and her entire focus returned to him as he lifted himself and tugged the quilt from her body. She gasped as he pressed his naked body along hers, careful to keep his weight from crushing her. Though his words sounded threatening, she also heard the desperation and romance as well.

She wrapped her arms around his huge shoulders and tugged until he was completely settled against her. She wanted to feel him crush her. Her belly fluttered in response when she felt his already hard cock press against her leg. Her pussy ached deliciously where he'd plowed into her earlier. She pressed her lips against the side of his neck and trailed her tongue up to his ear. Whispering, she said, "Then I'll just have to convince you to take me to dry land, won't I?"

He turned his head quickly, capturing her lips in a quick, hard kiss before pulling back to growl, "Don't know how you're going to manage that, *mujer.* Already know you're a sneaky little bitch."

She laughed and slapped him on the shoulder. Then she opened her long legs wide and wrapped them around his waist as far as they would go. She moaned in his ear at the feeling of his huge cock rubbing deliciously against her already wet core. Biting her lip, she arched her head back against the pillows and squirmed in his arms, using his body to build friction against hers.

She gripped his broad, tattooed shoulders tighter, widened her legs and climbed a little higher. In this position, she was able to gyrate against him and rub her clitoris against the hair of his muscular belly where it pressed delightfully against her.

"Sex!" she exclaimed breathlessly.

"What the fuck?" he demanded, confused, having lost the thread of their conversation while watching the sexiest woman alive use him to get herself off. The look on his face was somewhere between awe and shell-shock. She wanted to bottle it up and keep it forever.

"Going… to use sex to convince you… that I want to stay… forever!" she said the last word on a scream as she exploded in his arms, arching backwards. Her knees jerked inward, pressing hard against his waist for a few seconds while she rode the waves of her self-induced orgasm.

Her legs loosened at the same time as her eyes opened to find his staring down at her. His expression was fierce, but unreadable. She could feel his cock, hard and hot, pressed against her ass cheek. He pressed his thumb against her mouth until she opened for him. He held her tongue and leaned in to speak.

"Don't believe your words, Katie," he said gravely. He dropped his other hand down her body and shoved two fingers up into her pussy, so far inside her body she was sure he damn near touched her cervix. Pleasure and pain sizzled through her body, merging in her brain and short-circuiting everything until she couldn't have managed a single thought if she wanted to. She brought her legs up alongside his to ease the pressure, but her actions forced his fingers deeper. She arched her back and neck, choking on the thumb in her mouth.

He dropped his head to her neck and bit down on the tendon that was straining as she tried to ease some of the pressure building up inside her. She whimpered.

"I believe this body, baby," he growled against her skin, licking the spot that he'd just bitten. "It'll always tell me the truth."

He pulled his fingers from her body, releasing the tension from within her. A tiny explosion detonated throughout her body. A mini orgasm *just* from the removal of his fingers. She didn't really know what was happening to her, she just knew it felt amazing. She moaned as her body collapsed onto the bed. He didn't let her enjoy it for long.

He rolled her over onto her stomach and then forced her up onto her hands and knees. He kneed her legs apart on the bed and growled in appreciation as her glistening folds parted in front of his hungry gaze. He pressed his fingers back into her body, pumping them a few times. She moaned and arched her back, looking over her shoulder so she could watch every expression that crossed his dark face as he played with her. She loved that he couldn't hide behind his normally stoic expression when he was with her this way.

She was surprised at how quick she got over her shyness about her scars with Roman. Even with Colin, who she knew for years, she hated getting naked in front of him. Before the nightmarish year after their divorce, she'd always insisted on having the lights off for sex. After the divorce, he wanted them on. Colin rarely mentioned the tiny white lines, but when he did, it was never nice. He made her feel like a freak.

Roman scissored his fingers in her body, making her instantly forget about the scars. He pulled his fingers from her body and quickly moved them up to her puckered ass. She moaned in protest and automatically jumped forward in a bid to slide out of his grip. She panted and watched him helplessly. His dark eyes watched her every expression as he relentlessly used her own juices to slide one massive finger past the tight anal barrier.

"Roman!" His name was torn from her throat, half protest and half plea. She didn't know what she was begging for.

He dropped his head onto her ass cheek and continued pushing his finger remorselessly into her tight hole, enjoying the way she squirmed and cried out as he held her hips tight against his chest. Finally, he could go no further, his hand was flush against her red ass. She flexed around the invasion, making the fit even tighter and tearing a growl from deep in his throat.

"So fucking tight," Roman snarled against her, sweat dripping from his forehead onto her skin, scalding her. "This ass better be virgin, *mujer*."

Katie gasped and squirmed as he pulled his finger out and shoved it ruthlessly back in. "Yes!" she cried out. "Yes, Roman, it's all yours!"

"Good!" he said, with a slashing grin. He pulled out of her and brought his hand down, in a quick, vicious slap that she felt in every part of body. She screamed and would have lunged away from him, except he reached out and took a fistful of her hair, holding her tight. "Every part of this body belongs to me now. From now on any man that dares to touch *mi mujer* will die a very bad death. You understand this?"

He continued to hold her hair as he positioned himself behind her, ready to take her in one long delicious thrust.

"No, Roman!" she yelled, panic edging her tones so he knew she was serious.

He stilled behind her. The air around them seemed to chill in the luxurious cabin and she quickly realized he misunderstood her. His fingers were rapidly tightening in her hair, threatening to part the strands from her scalp if she didn't very quickly explain her sudden exclamation.

"I mean, yes I understand, Roman! Every part of me

belongs to you," she said quickly. His fingers eased. She was certain he didn't even realize he'd been hurting her. Roman had never been vicious that way with her. Just intense as hell. "What I meant was, you need to use a condom. I… I don't know if Colin was faithful to me… and I don't want you to catch anything."

She could feel his tension as he processed her words through a lust-filled haze. She knew it was going against everything he felt for her and everything he wanted in their future. Then she realized that was the key. Their future. If she could make him believe she wanted a future with him then he would be more likely to comply with her wishes. Sadly, she wanted nothing more than to have a future with this beautiful man.

"Please, Roman," she begged him breathily. "I need you to do this for me. I would die if anything happened to you. As soon as we get back to civilization we can get a doctor to check us both out."

She saw the moment his clever mind figured out what she was getting at. That she was talking about having a future with him willingly. She also saw the struggle in his dark features. He knew she was manipulating him, but unsure of the angle she was playing. He also knew how much this meant to her. It was their constant game of cat and mouse. Would he let her win this one or would he just take what he wanted again?

After a moment of hesitation, when his hips moved of their own volition and she felt the crown of his large penis touch her opening, he jerked back and rolled off the bed. When she would have collapsed onto the soft quilt, he slapped her ass again. "Don't you fucking move!" he snapped.

She stiffened her arms and tried to ignore the tremors that ran through them as she listened to him stride into the washroom and begin to search the cabinets. "Didn't come prepared," she heard him mutter. "Planned on taking my woman bareback. Don't think that idiot fuck of an ex-husband of yours would cheat on your beautiful ass. Or that he could, even if he tried."

Katie bit back a grin and glanced over her shoulder as he approached with a wrapper in one hand, rolling a condom down his penis with the other. "Damn good thing he kept condoms stocked or you'd be sucking a lot of dick before we got this thing to the mainland, baby."

Katie's giggle turned into a gasp as he leapt onto the bed behind her, went down onto one knee and shoved his cock all the way into her pussy in one long thrust. She screamed and clawed at the bed as she was forced to take the painful intrusion. She loved every second of it. She loved the way he read her body and knew exactly how much pain she could endure and dished it out accordingly. As if reading her mind, he took a fistful of her hair, forced her head back so that she was arched into his body and wrapped an arm around her throat cutting off most of her air supply.

Dizzy and dependent on him for both her orgasms and her life, Katie could feel herself flying high as he began pumping in and out of her body. She was helpless to do anything but hang on for dear life and choke in precious lungfuls of air each time he unflexed his bicep enough for her to take in a breath. Every time he cut off her breath she felt her body tighten and her orgasm build even higher than before. Every second felt intense and sharp, she was right there in the moment, with Roman.

"Oh god, oh god, Roman!" she gasped. "Please… please… need to come."

"Yes," he growled in her ear. "Come for me, baby."

She reached down her body, her fingers brushing his cock where it plowed in and out of her body. She felt the latex of the condom and wondered for just a second if it felt any different for him to fuck her with a barrier than it did without. Then she pinched the bundle of nerves that would help her reach her own nirvana and allowed the beautiful rhythm that Roman was playing out on her body to carry her over the edge.

Her scream was silent as the ridge of his arm muscle flexed into her throat, owning her screams for himself and pulling her head back into his shoulder. As she rode the waves of her orgasm, he shoved her forward into the bedding. He pulled her hips back and rode her fast and fierce. She felt the sharp pressure of something pushing into her again and realized he was forcing his finger back into her ass. The breath caught sharply in her throat as the dual onslaught of a cock in her pussy and a finger in her ass sent her back over the edge of another intense orgasm.

A keening scream tore from her throat. She fisted the quilt and yanked it toward her chest as she helplessly pumped her hips into the orgasm while she soaked Roman's cock. She felt him flaring impossibly wide within her. Her eyes flew open and she began to struggle in his hold. In that position, with her knees forced wide, his dick rammed up to her cervix and his finger bottomed out in her ass, she was positive she would tear wide open.

"Roman! It's too much!" she screamed, tears pouring down her cheeks as pleasure and pain merged to toss her toward an even higher peak she didn't think she was ready for.

"You take it all," he snarled from behind her. He threw back his head, tendons straining in his neck and continued to thrust into her, twisting his finger in her ass until she finally slammed headfirst into the orgasm she'd been resisting.

Roman joined her, his own grunt of satisfaction mingling with her screams. He slammed his hips hard against her ass and forced her wiggling body to hold still as he emptied himself into the condom. Wave after wave of the most intense pleasure she'd ever experienced washed over Katie, followed by a calming blackness. She collapsed in a boneless heap, the last thought she had was a sense of disappointment that the walls of her pussy weren't bathed in Roman's seed.

# CHAPTER SIXTEEN

Katie hid the syringe in the folds of her skirt, fisting it against her thigh as she approached Roman. She did her best to give him a beaming smile when he glanced over his shoulder. It really wasn't that hard. He was utterly, breathtakingly gorgeous. Even out on the water he wasn't dressed like a normal, casual guy. He went for the dark, shadowed look that gave sexy a new name. He wore black jeans that rode low on his hips with the same belt he'd used to hit her into orgasmic heaven. A black leather vest was all that covered his wide chest, leaving his rippling shoulder and pectoral muscles on display for her viewing pleasure. The back of his vest was covered in a large rust-red patch depicting a scorpion and the name Valdez.

He stiffened a little as her feet whispered along the deck toward him. She was probably the only person he would turn his back on. Sadly, she was the last person he should trust at the moment. She stepped up to him and leaned against his back as he steered the yacht. She pressed her lips against the tanned skin of his arm and peeked up at his clenched jaw. Tension vibrated through his big body. They were heading toward the mainland and he didn't like it. She knew he didn't completely trust her, but he was eager to start their lives together. Which included having sex without the barrier of condoms.

He would keep her under lock and key the entire time they were on shore, likely with the help of his boss and friend, Soloman Hart. After their checkups, she was fairly certain he intended to bring her back on board the yacht for a few more weeks until he was more sure of her feelings. Which was why she had to enact her plan immediately. As much as it made her heart ache to leave him after only one day – the most perfect day in her entire life – she knew she had to go. She needed to get her butt to Milan. She had to leave him before they made dock and he had reinforcements. At least now she knew where she was.

So, after pulling on a long chiffon skirt and pink blouse, she'd opened the safe and grabbed one of the syringes he'd stashed away. She was positive it was the same drug he'd used on her to get her on the yacht in the first place. He probably had more in case he needed to move her again and she was being uncooperative. Bastard. Well, she was about to see how much he liked his own medicine.

"Roman?" she whispered, raising her bright blue eyes to his.

"Yeah, baby?" he said, glancing down at her for a second before turning his eyes back to the open ocean ahead of them.

She took a deep breath and edged the needle up his back, threaded in between her fingers. It would feel to him like she was just rubbing his back when she was actually trying to get the needle closer to his arm. She didn't know what the drug was. He'd injected her in the thigh, suggesting it was safe to go in a muscle. It would act quickest in a vein, but she wasn't really willing to take the risk with his life. She would compromise instead and inject it in his bicep, closer to his head and heart. Maybe it would act quicker that way.

"You know I love you, right?" she whispered.

He looked down at her, studying her features. She hadn't actually meant to say that. She meant to keep the conversation light so his eyes would stay on the water. But somehow, she couldn't leave him without telling him how she felt. She was so focused on his face and the needle that she didn't notice the arm he wrapped around her waist until he jerked her hard against his body, lifting her right off her feet and crushed her lips beneath his own in a kiss meant to brand her soul with his. She was so surprised she damn near clenched her fist around the needle and injected herself. Apparently, Roman hadn't known how she felt about him.

Finally, he eased his hold a little and set her back on her feet. His obsidian eyes pierced her with such sizzling possession she thought she would burn up on the spot. Certainly, she wanted to rethink her, admittedly, pretty bad plan where just about a dozen things could go wrong and have more mind-bending sex with this bronzed man-God. Alas, more lives than just hers were on the line and the clock was ticking. Her big boss puppet master was benevolent, but also murderous when crossed. He had a soft spot for Katie, but not so much for Roman or XSource. She wouldn't allow others to get caught in her fallout.

Steeling her heart against the pain she knew was about to come, the kind she didn't enjoy, she waited for him to shift his eyes away from her. The moment he did, she brought her hand forward and plunged the sharp needle into his skin, pressing the syringe down just as his razor-sharp mind realized what was happening. The hand that had been around her waist came up to crush hers in a grip so tight she cried out in pain. He tore the needle from his arm, her hand still clutching it, and looked down at both.

She watched his face as he stared at the needle. Tears pooled in the corners of her eyes as she watched rage and betrayal tighten his features. His lips firmed into a hard line, his jaw clenched and every line of his body tightened in denial. His hand tightened around hers until she felt the needle snap under the pressure. She bit her lip to keep from crying out again. She deserved the pain. She would deserve it if he broke every one of her fingers.

Finally, he lifted his eyes to hers. What she saw terrified her. He was going to kill her. She saw it in his eyes. He had never looked at her that way before. She was certain the only people that saw that look were the ones he escorted into death. She made a tiny sound, halfway between a sigh and a whimper. She wanted to be brave, but she didn't know if she could. This wasn't what she'd planned. Why wasn't he passed out on the deck? God, she wished she'd at least been able to warn Source before getting sucked into this mess. Now, her beloved hacker buddy would no doubt die a grisly death too, because she'd gotten them both entangled in the grip of a psychotic international crime boss.

Roman crashed to his knees, nearly taking Katie down with him. His hold on her hand weakened. She tugged a little and he let go. He scrubbed a hand across his face and then looked at it in disbelief. She stumbled back, staring at him with wide eyes as though he was a wild dog that could attack at any moment. She tossed the broken shards of the needle behind her while he shook his head and then looked around.

"Katie!" he snarled, searching for her.

When he saw her, he reached out for her, swaying. She jumped back. He brought a knee up and rested his arm across it.

"Don-don't you fucking ru-run way from me, you little bitch. I'll hunt you down. No matter where you go. N-no place will be far enough," he slurred, trying determinedly to get off the deck, his dark eyes never wavering from his prey.

She shivered and continued to back away as he got clumsily to his feet. Every instinct she possessed told her to run from the angry drugged killer stalking her slowly across the deck, clutching at furniture as he neared her. But she couldn't just leave him. What if he fell over board? She would die if anything happened to him because of her. So, instead of running, she slowly backed away from him, allowing him to get close without actually touching.

She saw satisfaction flicker in his progressively heavier eyes right before she toppled backwards with a scream. Arms flailing wildly, she felt herself enveloped in the bubbling water of the hot tub. With a shock, Katie surfaced to find Roman stumbling right in after her.

"No!" she wailed. "You idiot! How am I supposed to pull your giant ass out?"

Then her concern for his safety became the least of her worries when his hands landed heavily on her shoulders and he shoved her backwards into the steaming water. She screamed as he pushed her under. She wondered for just a second if he meant to drown her in the hot tub when she realized he had actually lost his battle for consciousness when he landed on top of her. She shoved herself out from under him and then frantically began tugging at his shoulders. Thankfully, she was able to get him onto his back.

"Oh my god, you big moron!" she yelled at him, pulling him toward the edge. "I had it under control. You were just supposed to quietly fall to the floor like I did, while I called my friend and then steered us to safety. Instead, you freaking hulk your way across this damn boat with drugs in your system and try to drown us both in the yacht-tub? I mean, this is taking obsession to a whole new level, don't you think?"

She panted and moaned as she braced her feet against the edge of the tub and heaved, using every ounce of strength. Every time she managed to get him partway out, they would slide right back in together. She screamed out in frustration. Finally, standing up on the bench, she shoved her hair off her face and stood over him with her legs on either side of his wide chest. Pulling her arm back, she slapped him with everything she had.

"Wake the fuck up!" she screamed in his face.

His body jerked and his eyes fluttered open, long, black silky lashes sweeping up. His cloudy eyes immediately narrowed on her. He reached up and seized her by the waist, dragging her down into the swirling water until she was forced to straddle him. He tangled his fingers in the strands of her wet hair and brought her head down to his for a clumsy kiss.

Rolling her eyes, she sighed. "Trust you to have sex on the brain at a time like this. Okay, Roman, we need to get you out of here and I can't do it alone. You weigh an absolute ton!"

He grunted in acknowledgment and let her wedge a shoulder between his arm and ribcage. Leaning heavily against her, he used the last of his strength to help her get him out of the swirling water. He stumbled hard against her, taking her down to the deck.

"I... I'll come for you, Kat... rina," he mumbled, an echo of what he told her ten years earlier, his eyes drifting closed.

"I know," she whispered, running her fingers over his sculpted lips. She bent over and pressed a kiss against them. "But this time I'll make sure you won't find me."

# CHAPTER SEVENTEEN

"Mayday, mayday!" Katie called into the radio hysterically.

She was a pretty good actress at the best of times. Couple that with the nagging fear that Roman might wake up at any moment, her desperate need to depart the yacht *immediately* and her disgust over the fact that his phone had indeed been in his back pocket when they'd gone into the hot tub and was currently waterlogged, and the rising hysteria within Katie wasn't actually much of an act. After pulling the phone out and trying to turn it on, then double checking to make sure his breathing was regular, she'd dashed to the controls and made sure they were still on course for the mainland.

"This is the coastguard," came a quick, clipped reply over the radio. "What is your emergency?"

Katie sighed in relief and sent a quick glance toward Roman's prone body, making sure it was still, in fact, prone. "I don't even know what happened! My boyfriend just passed out!" she whined in the most helpless, kept woman voice she could manage. "One minute he was down on one knee next to the hot tub and the next minute he just fell over, knocking us both in."

"Okay ma'am," said the woman in a patronizingly soothing voice, "Can you tell me if he's breathing?"

"Uh huh, he sure is *and* he has a pulse. I learned to check from Grey's Anatomy," Katie said cheerfully. "But the *big* problem is I don't know how to drive his boat. What if we crash?"

Katie could darn near feel the eye roll over the radio. Normally, she'd enjoy this dumb blond role play, but she was feeling seriously jittery and just wanted to plant her feet on solid ground again so she could start putting distance between herself and the towering rage that would be Roman Valdez when he woke up. The coastguard was no doubt picturing Roman as some old millionaire and her as his play-girl. They were in for a bit of a surprise when they saw the giant Latino ex-gang, biker-looking guy.

*Please don't wake up, please don't wake up,* she begged over and over in her mind, eyes glued to his unmoving body.

"Alright, ma'am, we've located your position and have a craft headed your way for an intercept. Please stand by for further instructions. Let me know if there's any change in your boyfriend's condition."

"Yup, will do!"

They must have been a lot closer to the mainland than Katie realized. It only took fifteen minutes before she caught sight of a coastguard boat tearing toward them. Tugging down her top to sit low on her cleavage she cued up the waterworks and ran leeward waving her arms. Lucky for her, two men came to the rescue. Both appeared to be hetero-sexual and completely susceptible to her wiles. She threw herself sobbing into the first pair of arms that boarded the yacht.

As soon as his hands closed on her hips and his eyes landed on her cleavage she decided she was extremely glad, for both of their lives, that Roman was out cold. She managed to blubber her predicament out to her saviours and point toward Roman's sprawled body, laid out like a sacrifice in the sun. She peeked at their faces and hid a smirk behind her hand when they did a serious double take. His size alone would make a person pause, but the aura of sheer menace that surrounded the man was palpable, even when he was unconscious.

"Please, help me!" she begged, turning tear-filled blue eyes up to the man she was pathetically clutching.

"Of course, ma'am," he assured her, getting lost in her eyes for a moment before pulling back and kneeling next to Roman with his medical kit.

After checking his vital signs they loaded him up and moved him to their boat. The more sympathetic of the two medics, the man that Katie had targeted, helped her over with a hand on her waist. She clutched him gratefully and sniffed delicately, wiping a tear away from the apple of her cheek. His eyes followed every move she made. She smiled wanly and pressed a hand against her heart.

"I can't thank you enough for saving me, I don't know what would have happened," she said breathlessly, dropping her gaze to the deck.

She wanted desperately to break away from the guy and rush to Roman's side, but she was trying to distract them from looking too closely at him. He was clearly not your average guy. Glancing up, she realized her ploy had only partially worked. The other guy was on the radio. The sharp glances he was taking toward the medical cot on which they had laid Roman did not bode well. She heaved a sigh of annoyance. This definitely fell under the category of 'pretty bad plan' where a dozen things were definitely going wrong.

Sure enough, the ambulance that met them at the docks was escorted by a police car… which was escorted by an unmarked car carrying two detectives. She raised an eyebrow. Well damn. Did they already know who he was? She glared down at Roman from beneath her lashes as he was being loaded into the ambulance. She kind of wanted to slap him silly again. Only this time it was for getting her ass into this mess. She was about to climb into the ambulance with him and the paramedic when a hand circled her arm from behind, stopping her.

"Excuse me, miss."

She plastered on her favourite vapid trophy girlfriend look and turned around to look at the guy touching her. Yup. One of the detectives. He took one look at her and wrote her off as too dumb to breath. She kind of wanted to punch him in the throat for making assumptions, but that was the exact thing she was hoping he would assume, so she let it go. She was pretty sure he must have heard the mayday call, given the look on his face.

"Yes, officer?" she asked in a high-pitched voice that made even her want to gag.

"I'll need you to come with me."

"Are you going to the hospital?" she asked as sweetly as she could manage without gritting her teeth.

"Of course, miss," he assured her.

"Well sure, then I'll go with you!" she said, flashing him a big smile.

He blinked at her for a moment and then led her toward the vehicle. As she suspected, the entire ride to the hospital was the two detectives grilling her on her connection to Roman Valdez. Turned out they did indeed know exactly who he was. She hadn't counted on them figuring it out that quickly when she called the coastguard. Geez, they were organized. Good thing Roman's tattoos were pretty much a giant map of fingerprints. Freaking slang mafia guys.

"Umm, I dunno. I think we were just going out for a day trip," she said innocently, shrugging her shoulders when they asked if Roman had been intending to take the yacht into Mexican waters.

When they asked about her connection to Roman she told

them the truth. "He knew my brother. We've been friends ever since!"

The trip to the hospital felt like the longest twenty-five minutes of her life. She had to keep track of every word she said. Luckily, she really didn't know much about Roman's business and the cops weren't asking her questions about being kidnapped. Apparently, they had no doubts that she had been with him of her own volition. *Jerks*. She would be happy to set them straight about their line of questioning except she didn't want Roman to get in more trouble than he apparently was already in and she didn't have time to hang around and fill out a victim statement.

*Finally*, they made it to the hospital and she all but leapt out of the vehicle before it even stopped. The detectives escorted her inside and quickly ascertained Roman's whereabouts. Once she was able to reassure herself that he was okay and 'explain' what happened to a doctor, she excused herself to use a phone. One of the nurses at the nursing station closest to Roman's room was kind enough to allow her the use of one of theirs. She smiled as she reached for it, thanking him.

Her first call was to her best cyber friend, XSource. She was beyond pleased to find her friend healthy and safe from Katie's big, bad boss. Once she assured herself of a quick and invisible way out of the hospital when the time came, she made her second call. She quickly dialled her best friend, full stop.

"Katie!" Riley answered on the first ring. "I've been calling you for days. Where the fuck have you been? And don't you dare tell me Paris, because you promised me a gift and you never delivered, bitch. I want my mini monogrammed Eiffel Tower and I want to know what the fuck happened to my best friend right this instant!" she demanded, her angry voice betraying her concern. She always got meaner when she was upset. God, how Katie missed her.

"I'm fine Riles, but I need to talk to your scary-ass husband. Can I get his phone number?" Katie spoke as quietly as she could and made sure her back was to the nursing desk so no one could overhear her. Chewing nervously on her thumbnail, she watched the men in Roman's room through a window, positive they were going to figure out what she was doing at any moment and come running out to arrest her. Not that *she'd* done anything illegal. Well… not anything they knew about.

"You want to talk to the man you spent every moment of my wedding avoiding like he had the plague?" Riley said incredulously. "I mean, I don't think you even said his name once during your entire maid of honour speech, which is just impressive."

Katie snorted and tried to deny it, but thinking back she was pretty sure Riley was right. "Whatevs, dude gives me the creeps. I'm not joking though, Riley. If you don't let me call him then his guard dog is going to get arrested. After he gets out of the hospital… because I sort of drugged him and then called an ambulance…. but then the police showed up too," she blurted out the entire story all at once. Mrs. Pullman always told her children it felt better to get the truth out. Like tearing a band-aid off.

Yup. She felt better.

"Well, fuck," said Riley after a moment of silence. "You don't need to call him, he's right here. I'm handing the phone over to him now."

Katie could hear murmuring and assumed that Riley was giving him the rundown on her little 'oops' of a situation.

"Ms. Pullman," Soloman Hart's deep voice said coldly into the phone.

A shiver of fear slithered down Katie's spine. While Roman was just as tough and scary as his bad guy mafia boss, she knew Roman would never harm a hair on her head. She glanced guiltily toward his hospital room. Well, he wouldn't have before she drugged him, nearly drowned him in a hot tub and then got him arrested. Not so much with Soloman Hart. She was pretty sure this guy would kill her for coughing in his direction and not feel even a twinge of guilt. The only thing stopping him was the woman currently standing next to him. Which is why she really hated the idea of asking for his help.

"Ummm… so Riley told you… a-about our little predicament at the hospital?" she asked in a small voice and then rolled her eyes at herself. Like saying it quieter was going to make him want to kill her less.

"She did," he drawled, the chill in his voice dropping a few degrees.

A part of her wanted to remind him that she was the one that got drugged and kidnapped in the first place. But knowing how he'd forcefully wooed her best friend and his misogynistic views on women, she thought it best just to eat crow and let him get Roman out of the situation. Preferably without Katie dying in the process. Her eyes widened as she watched one of the detectives approach the bed with a pair of handcuffs. Damn it! Were they allowed to cuff an unconscious person? Didn't they have to read him his rights or something?

"Oh crap… they're handcuffing him," she said, rolling her eyes in exasperation. This was *so* not going how she'd hoped. "Please just get here quickly, Soloman, and take care of this mess."

"You keep your ass in that fucking hospital, woman," Soloman snarled coldly sensing her intention to take off.

She shivered, unused to being on the barking end of Soloman Hart's anger. She was actually not used to having anything to do with the man except that he was married to her best friend. Truth be told, she usually avoided the terrifying beast unless she had no other choice. She'd come to town for their wedding and stood next to Riley during the lovely ceremony, studiously avoiding Roman's relentless gaze throughout. Soloman usually had nothing to do with her too, thank goodness! He really only had eyes for his gorgeous wife. Who could blame him, Riley was a stunning handful of crazy. A person had to have both hands and eyes on her if they wanted to keep that one… and their car.

"You don't understand," Katie said sadly. The phone she'd borrowed from the hospital shook in her hand. "I would stay with him in a heartbeat if I could. I love Roman more than anything in this world, but staying will put him in danger and that's something I will *never* do. Well, not on purpose."

There was a moment of silence while Soloman digested her words. He was a powerful and intelligent man. He wouldn't underestimate her or the things she said to him. She wouldn't underestimate him either. His first loyalty would always be to Roman. And Roman wanted Katie under his power regardless of the consequences.

"Make me understand then, Ms. Pullman," he said in a tone meant to be more reasonable and less 'I'm about to murder you and everyone you know.'

She glanced up and saw one of the detectives looking down at his phone. A prick of apprehension slithered down her spine. She had no reason to believe that Soloman Hart might know these men or have one of them in his pocket, but she trusted her own instincts and they were telling her it was time to separate herself from this situation. To walk away from Roman. He was never hers to love anyway.

Without answering, she placed the receiver on the nursing desk, took one last look through the window into Roman's room and walked away.

# HUNTING FOR TREASURE

# CHAPTER EIGHTEEN

## One Year Later

Roman looked down at the photo. It made his guts burn with fury every time he saw her picture. Especially if she was smiling or doing something that made her happy. The soft, blond hair – longer now, past her shoulder blades – was cut stylishly with cute short bangs. Wide azure eyes that begged for help, sucking the rich into her schemes, begging to take their expensive goods, never knowing it was she that walked away with their paintings, eating up the foreign countries with those incredibly gorgeous legs. Yet still, he asked for these pictures. Every day he wanted confirmation of her movements. He still loved her. Unequivocally and without reservation. There was no other woman for him.

But he hated her also. Hated how she made him love her and then showed him that he couldn't keep her. Couldn't keep her… unless he could rise up to her level. Meet her on an equal playing field. One year ago, he had underestimated the bitch. Had underestimated her connections. He spent seventeen years placing Katerina Pullman on a pedestal rather than seeing her for the conniving, thieving, heartless woman she had been all along.

He should have taken her when he first decided he

wanted her. Fuck the rules. Fuck her age. He should have taken her across the border, risen up to his rightful place and dragged her along for the ride. He could have kept her much the same as his father had kept his own mother. It was the way of his family. Women were slaves.

So many times, it was tempting to snatch her up before he was ready. He hunted her across the world. He was close behind her, maybe not physically, but always watching. Waiting to grab her when the time was right. He stubbed out his cigar in the ashtray next to her beautiful face, pulled the cuffs of his expensive shirt straight and strode out the door in search of his second-in-command. He needed to ensure that everything was in place for his bride's arrival. He couldn't have his little artist escaping him this time. If he had to chain her to his side for eternity he would do it.

He wasn't going to act the lovesick fool this time. He would make sure she never escaped him again. The balance of power was on his side this time. Soon he would have her where he wanted her. Soon she would learn her rightful place. He would make her hurt. Not the way she wanted. Not like before. She was going to hurt bad. She was going to atone for *his* pain this time.

# CHAPTER NINETEEN

Annoyance flickered over Katie's features as she watched the huge yacht grow closer through the window of the helicopter. She *really* didn't like yachts anymore. Trust her benefactor to park his in the Mediterranean and insist she come meet him for her next assignment. She just wanted to get this meeting over with so she could get back to her apartment in Sidney and start researching with Source. Maybe digging up the details of her new assignment would give her *something* to look forward to. These days, even the rush of a good escape didn't do much for her.

The helicopter landed seamlessly on the yacht's landing pad. Katie sent the pilot a distracted smile, unbuckled herself, set the headset aside and slipped from her seat. As usual, the boss himself met her, taking her hand in his. *"Guten Morgen,* Katerina," he greeted her in a deeply accented voice, bending to brush his lips across her cheek.

"Good morning, Ivan," she said pleasantly, taking his proffered arm and allowing him to lead her down the winding stairs from the helicopter pad. She stiffened a little when she heard the helicopter lift off again. Apparently, she was staying for an extended visit. "And how long am I to be your guest this time?"

He chuckled and led her toward the breakfast table under the shadows of a canopy. Pulling a chair out for her, he leaned over to speak in her ear as he seated her. "As long as it takes to sort a few matters out."

He took the chair beside her rather than across from her. Katie glanced at the food spread across the table and, seeing a wide array of fruit, breads and cheeses, was reminded sharply of her breakfast with Roman. No popcorn though. Of course not. It was a silly detail only those closest to her knew. A sharp pang nearly stole her breath and she almost wished for the familiar numbness. She raised her eyes to Ivan and watched him fill a plate for her. He preferred to do the honours, no matter what she or any other woman in his life wanted. Why were all the men in her life such controlling jerks?

She wrinkled her nose a little when he set the plate in front of her and she saw a pile of grape tomatoes. Roman wouldn't have put them on the table, let alone on her plate. He knew how much she hated tomatoes. Ivan neither knew nor cared about such things.

"What matters would those be, Ivan?" she asked coldly, picking up a strawberry as far away from the icky tomatoes as possible and taking a bite. "I was under the impression you wanted to discuss my next heist."

He sighed and shook his head in silent admonition. She smiled ruefully. He considered the American word 'heist' to be crude and preferred she moderate her language. He'd head-hunted her from her university graduation at the age of twenty-two. He'd groomed her, lifting her from her rough beginnings to become one of the most renowned international players on the market. For a while, he thought he was grooming her to become his partner in all things until he realized he could not penetrate the ice encasing her heart. Now, she was much the same as the paintings she captured for him. Beautiful, cold, unattainable. To be watched and protected, but never touched.

"I want your XSource."

She stiffened under his laser sharp focus and dropped the strawberry top onto her plate. She dabbed her napkin carefully against the edge of her lips before speaking. "This conversation is getting old, Ivan," Katie reproved lightly, as though she weren't speaking to one of the most powerful criminal players on the international market. She knew he wouldn't hurt her. "XSource works for me and pretty much does his own thing outside of that. He takes the occasional contract in the States, but he chooses who he wants to work for. He doesn't want to work for you because he understands what that entails. You can't have him."

She lifted icy azure eyes to meet his grey ones. She could see the storm building and knew what was coming. No one denied Ivan. Katie had sold her soul to him seven years earlier. She felt she had nothing to lose. But she hadn't realized she'd be dragging others into her sordid life. The agreement she made with Ivan at the time extended safety to her family, but not her business contacts. And not Roman.

Though Ivan was Swiss, his dark brown hair and swarthy skin were more reminiscent of the Baltic nations. She wondered if perhaps his family tree extended closer toward Russia. Of course, she would never ask. The sinfully wealthy man was unpredictable and a little psychotic on a good day. He was downright sadistic when pissed off, which his current expression was leaning toward.

"You have been a good pet for over seven years, Katerina," he said cruelly, stroking his wide jaw. "It would be a shame for you to outlive your usefulness now."

She stiffened, more in annoyance than fear. She shot him a

look, much like a school teacher admonishing a particularly naughty student. "And it would be a shame for you to lose your steady stream of artwork because you murdered her in a fit of childish rage," she said steadily picking up her cup of coffee and taking a sip. She set it down quickly with a look of disgust. She did not enjoy Greek coffee.

He waved an arm around the luxurious room in which they were seated. "You think I couldn't do without the income you bring me? Don't be absurd."

She smiled coolly and replied, "No, Ivan, I think you can't live without the paintings you keep for yourself." She watched the slight flare of surprise on his handsome face before the shutters came down. "Don't think I don't know exactly which commissions you keep for yourself. We both know I'm a curious kitty. I watch the market, I know which paintings sell and to whom. I also know which ones stay with the master."

He studied her for a long moment, in which she wondered if she finally went to far with him. She just admitted to knowing he had at least eight priceless works of art hidden away worth millions of dollars on the black market. And she was a very accomplished art thief.

"Touché, my dear," he said finally. "And you are correct, I would never lay a hand on you. It would be like slashing the Mona Lisa. Impossible, to say the least. You are wrong about one thing though. I would not harm you myself, but I would let you go... for a price."

Katie frowned, toying absently with the food on her plate. Had she overestimated him? She thought she'd come to know him well over the years. Though he was often cold, and even brutal, he was her mentor, even a father figure, though he was only fourteen years older than her twenty-nine years. He was world weary in a way even she couldn't touch. Like he'd seen and known things she couldn't possibly understand. It made her ache whenever she saw the war building within him.

Whenever she saw him punishing himself physically in combat training so he wouldn't punish the world around him. In a way, it was how they'd come together. He recognized the girl that felt nothing, while she recognized the man that felt too much.

"What would you sell me for?" Katie asked, betrayal burning hot within her. It was hard to imagine her friend selling her out that way. Was that why he had brought her here and sent the helicopter away? Was he sending her on her final assignment?

He smiled gently and reached out to bring her hair over her shoulder. "You know me better than that, Katerina. There is only one thing I would sell you for."

"What is that?" she demanded, brushing his hand away impatiently.

"Your happiness of course."

She laughed bitterly. "Then I guess we don't have anything to worry about, do we? I'm not going anywhere."

He studied her for several long moments until, uncomfortable, Katie began eating again. She even choked down a disgusting tomato without realizing until it was too late. He chuckled low in his throat at the look of horror on her face when she realized what she was eating and then he joined her, wolfing down the contents on his plate.

"We will discuss your hacker friend over the course of the next few days, Katerina. I'm afraid I am not satisfied with this conclusion. He has been extremely useful to you over the years and I am convinced would be an asset to my organization. I have given you both the benefit of the doubt thus far and asked politely. I have accepted his 'polite' refusals to work directly with me and have not gone hunting. I will not remain so patient for long."

Katie dropped her eyes to her plate so he wouldn't read the panic that flared to life within. Damn it! She did not need this complication. She'd gone from fearing for Source's life a year ago when Roman grabbed her, to now fearing for her friend's freedom. One did not just go to work for Ivan in a typical sense. No, the man was a slave driver. Or more accurately, a slave owner. And as an elite hacker, her friend was not even remotely willing to become part of any organization. XSource worked freelance or not at all. The only reason Source became involved with Soloman and Roman was as a favour to Katie, so she could keep an eye on the home front. And, apparently, Soloman Hart paid extremely well and didn't mind the tech expert's insistence on anonymity.

Katie was forced to enjoy the perks of Ivan's yacht over the following few days. She had a bedroom complete with private ensuite and stocked wardrobe, so it wasn't necessary for her to bring any clothes or toiletries with her. Though Ivan grilled her a few more times on her best cyber friend, he didn't press the issue too hard. She wasn't sure why, but he seemed to be biding his time, as though he'd made a decision already. She wasn't sure what it was exactly, but she felt as though she should get a warning out to Source and then leave it up to the hacker what to do with the information. Source was perfectly capable of going to ground and had, from Katie's understanding, done it many times before. They both knew how to run and hide. It was the world they chose to inhabit.

Katie spent most of her time on the yacht sunbathing in the gorgeous Mediterranean sun and researching her next job. "Mexico," she sighed out loud, regret and yearning evident in her voice. She had only ever done one job there about five years ago and was not really looking forward to going back. It was a beautiful country, but somehow, being in the same country of Roman's birth and the death of his parents, felt too intimate. There wasn't much she could do, though. She didn't get to choose the jobs.

Ivan dropped onto the lounger next to hers and she

glanced over at him with a raised brow. "Bit overdressed for the weather, aren't we?"

He was wearing a tuxedo complete with black bowtie. His dark curls were smoothed back from his broad forehead tipping his already handsome appearance into the breath-taking category. Or it would, if she had eyes for anyone but Roman Valdez. She was stretched out on her lounger wearing a bright patterned bikini and wide-brimmed sun hat with a laptop open on her thighs. He was sitting on the lounger next to hers with his knees stretched wide and his hands clasped loosely between his legs.

"We'll be making dock in a little while," he informed her. "I have an event in Athens this evening and you, my dear one, have a plane to catch."

She studied him, wondering what was different about the tone in his voice. She wasn't surprised about the casual way he was telling her that she would be leaving. He always arranged her life like this. She was used to jumping at his bidding. The only times he didn't casually mess with her life was when she was at home with her family, knowing how much that time meant to her. Although, she hadn't been able to visit them for a year now. She knew Roman would be watching them, expecting her to show at some point. She had made the excuse that her current job was extremely demanding and that she just couldn't get away. She tried to soothe her mother's hurt by Skyping with her as often as possible.

Unable to pinpoint what it was about Ivan's demeanour that was setting off alarm bells within her, Katie impulsively leaned forward and brushed her lips against his cheek. Before she could settle back in her chair, he took her face between his hands and held it close for a few seconds.

"You will call if you ever need me for anything, my dear one, yes?" he demanded, pressing his lips firmly against both of her soft cheeks before releasing her and standing to tower over her.

She sat back in surprise. "Of course, Ivan," she assured him, "don't I always?"

He studied her for a moment. "Not nearly as much as I'd hoped," he muttered, before striding away.

# CHAPTER TWENTY

The building was a private residence on a massive plot of land outside of Juarez, Mexico. The hacienda was beautiful, though well-fortified. It wasn't the first time she'd had to break into a well secured home, but she had to be extremely careful in a country like Mexico where laws tended to be a little more... flexible. Especially out in the area she was working in. There were few people that would miss a blond *gringa* if she was caught breaking into a home in this area. Chances were, such a gorgeous hacienda belonged to a drug dealer, or worse.

Katie was actually surprised she wasn't having to dodge more physical security. She had been expecting to slip by a few more obstacles on her way over the southern gate, but so far she'd seen no one. Perhaps this particular fat cat had enough local law in his pockets that he felt safe without the added expense. So much the better for her. She'd be able to get in and out with fewer potential run-ins.

She had no idea who actually owned this particular painting Ivan had commissioned her retrieval services for. She'd done extensive research on the building, the grounds and the local area, but hadn't been able to uncover a peep about the mark him or herself. Even XSource, an information genius, hadn't managed to turn anything up. She felt like she was going in blind, but she'd run out of time and didn't have a choice. All she knew was that this particular mark had a priceless, well-preserved seventeenth century painting of the Virgin Mary that would net Ivan, and subsequently Katie, bucketloads of money.

She noiselessly approached one of the servant entrances and threw a nervous look over her shoulder even though she knew she fit seamlessly into the darkness. She wore tight black pants that moulded to her legs so they wouldn't catch on anything as she shimmied and climbed, a long-sleeved black shirt, black gloves and a thin black mask that hid her pale face and blond hair. She also wore thin-soled black shoes on her feet so she could move easily and run if she had to.

She easily broke in through the side entrance and disconnected the alarm that she knew would be there. She held her breath as she listened for any indication that she'd been heard. This job was making her a skittish kitty. She wasn't used to having so little information on a client. Normally she would make sure her mark was out of the building before she moved forward with the lift. Unfortunately, she had no way of knowing who lived in the hacienda, let alone who was going to be at home. Luckily, she did know that the painting she was after was housed in a separate section from the living quarters that, especially at 3:00 am, should be unoccupied.

Following the internal map she'd build after relentlessly studying the blueprints Ivan had provided her of the huge house, she made her way through the darkened, deserted hallways. Again, she was a little surprised at just how quiet such a large home was. She supposed that any security that may be on premises were just rotated to another part of the house. Or perhaps, given the time of morning, they were napping on the job? Well, that only made *her* job a little easier.

She found the door to the Virgin's room easily and

grinned happily when she discovered it was locked with a Baldwin smart design. Finally, an obstacle! She thought the damn ten-foot-high fence around the property was the worst thing the reclusive homeowner was going to throw at her. Taking a quick peek around, she took out her phone and snapped a pic, sending it to Source. Then she sat with her back against the door, waiting for her friend to figure something out. Good old-fashioned locks? Katie had it in the bag. A techno lock? Nope, no way.

A few seconds later her phone vibrated in her hand. Katie lifted it to her ear in surprise, answering with a whisper, "Holy crap, buddy! I don't often get the pleasure of talking to you in person, this must be serious."

"Yeah, well, you present a challenge and I deliver," came the slightly husky and always lovely voice. "Okay, Kitty Kat, time to get cracking, here's what you need to do…"

Ten minutes later, Katie was finally in the sealed and chilled room. She was careful to heed her friend's instructions and keep the expert on the line for when she needed help getting back out. She knew the room was sound-proofed and didn't intend to die in there before the homeowner came to check on their painting. Keeping the phone on, she slipped it into her pocket until it was time to exit.

Katie retrieved a flashlight from her other pocket, flicked it on and turned to point it at the only thing in the room, the painting of the Virgin Mary. Her loud gasp echoed in the room, so loud she was certain even Source heard her. Instead of the seventeenth century Virgin Mary, piously praying over clasped hands, Katie found herself facing another painting entirely.

Unable to believe her eyes, she stepped slowly forward, hand outstretched. She stopped within inches of the painting and stared, eyes wide and unblinking. Positive that it was, in fact, the original, she moved her hand to cover her mouth. But how was it possible? This painting had been sold at a private auction in New York for millions of dollars. She followed the purchase closely, toying with the idea of picking it up for herself. How had Picasso's Woman with Folded Arms ended up in Mexico?

She felt his presence like the electrical surge before a storm as he approached her soundlessly from behind. She must have missed his presence in the perfectly chilled room from her buzz of breaking in and her focus on the painting. Now there was no missing him. Nor was there any missing the swirling rage that enveloped him. She should have known Mexico was a trap.

She never in a million years thought her beloved bene-factor would so heartlessly set her up this way. It hurt her badly to realize that he must want the resources XSource could bring him more than he wanted his favourite cat burglar. The door lock had been a set up to get Source on the phone. Katie's throat ached and her eyes burned, knowing she was probably too late. Ivan would have people ready to mobilize all over the world once he pinpointed the signal. Still, she had to try.

"Source, get out n…!" she screamed.

Roman's scent enveloped her just before a bag went over her head, cutting off her senses. She continued to scream until his huge arm slipped around her neck, cutting off her air supply. His other arm slipped around her middle and crushed her against him, lifting her off the ground. She kicked out at him, but her thin-soled shoes were no match against his muscular legs. Though she knew it was Roman that held her, his silence combined with the bag over her head terrified her.

Finally, he spoke, his deep, familiar voice sending a chill slithering down her spine. "Stop moving or I will snap your neck."

Katie relaxed against him and allowed him to hold her body weight off the floor. She could feel his erection pressing intimately between her ass cheeks and wondered if that was a good or bad sign. He still wanted her. He wasn't even breathing hard after their brief struggle, even though she felt like she'd run a race. Her chest was heaving against his thick arm and she was sure her ribcage was going to be bruised.

He slipped his hand into her pocket and retrieved her phone. She felt his fingers slide along her pubic bone as he pulled his hand away from her pants. A spark leaped to life within her belly and she wanted to scream at the unfairness that the only man who could pull any kind of response from her was a ruthless, kidnapping asshole. She felt him lift the phone to his ear and then make a grunt of satisfaction.

"It sounds like your friend is finally done running, *mi chica.*"

Katie slumped against him, a whimper of despair escaping her lips as he disconnected her phone and tossed it on the floor. He turned her around abruptly, setting her back on her feet so she was facing him. She nearly crumpled to the floor, but his harsh hold stopped her. He yanked her hands together in front of her and began winding something that felt rough, like rope, around her wrists.

"Roman, please!" she begged him in a muffled voice through the bag.

"Do not speak," he commanded sharply.

Her breath caught in a painful gasp at the coldness in his voice. He pulled her roughly from the room, impatiently hauling her to her feet by the arm when she tripped and lurched forward, unable to see where she was going. Once they stepped out of the gallery room he handed her over to someone else with a grunted command. "Take her downstairs and hook her up."

A new set of hands took Katie impersonally by the arm and led her into the bowels of the huge hacienda. Katie was too stunned to protest. Never in the time that she'd known Roman had he ever willingly allowed another person, let alone another man, touch her in his presence. This act of coldness told her more eloquently than words that his love for her had died. He had maneuvered her capture instead for revenge.

Tears flowed freely from her eyes, soaking into her mask as she stumbled alongside her guard into the chilly depths of Roman's home. They stopped walking abruptly and she was left standing alone for a few seconds, shivering in terror, wondering what they were going to do to her. She thought about attempting to run, but knew she wouldn't make it far.

She jumped and let out a muffled scream as her hands were seized and jerked abruptly over her head. She was stretched upward until she was forced to stand on the very tips of her toes. The guy holding her grunted and she felt the rope binding her wrists lifted up until her feet left the floor completely and then she was dropped back onto her toes. Her heart pounded painfully as she swung forward and then around in a circle until she realized she was hanging from an actual hook. Terror swelled within her until she thought she would choke in it.

As she heard the man walk away from her, she fought the rising panic that was threatening to claw its way out of her chest. She was hooked up in the basement of a very pissed off Mexican mobster with a grudge against her and a bag over her head. She didn't really see how things could get much worse.

About twenty minutes passed (though, with her arms tied over her head, it felt more like hours) when she heard the unmistakable sound of the crack of a whip slice through the air beside her body. Katie decided her plight could actually get much worse. *What the fuck had Ivan set her up for?*

Eyes wide and breaths coming out in whimpering gasps under the hood, Katie twisted and struggled helplessly in her binding. The whip continued to crack ominously, echoing loudly through the concrete basement and making her flinch to the side of where she thought it was landing.

"I would not move like that, Katerina." Roman's voice finally stopped her struggles. He sounded much closer to her than she had thought the whip yielder was. "You might accidentally push yourself into the path of my whip. Wouldn't want to accidentally mark you… yet."

She'd been holding her breath, trying desperately to hear his words through the rush of blood beating in her ears and the hood and mask over her head. A choking gasp escaped her lips when she caught the last word. Roman intended to hurt her bad. He'd had a year to contemplate his revenge on the woman he thought he loved. Now that he had her, there would be no mercy.

"Please… Roman…" she tried appealing to him, twisting her body in the direction she thought he was standing.

"What?" he roared, his voice a loud echo throughout the room.

Katie flinched away from the sound.

"I can't hear you?" he snarled and reached out to roughly tear the hood away. He did the same with the mask. "Do you have something to say to me, Katerina *mia*?"

With no barriers left between them, they were once more face to face for the first time in a year. Her terrified gaze met his. She saw only triumph in his face. The same blazing possession she saw the last time he had captured her, only this time the demonic look on his face wasn't tempered with the love he had felt for her since they were little more than teenagers.

He took her chin in a brutal grip and shook her. The chain above her head rattled as she swayed. "Answer me," he snarled. "You have something to say, *mujer*?"

She flinched again, but continued to hold his gaze. Roman Valdez had always been a hard man. From the day she met him she'd known he was a killer. But this man that stood before her now? He was so much worse than anything she'd ever been confronted with before. Her betrayal had changed him in ways she never anticipated.

Physically, he was even harder, more dangerous looking than she remembered. He wore a suit that fit him to perfection. He'd ominously removed the jacket and rolled his shirtsleeves up extremely muscular forearms. His usual long, rangy form had been honed into muscular perfection, as though he spent much of his time away from her punishing his body in anticipation for the day he would get his hands on her.

"Speak!" he shouted in her face when she refused to say anything.

Tears formed in the corners of her eyes and spilled over. Fine, if he wanted her to speak, she would speak. She would give him the truth. She wasn't going to blubber and beg like he wanted. She was better than that. She stared into his dark eyes, lifted her chin and whispered, "I never stopped loving you."

# CHAPTER TWENTY-ONE

Rage exploded in his chest and before he could think to stop himself he'd backhanded the lying bitch. "Fuck you!" he snarled, rearing back.

The hit didn't have much power behind it, but still, he regretted the action. He didn't beat women. If he had to deal with one within the organization, they were killed swiftly and humanely. Katie swung wildly on the hook, crying out in shock. She sobbed, her feelings likely hurt more than her face.

"You do not speak to me about that shit again, understand?" he snarled.

When she didn't answer, he took a threatening step toward her, lifting his hand again. She watched him warily and whispered, "Yes."

He stalked toward the table on which he'd set his whip down earlier. He could feel her terror-filled gaze following his every move. He picked up his special knife, the one with the wolf carved into it. He held it up so she could see the metal glint in the dim lighting. Another tear slid from her eye. He brought the knife up to her face. When she flinched away he cupped the back of her head in a big hand and swiftly captured the tear on the edge of his knife. She held her breath, barely moving as the razor-sharp blade slid along the silky skin of her face.

He licked her tear from the blade, savouring the look on her face. Fuck, one more year of age had made her even more heartbreakingly beautiful that she'd been before. Her cheeks were sharper, but her hair softer and longer. His balls ached as blood pooled in his cock. Soon he would find his way back home in her sweet pussy. But first, she would learn a lesson in submission. No more patient wooing for this one. She would know real pain at his hands. She would know what it was to be owned by the Valdez cartel boss.

Suddenly, he needed to see her naked body more than he needed his next breath. He wanted to see what else had changed in their time apart. He despised these fucking years apart she kept demanding from him. No more. Now there would be only minutes separating their time together. If even that. He would keep her close. So close she would begin to wonder how she ever survived without him. How she made decisions without his assistance. He would become her every-thing. There was no other choice. Because he would never trust her again.

"It would be very dangerous for you to move right now, *mi querida.*"

Her eyes widened and when he took a handful of her shirt, placed the knife at the neckline and slid it down the front, cutting right through the fabric like it was butter. Her mouth fell open and she made a small sound of protest. He gave her a quick look that told her she better not start protest-ing. She closed her mouth and stood stiffly as he continued to cut away her clothes.

Roman spoke as he stripped her, his voice cold and clipped. "I could have taken you back a year ago if I'd wanted to, but I knew I would not be able to keep you. You have powerful friends that you neglected to tell me about while also refusing to tell me the details of your job."

His eyes flicked to her, giving her a taste of the rage that was soon to come. He slid the blade through the front of her bra, easily parting the material in two. He peeled one of the cups aside and carefully applied the flat of his blade to her nipple, never taking his eyes from hers.

"There it is," he murmured, satisfaction tempering a little of his perpetual anger as he recognized the flare of pleasure lighting in her expression as he applied a bite of erotic pain to her flesh. She may fear for her life at the moment, but her body still responded to him the same as it always did. He would bet his empire that her pussy was growing wet as well, whether she liked it or not.

He reached up to cut the sleeves away from her arms. "Knew if I wanted to keep you this time, I would have to reclaim what is mine. I would have to reclaim the Valdez name. Offered Hart a cut of the border action if he helped me take down the bastards that murdered my family and reclaim my inheritance."

"What?" Katie gasped in surprise, jerking in his arms. "You mean the cartel?"

"Careful!" Roman snapped, glaring down at her and forcing her to stand still in his arms. He'd come very close to cutting her skin with her sudden movement. "Yes, the cartel. It's mine now. This hacienda is mine, along with the land, the town, the law, the people… everything."

He brushed the last shreds of her shirt and bra away from her and stood looking down at his handiwork as she looked up at him with fear and awe. "But Roman," she said in a shaky voice, "I don't understand. If you could have done all that, why did you never do it earlier? Why now?"

"Not listening, are you?" he growled, going down onto his knees in front of her. He was so tall his mouth could easily reach her nipples in that position, but he needed to get her pants off before he could start playing. He slid his dagger into the waistband of her pants, savouring the sound it made as it sliced away the barrier between him and her delectable self.

"Never wanted the responsibility of a region or a people. When my father fell, a lot of people fell with him. Families torn apart and allegiances splintered. Was better off going it alone in the States. Pledging my loyalty to whoever would have me. I've killed for money my whole life. For you? I have gladly killed for pleasure, cut the throat of your *culero* ex-husband with this very blade."

He enjoyed the shudder that rippled through her at his words. It was dirty talk to him. Talking death with the love of his life held safe in his arms once more. Yeah, he was a sick bastard, but he owned it. Like he was going to own her once more. He yanked the fabric of her pants away from her, taking the shoes with them. He peeled the socks from her feet until the only thing left was a pair of brief cotton panties. They were the same light blue as her eyes.

He looked up at her as he spoke, loving the way she tilted her head down to watch him with those sexy eyes, wide with fear. The way her blond hair swirled around her restrained shoulders. It made him so fucking hard seeing her like that.

"The only thing I ever wanted for myself was you, Katerina. But you kept running from me, over and over again. This last time has taught me a hard lesson. That it was time for me to become a man equal to your challenge. And what kind of man is that, your gorgeous eyes are asking me?"

He brought his hands to her hips and squeezed, mindful that he still held the sharp blade in one hand. He buried his nose against her cunt, taking her scent deep into his lungs. She made a sound of distress combined with a whimper of pleasure as her pussy creamed warm fluid against his nose. He hadn't intended to give her any kind of pleasure so soon after her arrival, but he couldn't help it. He needed one little taste, just to tide him over until he got to bury himself in her.

Fuck, he felt more like a teenager with a raging cockstand

than a grown 36-year-old man. Spreading his fingers and holding her tight, he rammed his tongue against the thin fabric of her panties, tasting her through the material. His responsive little runaway gushed right against his chin and mouth, giving him exactly what he wanted. He opened his mouth wide and devoured as much of her as he could, soaking her panties in his saliva. She filled the room with her echoing cries, rocking her pussy helplessly against his face, begging him wordlessly for more. But just as she was approaching some semblance of orgasm, he released her.

"I think the cartel boss can tame the international thief, do you not?" he asked, pushing away from her and standing once more to tower over her. Her dazed eyes watched his movements with disbelief. With two quick flicks of his wrist he cut through her panties and pulled the wet garment from her body.

He balled it up and held it up to her face, growling, "I would shove them in your lying mouth, but I want to hear your screams."

"Roman!" she cried out when she finally found her voice. "Can we talk? Please? I didn't mean to hurt you like this. This... this is crazy! That you would start an entire criminal organization just to get back at me..."

He dropped the knife on the table and picked up the whip. Turning back to her, he raised an eyebrow. She fell silent, her horrified eyes on the whip. He approached her, lifting the instrument so she could clearly see the long black leather whip and handle. It certainly *looked* and sounded terrifying. It could do real damage if he wasn't careful and he certainly intended to hurt her. But he had more than enough proficiency with the weapon to let it kiss her tender skin without actually causing lasting damage. "Not to get back at you, Katerina. I avenged the Valdez name twenty-four years after it fell so that I could hold onto you. Since you've made it clear to me this is the only way I can do it. I intend to lock you up so tight you'll have nowhere else to run."

He took a handful of her hair in a painful grip and pulled her head back. She cried out in protest. He placed his lips next to her ear and growled, "I will burn your childhood home to the ground if it means you no longer have any place to run from me."

He stood like that, holding her for several long minutes as he let the words sink in. Her chest heaved where it was thrust out into the cold air. Finally, he whispered, "Don't fucking move, or *you will bleed*."

"Roman, no!" she cried out when he let her go and shoved her away from him, snapping the whip in the air, amping up her terror.

"You still like the pain, baby?" he snarled. "You letting other guys give it to you these days?"

"No, no!" she screamed as the whip sang through the air slapping against the skin of her stomach. As promised, it left a red mark against the pale flesh, but didn't break skin.

He stalked forward and ran his thumb over the mark, enjoying his handiwork as she sobbed and flinched away from him. He grabbed her chin and forced her to look at him. She needed to know what it was going to be like living with him, what she could expect if she ever tried to leave him again. He could make her life heaven or he could make it hell. It was her choice.

"We're going to count, Katie. Eighteen lashes. You got that?" he asked her, pinching her chin to see if she understood. When she nodded, he asked, "What does it mean, *mi mujer*. Why eighteen?"

Tears ran over her cheeks and her voice quivered as she answered, "E-every year we've known each other."

He stepped away from her. "As intelligent as you are beautiful. Except this is punishment for the crime of eighteen years apart. Years that you have kept us separated."

He cracked the whip again, allowing it to bite into the flesh of her thigh and curl around to mark her ass cheek. "Count it!" he snapped.

Tears dripped from her eyes, but she managed to glare at him and say from between gritted teeth, "Two."

He nodded his head and, walking behind her, cracked the whip fully against her ass. "Three!" he shouted, startling her. "If you forget, I will hit you harder, Katerina."

"Three," she hurried to comply.

Still so beautifully submissive. He reached around her body and plucked at her already stiff nipple, cold from the chill in the room. She arched her back and moaned at his touch, responding immediately to the heady combination of pleasure and pain only he knew how to give her. He gently rolled the distended nipple between his thumb and forefinger until she was squirming in her bonds and moaning, arching her head back into his shoulder.

He stepped away from her and cracked the whip in three successive hits, striking her harder each time until she was screaming and counting, recoiling with each hit. Red streaks formed along her body, up her side, along her breast and hips. Tears dripped from her chin onto his head as he took her nipple deep into his mouth and alternately soothed and tortured the distended object with his hot tongue. She cried out and arched her back, forcing her small breast into the back of his throat. The sounds coming from her mouth were more carnal than he'd ever heard her make before.

He backed up and took in the fear that immediately flashed across her face as he lifted the whip. She shook her head and he could see a denial forming on her lips. She wanted to beg him to stop. Sadistic pleasure flowed through him as he remembered the way he'd woken up at the hospital handcuffed to a fucking bed. Questioned by detectives. Humiliated, while his boss maneuvered him out of the situation. If he'd been able to wrap his hands around Katie's neck at that time, she may not have survived.

He brought the whip down on her thigh harder than he meant, nearly drawing blood. She screamed, "Eight!"

But having lost her had given him plenty of time to figure his shit out. Sort out his priorities and life goals. Realize it was time to stop doing the lone wolf thing if he intended to keep his woman. He clearly needed the backing of an entire cartel if he intended to lock this woman down. It was time to rise up and claim the Valdez mantel, become the man he was born to be. And take the woman meant to be by his side.

He realized as he slapped the whip against the flesh of her ribcage on either side of her body that she'd gained some much-needed weight. Probably less stressed after he'd taken care of her douche of an ex-husband. So, he'd done something right during their last encounter. Now that she belonged to him, he would make sure she continued to eat right and take good care of herself. Take some vitamins and shit, too.

He paid particular attention to her toned, fleshy ass as he continued to lift his arm and snap the whip against her helpless flesh while she screamed numbers at him. He loved the way it jumped and jiggled as the whip slapped against her, turning bright red with each hit and then evening out into a gorgeous line.

"Fuuuuuck!" she howled, tears dripping relentlessly onto her reddened breasts, and then yelled, "Fifteen!"

"Such a good fucking girl when you want to be," Roman growled, still stalking circles around her. "But you just got to go and use that powerful brain against me every chance I give you? Well, that won't be happening this time, *hermosa*. Open your legs."

Her eyes flew open, fear twisting her beautiful features. "No, Roman, please!"

"Open. Now, Katie, or I will make you hurt like you've

never hurt before," he snarled in a voice gone quiet with menace.

"Oh god," she whimpered.

She opened her legs a little. He brought his hand down on her abused ass and yelled, "Wider!"

She yelped in pain, but quickly complied, opening her legs as wide as they would go while still keeping her toes on the concrete. He noticed the nails were painted silver. So pretty. He stood in front of her, watching her pert breasts jerk up and down as she heaved laboured breaths into her lungs. Her blond hair was a sexy, fluffy mess around her head. Her body decorated in his stripes, her pupils dilated in fear. She'd never looked more beautiful to him.

He cracked the whip against the floor, drawing her startled attention to him. He could see her eyes go from the whip to his tattooed hands, up his arms and shoulders to finally settle on his face. He gave her a sinister smile. She could see the monster she'd created.

"I had this room cleaned up for you, *mi amor*. It was a little gory before you arrived. You see, Katerina, reinstating the Valdez cartel was, and occasionally still is, a bloody prospect. It has not been easy ensuring loyalty to the last man. I could not have my woman seeing such filth, so I made sure the… accommodations were befitting my princess."

Her eyes widened in fear and disgust. She'd always known what he was about, but he had protected precious Katie from the real Roman. Now that she was going to be living this life by his side, she would have to get used to a few harsh realities. His cold eyes searched her face before he spoke again.

"I will not make the same mistakes my father made. There will be no leniency for disloyalty or betrayal. There will be no second chances. Any man who is my enemy will die a bad death. Any woman who disobeys will die, period. If it is *my* woman that fucks me over," he took a step closer, drawing a shudder of fear from her, "I will hunt her and I will beat her, lock her up forever and remind her every day, using the harshest methods, who she belongs to. You ran once, Katerina, you will not run again."

Her wide eyes traced his face as though truly seeing him for the first time. He stepped back and lifted the whip bringing it down on her right hip harder than he'd done before, drawing a thin line of blood and shouting, "Seventeen!"

"Seventeen!" she screamed back, eyes locked with his. He was surprised that she had enough wits left to keep counting. Something about what he'd said to her persuaded her to stay with him in the moment.

She kept her eyes on his face as he lifted the whip high and brought it down on her other hip, drawing a matching line of blood on her other side. As she whimpered the word, "Eighteen," he reached out, snatched a fistful of hair, jerked her forehead to his and snarled, "Mine!"

# CHAPTER TWENTY-TWO

Her entire body was on fire. Flames licked over her sides, her belly, her ass, her back and her thighs. She shook with the effort to keep her legs open, but knew he would bark at her to keep them open if she dared to move. Roman was dominant on a good day. Tonight… tonight, after recapturing his prey, after a yearlong hunt, he was downright sadistic.

He approached her, brushing the tail of the whip over his long, blunt fingers as though contemplating whether or not he was actually done hitting her. Tears trickled from her eyes at the thought. She didn't know if she could take any more. The pain was intense, unbearable, insane. It was also breathtaking… and maybe a little wonderful. But she couldn't handle more. Not like this. Not with the boiling anger and hatred barely leashed under the surface of Roman's control.

He brushed the leather across first one painfully distended nipple and then the other until she was crying out and biting her lip to keep herself from begging. She had no idea what she would be begging him for anyway. Her wrists and shoulders ached unbearably. Every time he touched her, he took her attention away from the pain. But each ache was a new, even rawer pain that she didn't know if she would be able to withstand without breaking.

He trailed the whip down her body, scraping it over some of the burning stripes. She tried to arch away from the pain, but he looped an arm around her back and forced her forward so that she would feel everything he chose to dish out. He twirled the braided leather handle of the whip around in his hand and pressed it against her clit. She jumped and arched into him, tossing her head back restlessly.

"That's right, baby," he growled, "show me what you like. Just like last time."

Katie was dimly aware of what he was saying. She wanted to deny his words, deny what his touch was doing to her, but it was like electricity when he touched her. He was the only person in the world that could draw this kind of response from her. She arched her hips into him and tried to press her clit harder into the whip, seeking more of the mindless pleasure he was offering after bringing her body painfully alive from the whipping. Now he was also holding her up, relieving the pressure on her poor arms as well.

Then he did something both horrible and incredible all at once. He moved the handle further down her slit and pressed it up into her dripping pussy. The braided leather was rough against her tender passage, causing her to cry out and arch her back to relieve the pressure.

"You can take it!" he growled, tightening his arm around her middle and forcing her against him. He pressed the handle further into her body.

Katie's mouth fell open. He took advantage, swooping in to take her lips in a savage kiss, claiming the hot recess for himself for the first time after a year of abstinence. She knew with every fibre of her being that, once more, Roman had been faithful to her. That Roman would always be faithful. His obsession with her ran too deep for him to even consider another woman.

"Oh god, oh my god, Roman… it's too much," she wailed as soon as he released her lips.

"Shut up," he snarled savagely, dropping his head to bite her collarbone. "You'll fucking take everything I give you. You were made for this, for me, Katerina."

"Yes," she moaned mindlessly, as she felt the leather slide another inch further. "I'll take it…"

He took her mouth again, forcing her head back and fucking her with his tongue until she choked. She was completely overwhelmed by him. He was pushing her to her limits and beyond… but it was Roman. He would never actually hurt her, would he? Had she fucked up so bad a year ago that she'd pushed him past the pointing of caring what he did to her? The thought brought fresh tears to her eyes.

Her tears spilled over and touched their lips as he savagely kissed her. She felt the moment he realized she was crying. He hesitated and pulled back, looking into her eyes. She thought for just a moment he might take pity on her, but then triumph blazed hot in his obsidian depths, leaving her in no doubt that she had truly broken the one man that was meant to love her unconditionally. She sobbed helplessly in her bindings as he gripped a handful of her hair and forced her to look at him.

He pulled the whip handle partway out of her tender pussy before thrusting it ruthlessly back in. She screamed, her face twisting, and went up as high as she could on her toes in an attempt to relieve some of the pressure inside of her. Tears poured from her eyes. Her fingers opened wide and she reached high above her as if reaching for heaven.

He took her chin and turned her face to his, licking her cheek. "I love your tears, *mi amor,* they are so beautiful. They make my dick harder than it's been in a year."

Her tear-stained eyes turned to him, wet, spiky lashes fluttering as she tried to focus. "H-how… can you call me y-your love? After everything that's happened. You should hate me," she whispered, her lips inches from his.

He considered her question carefully. She was half afraid he would fly off the handle at her mention of love again, but she needed to know. She had to know where they stood. He clearly enjoyed torturing her. Although she was no fool. Even while her body stung and hurt, and she was utterly exhausted, she understood this wasn't real torture. She was in one piece. She had pissed off a killer. The boss of the Valdez cartel. What she was experiencing, though it felt all kinds of terrible, was probably a slap on the wrist when it came to men like this. A light punishment for the girlfriend of a cartel boss. His next words confirmed her thought.

"I tried hating you," he admitted bleakly, his dark eyes meeting her bloodshot ones. "Truth is, you're *mi mujer* and you always will be. I might not trust you, but I can never hate you, Katie, *mi amor.*"

"Oh god, Roman," she whispered, wishing she could touch him, wipe away the pain of betrayal she saw in his eyes. "I'm so sorry I hurt you."

She watched in dismay as the shutters slammed down over his eyes. He shoved her away from him, ignoring the cry of fear that leapt from her throat. Without warning, he yanked the handle from her pussy, ripping another scream from her. She clenched her knees together and let her body hang from her wrists, uncaring of his stupid orders or the pressure on her arms. Her tender vagina needed her now. She drew her legs up to relieve some of the pressure and cried softly, completely unaware as Roman approached her once more.

"Ro… ooooman!" his name quickly turned into a scream of agony as he hooked one arm around her waist and reached up to guide her wrists from the hook. The pain increased as blood rushed into her arms.

"Shhh, it'll stop hurting in a minute," he murmured

against her head, lifting her in his arms and carrying her to the table as if he weren't the cause of all her current suffering. She glared at him as he set her bare ass on top of the table. She yelped as the welts on her ass hit the table, but then settled when the cool metal soothed the pain of the stripes he'd given her. Remembering his earlier words she wondered how many people had been killed in this room, perhaps using this very table. She shuddered and squirmed on top of the possible torture table.

He brought the bone handled knife up between her hands and easily sliced through the tight rope binding her wrists without touching her skin. She spared a brief moment to marvel at how skilled Roman was with a knife. Though a little unsettling in the context of this room and his position as a cartel boss, she had to admit, her guy knew what he was doing.

He stood next to the table, towering over her, a knife still held loosely in his long, tanned fingers while she sat naked on the table he used to torture people. Yet she was still turned on. What was it about this man that just pushed all of her buttons?

"Going to fuck you now," he said, his dark eyes relentlessly focused on hers.

Her breath caught in her throat. She wondered what would happen if she said no. She'd done it once when she was eighteen and gotten away with it. He'd politely, or as politely as Roman had been capable of, tucked her into bed and walked away. Now, she was in a lawless land, kidnapped and at the mercy of a man that owned everything around him, including the local law.

He took her abraded wrists in his big hands and ran his thumbs over the red marks. She moaned as he massaged the wounds, soothing the sore skin and stroking the blood flow to life. Her head fell back and her eyes closed. She was completely helpless to resist his brand of gifting her tiny bits of pleasure after subjecting her to so much pain. He let her wrists go and dropped his hands to her thighs causing her to jump and yelp when his warm hands landed on the stripes of painful flesh.

"Easy, baby," he murmured.

Memories of their time on the yacht flooded her mind at his words and she jerked in his hands as though to get away from him. Of course, Roman would have none of that. His fingers tightened around her slim thighs, dragging a pained groan from her. He dragged her forward to the edge of the metal table and snarled in her ear, "Not going anywhere."

"Roman!" she whimpered as pain and need merged within her. He fucked with her head just as much as her body, playing a dangerous game with her emotions.

He yanked her off the table and turned her over, admiring the red welts crisscrossing her pale ass for a moment before kicking her legs apart and opening her up to him.

"You wet for me, *mi hermosa mujer*?" he growled, unbuckling his belt and pulling his cock from the confines of his pants.

Katie looked at him over her shoulder, wanting to see him, needing to see what she did to him. "You know I am, Roman," she told him, meeting his eyes. Her body was on fire for him. Lit up from the whipping and from every touch he subjected her to.

He took a handful of her hair and, without warning, lined himself up behind her and slammed himself home. If he hadn't used the whip handle first, he might have hurt her more. As it was, Katie had enough trouble adjusting to his size, going up onto her toes with a shout. She gripped the edge of the table and tilted her hips forward. He leaned over her, kissing the welts that marred her beautiful back before biting savagely into her shoulder and pulling back to slam his hips into her again and again.

Katie shrieked and clawed the edge of the table, helpless

to do anything but take his ruthless siege on her body as he relieved some of his yearlong obsession with finding and punishing the woman that escaped him. His penis angled into her g-spot with such force that she had no choice but to hurtle forward into an orgasm of such magnitude that she was barely able to hold onto consciousness as she came. Wave after wave of painful joy in the cruel arms of the lover that had reclaimed her for himself.

Satisfied that Katie was taken care of, Roman followed shortly behind her with a grunt of release, pumping into her over and over, scalding her bare pussy with a year's worth of pent up semen. He held her so tight she could barely breath. Not that it mattered. She had nothing left to give. She lay limp in his arms as he turned her over against the metal table.

She could barely manage to open her eyes and look up at him, her eyelashes fluttering. She was so completely done. He'd won. She would give him whatever he wanted if he just let her sleep for a million years. She thought she saw the ghost of a smile cross his hard lips as he gently brushed her short bangs off her forehead and pressed a kiss against her skin. He hefted her against his strong chest and carried her naked out of that god-awful torture basement.

Katie was too tired to open her eyes as he ascended the stairs and took her into the main part of the house. She felt the air become noticeably warmer though, which she defi-nitely appreciated. She snuggled closer against Roman and felt his arms tighten around her. She heard his shoes click against the floor. Her own bare feet bounced as he carried her through his huge hacienda. And then they were going up again. Up and up, high up into his castle. She was beginning to have a nagging suspicion in her too tired mind that he was going to lock her in a tower so she couldn't escape. Like Rapunzel. Because Rapunzel had blond hair, right? Only Katie's hair wasn't long enough to get her out of trouble this time.

Then she was being placed gently on a bed and her dark captor was stepping away from her. She was able to slit her tired eyes open enough to understand that there was a window in the room and that dawn was approaching. Then she blinked. And blinked again. And narrowed her eyes. There were bars on the window.

Deciding she was just too tired to deal with it she sighed and closed her eyes again. She felt the weight of covers drift over her naked shoulders and snuggled into the warmth. She could hear voices murmuring in Spanish from the doorway and latched onto Roman's as her sense of comfort, hugging it to her heart as she drifted off.

"You are to see to her every comfort, Lana. She will need a warm bath and cream for the welts, then you can prepare her for the ceremony…"

# CHAPTER TWENTY-THREE

Katie woke to the pleasant aroma of pancakes and coffee. She thought for a moment that she was back home in the United States, tucked into her childhood bed, smelling a home cooked breakfast prepared by mom. Then she stretched and the soft blanket slid along bare skin, touching the wounds Roman had inflicted the night before. Katie flinched and curled into herself as memories of the night before flooded through her. The chill darkness of the cellar he had her strung up in, the fiery heat of his angry gaze licking over her exposed flesh and the painful strike of the whip biting into her while he forced her to count out her own punishment. The deep ache between her legs reminded her that Roman's brand of torture was both erotic and terrifying.

"*Hola*, miss," said a quiet but cheerful feminine voice behind her. The woman spoke in soft Spanish as she approached the bed, "If you are ready to get up I have some breakfast here for you and then we can see to your wounds."

Katie decided she had no choice but to open her eyes and face this day. And whatever further horrors Roman had in store for her. She sat up slowly, mindful of the stretch and ache in each part of her body. She held the light hand-woven white blanket up to her chest as she turned slowly on the mattress and faced the woman who'd been sent to care for her.

"My name is Lana. I'm the wife of Jorje, Mr. Valdez's second-in-command. I will be your companion while you stay in the hacienda," said the woman, her eyes taking Katie in curiously. She was probably somewhere in her forties, short and full-figured with a head full of glossy black hair and gorgeous round eyes. She was wearing a pretty pink chiffon dress that looked a little too formal given the occasion. Her expression was friendly though, so Katie held out her hand.

"Katie Pullman," Katie said with a smile. "International art thief and two-time kidnap victim of Roman Valdez. Nice to meet you."

Lana's mouth opened slightly. Then she took Katie's hand in hers and gave it a squeeze, the corners of her lips twitching up. She studied the beautiful blond with a critical eye. Even tousled from sleep she was stunning. Cleaned up and dressed to kill, she would be irresistible. It was easy to see what had kept Roman Valdez in the United States for all those years and away from the local girls this past year. His heart clearly belonged to this one. If they wished to keep his insane blood-thirst reigned (a trait inherited from his crazy papa), then they'd best keep his precious treasure safe under lock and key. Lana would have to have a conversation with Jorje about ensuring security around this one. Sometimes women's minds worked a little differently than men's.

"Come, *niña,*" she said softly, clicking her tongue in sympathy when Katie stepped away from the bed still clutching the blanket and Lana caught sight of a red stripe across her back. "Let's get you fed and bathed. You must be starving after your ordeal yesterday."

"Oh, yes," Katie moaned as she approached the breakfast tray that Lana had set on the vanity table. She sat in the chair and began eating as fast as she could get the bites in her mouth. Between her usual nerves at doing a job and Roman's punishment, she eaten almost nothing the day before.

Lana drew a bath for her while Katie ate and gulped down the delicious coffee prepared just how she liked it. She eyed a small crystal bowl of strawberries with longing. She knew Roman had added them because he knew how much she loved them. What next, popcorn? The bastard knew the way to her heart was through her stomach. She briefly considered not eating the strawberries. But the childish gesture would harm no one but herself. So, she took the bowl and pushed the tray aside, keeping them for a snack. She would savour them at her leisure.

Lana encouraged Katie to drop the protective barrier of the blanket when she entered the washroom. She left for a moment so Katie could have some privacy, which Katie was very grateful for. She wasn't used to having anyone in her space, though she had to admit she was happy for the company this morning. She didn't want to be alone with her confused thoughts and emotions. She didn't want to have to think at all if she could help it. Not about how Ivan had so cold-heartedly handed her over to Roman. Or how Roman's love for her had turned into such a twisted, bitter thing that he'd gone and restarted a long dead cartel just to get her back. Nor did she want to think about how her body betrayed her into responding to a man that had beaten her so viciously…

"Katie, *niña*, are you okay in there?" Lana's voice drifted worriedly through the partially cracked door.

Katie flicked away the tear she hadn't even realized had fallen and called back, "Yes, I'm fine, thank you."

She stepped into the warm water and sat down in the big ceramic tub, hissing in pain as the water enveloped her abused body. The painful reminder of Roman's anger brought a fresh bout of tears to the surface. Her sound of distress drew Lana quickly through the door. The older woman was quick to sit on the edge of the tub and take Katie's face in her hands.

Anger flickered in the dark depths of her beautiful eyes as she looked over Katie's naked body. As always, Katie felt self-conscious when she was exposed to anyone. It was not her old scars, however, that drew Lana's wrath.

"That man loves you very much, but this is too much I think," Lana said shaking her head. She gently wiped a tear from Katie's cheek. "Ah, poor *niñita*, you miss your people?"

Katie nodded, more tears spilling from her eyes as she thought about her family and friends back home. Would she ever see them again? Or would Roman keep her locked up in the hacienda forever, punishing her over and over for daring to leave him?

"Come, come, there is nothing to be done for now. Perhaps he will relent in time," Lana said gently. "Let us wash your lovely hair and then we will soothe the pain of your marks."

They spent the next few hours getting to know each other as Lana took care of Katie much the same as her mother would have if Katie had been sick or having a really bad day. Lana blow dried and brushed out Katie's hair until it shone pale golden in the light filtering through the bars of the window. Then, she insisted Katie take her robe off and lay back on the bed where she applied a soothing cream to each welt. The only ones that had actually cut into her skin were on each thigh. The last two. She sucked in her breath as Lana applied the cream to them.

She waited for Lana to ask about the old white scars littering her skin, but she never said a word. Katie wondered if Roman had warned her not to. It didn't seem like him to discuss something so private. He was very possessive when it came to Katie. But then, he also seemed somewhat able to set that possessiveness aside when it came to her ultimate welfare.

"Thank you," she whispered when Lana finished and helped Katie back into a lightweight robe.

Lana gave her a genuine smile and said, "You are welcome, my dear. Most of your wounds probably feel much worse than they actually are, I am relieved to say. You must be one brave *chica*. I think I would have fainted at the first sight of that whip before it even touched my skin."

Katie shuddered as she remembered the bite of the whip against her flesh. She smiled weakly and admitted, "It's definitely not something I want to experience again. Lana, I'm still very tired. Do you think I could take a nap? Or… or is R-Roman expecting me soon?"

She could barely say his name. A flood of emotions hit her when she thought of seeing him again. Excitement, fear, anxiety. Fear. Lana must have read some of the crazy going on in her head, because she checked her phone discreetly, looking at the time, before turning back to Katie with a kind smile. "Yes, of course. I will come wake you when it is time."

Katie chose not to ask the obvious follow up question. She was a firm believer in 'what you don't know can't kill you.' Instead, she lay down, stretching out on her back, which hurt less than her front, though the cream helped sooth away most of the pain. She watched through eyes that were already closing with fatigue as Lana knocked on the door. It was opened for her and she was escorted out by a burly guard before the surprisingly heavy sounding door slammed shut and a lock engaged. Wow, these people were serious about keeping her locked in.

*Well, lucky I'm a master escape artist,* she thought as she drifted off.

Just as she said she would, Lana woke Katie after letting her rest for a few hours. The older woman was standing over her with a garment bag and a smile on her face. Confused, Katie sat up and shoved hair off her face. She blinked sleepily at the woman and asked, "Are you wearing more make-up than before? And jewelry, you're wearing earrings and bracelets."

"*Si niña,* I have dressed up for the occasion. Now it is your turn to get that beautiful butt out of bed and get yourself ready," Lana said with a laugh.

Katie closed her eyes and pressed the heel of her hand against her eyebrow for a moment before opening her eyes and giving Lana her best glare. It was hard because she genuinely liked this woman, despite knowing her for less than a day. She was beginning to think there was a conspiracy going on within the household, with all this 'let's take care of Katie after torturing her first' bullshit. Nope. She wasn't having it. Time to ask the question.

"And what occasion would that be exactly, Lana?"

The other woman gave her a big, bright smile.

"Why your wedding of course!"

# CHAPTER TWENTY-FOUR

"She did what?" he asked incredulously.

Roman looked up in surprise at the woman who was standing in front of his desk wringing her hands worriedly. The ice around his heart melted slightly over the fact that she was not concerned for herself at having to bring him the news that his soon-to-be bride wasn't cooperating. No, she was worried for the woman on the top floor, locked away in the tower room he had specially built for her. A concrete and reinforced steel cage meant to hold her. Keep her forever if need be.

"She threw strawberries against the wall," Lana answered in hushed tones, as if saying it quieter would take some of the violence out of it. She clearly did not want to get her charge in trouble. Good, the women were bonding. He wanted Lana entirely loyal to Katie. "Then she threw whatever else came to hand. She was screaming and crying, too. I… I was afraid she may hurt herself, perhaps tear one of the wounds open so I had to ask Miguel to come in and restrain her."

At the look of barely restrained rage that flickered across Roman's dark features over the thought of another man putting hands on Katie, Lana was quick to reassure him. "I was in the room the entire time and made sure he touched her as little as possible. She is handcuffed to the bed, Mr. Valdez, and unable to harm herself. But I am afraid she refuses to get ready for the wedding."

He gritted his teeth in an effort to bring the anger back under control. Only Katie could do this to him. She fucked with his head in a way no one else could, made him unpredictable. She'd been doing this to him since she was a long-legged, gangly 13-year-old with braces on her teeth. She would be doing this to him when they were in their eighties, if God were kind enough to allow them that much time together. Now it was up to him to ensure they were bound together so they could pass those years as man and wife.

When the rage passed, he glanced up at Lana. She was a lovely woman. Perhaps ten years older than Roman, she was a combination of old-fashioned homey and sultry. Jorje, his second-in-command, was a lucky man and he knew it, nearly as possessive of his *hermosa* Lana as Roman was of Katie.

Roman's lips twitched in humour. "She really threw a tantrum?"

Eyes wide, Lana nodded. "It was like watching a dust devil in action, Mr. Valdez. I had no idea she had such a temper!"

He chuckled, startling the woman. She couldn't remember hearing him laugh before. Certainly, none of his men had ever heard such a sound from him. The blond beauty brought out myriad emotions in their cartel boss. It would be both unsettling and magical to watch their love unfold. Like one of those Spanish telenovellas she loved to watch.

"I have known Ms. Pullman for almost two decades and have never known her to get as angry as you've described. She is usually manipulative and sneaky when it comes to getting what she wants. This is good, Lana… this tells me she is finally running out of options."

Lana stared at him like he was crazy. But he was the boss. What could she do except nod and go with him when he beckoned for her to follow him out of the room, back up the winding stairs and into the fortified tower holding his reluctant fiancé. He nodded coldly at Miguel as they approached the door to her cell. Miguel was a huge man, ideally suited to the job of watching over Katie. He was fiercely loyal to Roman, having pledged allegiance as soon as he'd found out there was a new Valdez in residence. He was also much faster than he looked, and just as strong. And just as cunning as his lovely charge.

He unlocked the door and stepped aside, keeping his eyes wisely averted from the beautiful blonde restrained to the bed. She'd twisted and turned until her robe had given way, opening to reveal one creamy, pink-tipped breast, her nearly hairless pussy and one long leg. With a curt instruction for Lana to wait outside until he was ready, Roman entered her room and slammed the door shut behind him. Her head jerked around in surprise, her wary gaze clashing with his.

Any amusement he'd felt earlier fled to be replaced with blazing fury. What if she'd needed help while she was tied up like this? Miguel would have had to enter the room and he would have seen her like this. Miguel was loyal and well trained, so he would have looked away and done his job professionally, but Miguel was still a single, heterosexual man and Katie was a stunningly beautiful woman. If Miguel had to put hands on Katie while she was in such a state, well, it was more than Roman could handle. He needed to convince her to settle down and accept her situation before he left a trail of body parts in the wake of their fiery love affair.

He approached the bed, his hands going to the buttons of his shirt. He'd dressed in his finest suit for the occasion of their wedding day, but had left off his jacket since he expected to work until the ceremony. Her gorgeous blue eyes burned with fear and defiance as she silently watched him remove his shirt, baring his chest. Those eyes of hers, so full of emotion, turned his dick to stone more than any other gorgeous feature she had. Her gaze strayed to the large, ornate tattoo of her name, scrawled across his pectoral muscle. He'd had some embellishments added to it over the past year.

She licked her lips and lifted her chin defiantly when he reached the edge of her bed. "I won't marry you, Roman," she said in a voice shaking with emotion.

"You will," he said simply, his hands going to the buckle of his pants. Her eyes followed the movement and she flinched, thinking perhaps he meant to beat her into compliance. His poor *mujer* had been through a lot in the last twelve hours.

He unzipped his pants and pushed them along with his underwear down his legs. Her chest heaved in relief when he simply placed them neatly over the same chair he'd set his shirt. He didn't want his outfit to wrinkle before the ceremony. He turned back to her, fully naked and erect, ready to anticipate his vows before they were made. But then, he and his little fiancé were anything but conventional. He would fuck her before the wedding and she would stand at his side and become his wife with his seed wet between her legs. A reminder of whose property she was.

"No, Roman!" she protested when he kneeled on the bed, knocking her legs apart. "I won't be forced into marriage this way. You can't keep doing this to me! You can't keep kidnapping me, beating me and fucking me and then expecting me to forgive you. I don't want this!"

He pressed one long finger into her wet heat while dropping a kiss on top of the worst welt he had given her, a long thin stripe that had bled a tiny bit. His tongue snaked out to lick the line. He could see the moment that heat, pain and pleasure merged as he curved his finger into her g-spot and massaged her. She moved her knees back restlessly on the sheets, giving him better access to her sweet pussy. He moved to her other leg, treating her other wound to similar care, apologizing with his lips and tongue until she was writhing underneath him.

"You think I can't force you into marriage, Katerina *mia*?" he growled, forcing another finger into her slick passage until she was panting and pressing her hips up into the incredible heaven he was promising. "This is my land, baby girl, my laws. You just have to show up, I'll do the rest. Now, I want you to come on my tongue and then beg me for more."

He flicked his tongue against her clitoris, teasing the tiny flushed nub from its hood until she was squirming and begging underneath him. He had to hold her down with one hand on her belly so she wouldn't buck him off with her wild movements. She jerked so hard on her arms, the handcuffs Miguel had used to secure her to the bed frame rattled over her head. Roman hoped she wasn't damaging her wrists even more than he had the night before. His poor *mujer* was having a rough first day in his care. After she settled down, he would make a point of giving her the princess treatment she deserved. He would only bring his dark side out to play when she was bad.

"Oh god, oh my gooooood, Roman!" she shouted, gushing all over his mouth and hand as she came hard, her hips jerking against him.

He frowned as she screamed loud enough for the occupants in the hallway to hear. He had chosen not to sound-proof her tower room in case she ever needed help. At the time of its building he had made the choice, knowing her guards would hear them having sex when he visited her room. He hated the thought, but he didn't see a way of reconciling. He could have given her an intercom, but if she ever hurt herself and couldn't get to it in time to receive help, he would not be able to forgive himself. Ultimately, he chose the lesser of two evils in the hopes that one day he would trust her enough that her tower room would no longer be necessary and she could join him in the master suite.

He moved over top of her, caging her face with his palms and taking in the dazed post-orgasmic expression on her face. He loved the soft glow she emitted after he made her come. She became his mindless wanton when she was like that. She lifted her hips and wrapped her gorgeous, long legs around him, pressing herself up.

"You want me to fuck you, baby?" he growled, sinking his teeth into the edge of her lip.

"Yes… yes," she moaned, arching her neck back so he could nip his way down her throat, giving her the stinging bites of pain she craved. "Please, Roman… I want you inside me so much!"

He reached up and gripped her wrists where they were shackled to the bed, squeezing them hard, enjoying the feel of her shackled with steel. He loved knowing she couldn't run from him this time. He had complete control over her and she was begging him to fuck her anyway. He gripped her thigh and pulled it up high so he could plunge into her at a tight angle, throwing her headlong into another orgasm.

She screamed as she came, her pussy clamping down on him like a vice. It was everything he could do not to come right along with her, but he wanted to stroke her higher until she was mindless with pleasure. Forcing his way through her spasming channel, he ruthlessly fucked her while she screamed and begged for him to both stop and keep going. Placing her ankle on his shoulder, he reached between their bodies and swirled his thumb over her clit, enjoying the jerk of her hips.

"No, no, stop, it's too much!" she gasped, her eyes wide as she begged. She was helpless to stop him though, with her arms over her head and her legs forced wide. He continued to plunder her clit and thrust into her slick channel until she was once more coming apart underneath him.

"Mine, Katie," he grunted, dropping her leg and pressing his body into hers, crushing her against the mattress while he continued to thrust his cock deep inside her body. He came while she was still shuddering from the intensity of her orgasms. He roared in her ear while pumping hot jets of semen against her cervix, "I'll never let you go!"

# CHAPTER TWENTY-FIVE

Katie barely had a chance to process what had happened before Roman was rolling off the bed. She stared in horror and gasped for breath as he stalked to the door and jerked it open. She scrambled up against the headboard, attempting to yank the now seriously disheveled robe over her body. Naked, Roman demanded the key to her handcuffs before slamming the door shut and stalking back to her.

He loomed over her, a dark frown once more marring his rugged features. Geez, they'd just engaged in seriously mind-blowing sex. Couldn't he lighten up a little bit? Once her wrists were free, he cradled them in big hands and ran his thumbs over them, his gentleness somewhat at odds with his fierce expression. Finally, he let her hands go, apparently satisfied that she hadn't sustained further damage. Without a word, he redressed, his eyes never leaving her face.

God, Roman Valdez was one intense man. She didn't know what to do with him. This is exactly why she couldn't stay. He mixed her up inside and made her feel crazy. Well, crazier than she was and *that* was really saying something. His intensity frightened her. They needed to sort out what it was they were doing if they were actually going to move forward with their lives. And she needed to show him he couldn't do that by acting like a caveman every time he got his hands on her. She tried to move away from him when he approached the bed once more, but he took hold of her chin and forced her to look up at him.

"You will allow Lana to help you dress," he said coldly, his eyes lashing her with the promise of more pain if she disobeyed him. "You will *not* throw another tantrum. Do you understand Katerina?"

When she only pressed her lips together and glared defiantly up at him he sighed heavily and pinched her chin, giving it a shake. "You think it is wise to test my patience, *mujer?* Believe me, my beautiful lady, after last night, I want nothing more than an excuse for a repeat performance. That was… fucking *caliente*, baby." His voice dropped an octave and his eyes turned to hard obsidian pools of desire at the remembrance. "Only this time, maybe I use a horsewhip instead, no? I think I like it with a little more blood than you do."

The blood drained from her face as she watched the sadistic pleasure gleam in his eyes while he pictured the scenario. "I will do what you want, Roman," she whispered, dropping her eyes.

He released her chin and caressed her cheek before stepping away from the bed. Her shoulders relaxed when he turned to leave the room. Before he opened the door, he glanced back at her and said in a low, heated voice, "One more thing, Katerina. You do not wash between your legs before the ceremony. You will marry me the way you are, with my seed wet between your legs. Every minute you are down there listening to our vows you will remember who owns you."

She gasped, her mouth falling open as he left the room. She sat just like that, contemplating how she could possibly get out of marrying such a crazy, obsessive, totally controlling male when Lana entered the room, took one look at her and blushed. Katie blushed back and then they both started laughing while Lana hurried to close the door.

"Please tell me he didn't leave any fresh marks on you," Lana said in a scolding voice. "That man, he is worse than my Jorje!"

Katie shook her head and then submitted herself to Lana's capable hands, allowing the other woman to prepare her for her wedding ceremony. She quickly found out that was why Lana had come to the hacienda essentially wearing her best dress and all her finery. Katie was flattered that her wedding was so important to the other woman, though she was a little embarrassed that Lana knew she was getting married under duress.

As if understanding Katie's flustered state of mind, Lana kept up a steady stream of mostly one-sided conversation while helping her charge prepare for her wedding ceremony. Which was apparently to take place in a little over an hour. Lana chattered away as she brushed the fresh knots from Katie's hair, curled the glossy locks and then pinned the sides up with two beautiful pearl combs.

"I was not a young girl when my Jorje decided to pursue me. I had decided long ago that marriage was not for me, having watched my parents fight and my papa come home drunk all the time. Instead, I wished to work and remain independent. Not a common idea in this area, but there you are. Anyway, I was not opposed to flirting and messing around when Jorje first approached me. But he was an old-fashioned guy and he would have nothing less than marriage. So, I refused and went my own way."

"I'm so sorry about your parents, Lana," Katie said, meeting Lana's gaze in the mirror while the other woman worked on her hair. "Sometimes my dad drank too much, too, if things got stressful at work. I guess we were lucky though, he wasn't a mean drunk and he usually stayed at the club to sleep it off. So, what happened with Jorje? If you walked away from him, how did you end up married?"

A small smile curved Lana's lips and she patted Katie gently on the shoulder. "There is a reason my man works for the Valdez, *niña*. Much like yours, my man does not take no for an answer. He quite swept me off my feet."

"B-but you seem so happy?" Katie spluttered, taken aback.

Lana chuckled and patted Katie's hair after putting the final touches on it. "Of course, I was not happy at first. I kicked and screamed and fought even angrier than you. But that was many years ago and we have settled into a happy marriage with many blessings. I would not trade my Jorje for anything in the world."

Katie was smart enough to realize that Lana was trying to reassure her that her own story may work out the same. That Katie could learn to find happiness in her captivity. Katie gave her a tremulous smile. Right now, she didn't know how to think or feel. All she knew for sure was that it wasn't right for Roman to tell her what she was to think, feel and do. That she had to decide for herself what she ultimately wanted, and the only way to do that was to leave. Perhaps it was a good thing Ivan essentially sold her to Roman and took Source for himself. As terrible as it was that one of her good friends was at Ivan's sadistic mercy, it freed her to leave Roman's control and, for the first time in a long time, make a decision for herself.

"I can't believe I haven't asked you earlier, but do you and Jorje have any children, Lana?" Katie asked, turning on her seat.

The sadness that leapt into Lana's eyes was impossible to miss and she instantly wished that she could take back her words, no matter how innocently spoken. She took Lana's hands in hers and squeezed them compassionately.

"No, we were not so fortunately blessed. It is part of the

reason I was eager to work in this house when I found out Mr. Valdez was to bring home a wife," Lana said, brightening. She patted Katie's cheek when Katie visibly blanched at the idea, suddenly remembering her birth control pills, tucked inside her carry-on bag at the motel room she'd rented in town. "Do not worry, *niña*. You are young and healthy. There will be many children in your future. Come now, let's get you up. We only have a few minutes left for the dress."

Katie stood silently, trying to figure out the odds of pregnancy from one missed birth control pill and two bouts of sex, while Lana pulled the robe from her and handed her a pair of white sink panties and a matching bra. Katie squirmed and blushed when the crotch of the panties became instantly soaked with a combination of Roman's semen and her own juices. Just the way he'd planned it, the barbaric bastard.

Next, Lana had Katie step into a beautiful silk and lace white dress. It was modern in that it was cut to just above her knees and hugged her every curve, but was traditional in every other way. It was long sleeved and high in the front and back, covering her to her neck. It also covered any evidence of the whipping. Clearly Roman had planned her entire abduction well in advance. The dress looked both classic and chic. Lana provided Katie with a pair of four inch white stilettos, that added even more length to her already long legs and finished off the dress perfectly.

"Pardon, but the *niña* will have to sit for the next part, as you are much taller than me at the moment," Lana chuckled with a twinkle in her eye.

Katie smiled and graciously sat so that Lana could add a small wedding tiara just above Katie's bangs with a short fluffy veil attached. Then, taking Katie's arms, she helped the younger woman stand in front of a long mirror. Katie stood for a moment looking at herself, and then her shoulders began shaking as she fought valiantly against crying. This was actually happening to her. Today was her wedding day.

"I want my mom," she whispered, her voice cracking.

Then Lana was in front of her, hugging Katie tight against her and rocking her gently. Though she was tall and beautiful, with the presence of a queen and the courage of a lioness, this young lady was still very fragile.

"Shhh, it will be okay my *niñita*. I know you miss your mama, and perhaps one day you will share your special memories with her. But for today I will be your mama if you will allow. Now look at me and dry your eyes. Your man out there will marry you no matter what you have to say about it. Be the brave woman I have seen and go with dignity, *si*?"

Katie looked down at Lana, drawing on her strength. She took several deep breaths then reached under her veil and ran the edge of her fingers under each eye to make sure her mascara hadn't run. Lana gave her an approving nod.

"*Si*," Katie agreed, "I will go with my pride intact and you will be there with me."

They sat quietly together while Lana did a few last-minute touch-ups on Katie's make-up. Ten minutes later a loud bang on the door interrupted them. Katie jumped and stared at it like the boogeyman was on the other side come to get her. Lana gave her a reassuring smile. "It is time."

They stood together. Lana took Katie's hand and called out that they were ready. They were escorted through the hacienda by both Miguel and Lana's husband Jorje, a broad, stocky man that looked like he ate poisonous snakes and nails for breakfast. After meeting the man, Katie could *definitely* see Lana's hesitation in marrying him. She could also see why Roman had made him second-in-command. They probably sat around the breakfast table eating scorpions and discussing their daily agenda of mayhem and killing.

Jorje took Katie's elbow in a firm but impersonal hold as they descended the stairs, ensuring her safety while she took the steps in her sky-high heels. At first, she was confused that he wasn't helping his own wife and leaving Katie to the care of her guard, but the more she thought about it, the more she realized how cartel mentality would work. Katie was soon to be Roman's wife, which made her second highest in his organization, whether she liked it or not. Jorje was next in line below Katie. By ensuring her safety first, he was showing allegiance and loyalty to the Valdez cartel. He was also a married man, likely twenty years Katie's senior. His touch would be the least likely to set off her extremely possessive soon-to-be husband.

*Good thinking, Jorje. I'm sure Miguel enjoys keeping his body parts*, Katie thought cynically as they stepped off on the main floor. Jorje, an even smarter man than he looked, dropped Katie's arm entirely and waved her down the corridor. Remembering the blueprints, Katie glanced longingly toward where she knew the front doors were situated before preceding their small group in the direction Jorje had indicated.

Katie's heart beat faster and faster as they approached the end of the hallway, where Jorje indicated she should stop and wait while he knocked on the door. Roman's voice bade them enter. She stepped back as the door swung open to reveal Roman's office. A large, darkly furnished, masculine room. He wore the same suit he'd removed earlier in her room, only he'd added a jacket and tie. He was so incredibly handsome. A dark Mexican prince who stole his princess one night and married her the next.

He moved forward, taking her hand and drawing her into the room. Katie noticed another man, a priest, standing to the side of Roman's large desk. She looked around, panic beginning to swell in her chest as she caught sight of the marriage certificate on the desk.

She raised her eyes to Roman's, trying to see him from beneath the veil. He reached underneath and brushed his thumb across her bottom lip. Then he smiled. Not a sinister or a threatening smile. An intimate smile. One that was for Katie alone. The smile, combined with the soothing touch of his thumb against her lip, calmed her enough that she knew she would be able to take this step with him.

"Come, Katerina, it's time," he said, his deep accented voice washing over her.

She nodded and sucked his thumb into her mouth, swirling her tongue around the thick digit, knowing that no one could see what she was doing beneath her veil. She enjoyed the surprised flare of his eyes, followed by the contemplative narrowing as he jerked his thumb to the edge of her mouth and then almost unwillingly back in the moist depths, before finally pulling out. She would marry Roman because she had no other choice. But her tiny revenge for this shotgun wedding was that her groom was going to say his vows with a hard-on.

# CHAPTER TWENTY-SIX

The ceremony passed quickly. Roman was correct, Katie barely had to do anything except stand silently by his side. Perhaps he'd paid off the priest, or maybe he really did have this kind of power in the area, but no one seemed surprised or dismayed when the bride said nothing during her wedding ceremony. He lifted her veil at the appropriate time and took her lips in a chaste kiss that felt strangely obscene given his treatment of her earlier, and his semen still slick between her thighs. Then, he held her hand while she signed the register and placed his name boldly next to hers. And, just like that, they were married.

Katie looked up at him in stunned disbelief. He had actually done it. This man that she'd known for more than half of her life had taken her in marriage without her consent. She searched her heart and realized she couldn't find true disappointment at being tied to him in such a fundamental way. She did love him, after all. But she couldn't be pleased that he was going about things in such an ass backwards way. Where was the proposal? The declarations of undying love? Where were the flowers and bridesmaids forced to wear ugly dresses? This is not how her dream wedding was supposed to go. Not that Katie had ever planned on having a dream wedding. This was her second time down the aisle and neither had really been her choice.

*Fucking men!* she thought with disgust, narrowing her eyes at her brand-new husband.

He stared back at her, his emotionless eyes as unreadable as ever, giving none of his thoughts away. Well, she supposed that was better than the triumphant expression she had been expecting. He took her arm and together they thanked both Lana and Jorge for standing with them and the priest for performing the ceremony. Roman discussed some kind of formal meal with the other couple before leading Katie from the room.

She followed him down the hall and around the corner, tracing the corridors in her mind through the blueprints she had spent so much time studying. She knew exactly where he was leading her when they finally stopped. He entered the code into the door and pushed it open. Katie gladly welcomed the chill air as it rushed at her, hungry for a glimpse of the gorgeous painting. Her heart pounded in remembrance of the way Roman had captured her while she had been standing in front of it, staring in shock. Hard to believe that it had only been the evening before when he had lured her into his frightening trap.

She shuddered and glanced back at him before returning her eyes to Woman with Folded Arms. "She's so beautiful, isn't she?" Katie asked, her heart breaking as it did each time she looked at the painting. Seeing it up close and in person was a magical treat she thought she'd never achieve.

"She's yours," Roman's voice rumbled from behind her.

"Mine?" Katie whispered.

"A wedding present," he confirmed.

She tilted her head in acknowledgment, her eyes following each harsh, sad line of Picasso's famous painting. The tortured emotions were there to see, starkly laid out, oil on canvas for their private viewing, the misery of both subject and painter so heartbreakingly evident. It had called to Katie from the moment she first laid eyes on a tiny replicated thumbnail in one of her art history textbooks eight years ago. They stood that way for a long time as she simply soaked in her new painting. It was the first one she would be allowed to keep for herself. Fitting that it was also her favourite.

Finally, she spoke, her voice low, shaking with emotion. "God, Roman, I don't even know what to say about all this. Your level of planning and… and motivation, it's too much, too intense. To find and acquire this painting… *my* painting. To resurrect an entire criminal empire that fell more than twenty years ago. To contact my boss and heartlessly hand over my friend – *our* friend – to him."

His voice was sharp as a whip and just as brutal when he spoke. "XSource stopped being a friend to me when he chose to hide you and not reveal the extent of his duplicity. I hope I never cross paths with him, Katerina. Because I will gut him on the spot for playing me."

She shivered as he stepped up behind her and drew her against his chest, his gentle actions in direct opposition to his brutal words.

"Source saved Riley's life when he helped you and Soloman hunt down her kidnapper. Doesn't that count for something?" she asked softly.

"Not when he's been putting your life in danger for years while playing me and the boss," he growled, leaning into her, letting her feel his hardness against the curves of her ass. "Now why would he do that, Katie? Why would he allow us to think he was working for us, when he was really working for you the entire time?"

Katie rolled her eyes and replied sharply, "That's not how independent consultants work, Roman. Source works for h- himself. He chooses his own jobs. We work well together, which is why he consistently chooses to work with me. Yes, sometimes he told me what you were up to, but only because he knew I cared about you and wanted to know you were safe."

Roman's growl reverberated through her back and his arms tightened against her. She could feel his jealousy thicken in the air. She was an idiot for not telling him the truth about Source. There was no reason now not to reveal Source's true identity, unless the hacker was able to somehow slip away from Ivan. Until she had definitive confirmation one way or the other she was keeping her lips sealed. She didn't need to make more trouble for someone who had stayed true to her over the years, helping her out of more jams than Katie could count.

"You love XSource, don't you?" Roman demanded suddenly, his arms tightening to the point of pain. "Don't bother denying it, I can tell from the way you talk about him. How many times have you fucked him?"

"Roman!" Katie gasped, twisting in his hold. "Of course, I've never been with Source! Don't be ridiculous! Where is this even coming from? You know I've only ever been with you and Colin."

He slid his fingers in her hair and tilted her head back. Because of her high heels, she was tall enough that her head rested against his shoulder giving him access to her delectable lips. He held her firm against his body, taking the occasional bite and sip from her gasping mouth as he studied her painting.

"Wanted to burn it you know," he told her, his deep voice an angry growl.

Katie gasped, going rigid in his arms as though afraid her precious masterpiece might be in danger at that very moment. She would fight him tooth and nail if he were to try anything with her new baby. She glared up at the ceiling. He was holding her too tightly for her to level an appropriate look of censure his way. The painting was literally worth millions!

"Why?" she asked him, her voice trembling with the perfect amount of aghast disgust his remark deserved.

He pressed his lips against her jaw. "Because I look at her, your Woman with Folded Arms and see my Katerina when she is left alone in the dark. She is sad and lost, huddled in on herself. She hurts herself and goes slowly insane with the bad thoughts in her head. That is why she needs her man, whether she likes him or not."

Katie's chest lifted and dropped with each breath she took as she processed his words. A tear escaped her eye. He captured it with his tongue before it could drip off her cheek. This man saw her better than she saw herself. He turned her slowly in his arms so she was facing him. He used his grip on her hair to tilt her face up to his. He studied the vulnerability shining through as clear as day and nodded his head. She knew he had brought her here to prove something, perhaps break down some kind of barrier.

"We are so messed up, Roman," she sighed, leaning against him, absorbing his strength.

A slight smile twisted his lips. He gently set her away from him and straightened her wedding dress and veil, smoothing the latter back over her shiny curls. His gaze was hungry, but he clearly intended to savour both the evening and his new bride. He took her arm and escorted her back to the door. Katie was surprised when he gave her the code to get in, but he explained that both the painting and the room were hers to enjoy.

"Y-you won't harm my painting?" she asked anxiously, as though she were protecting a child.

He shook his head with a frown. "You should know by now, *mi amor*, I could never harm something that you loved."

She smiled brilliantly, and then a mischievous glint

sparkled in her blue eyes. "Unless the object was another man."

He growled, his hand tightening on her arm. "You better stop playing with me or you'll miss your wedding feast and instead spend the time in my basement apologizing for such remarks."

"Yes, Señor Valdez," she murmured, dropping her eyes.

He led her through the corridors toward the back of the hacienda and out into the warm evening. She was surprised to see that it was just starting to grow dark. What an eventful day! Katie tipped her head back and searched out the Southern Cross. Seeing the beautiful stars that each part of the world had to offer was one of her favourite parts of being an international traveller. They walked together with Roman's hand warm at the bottom of her back.

He led her across the hard-packed dirt yard toward another home, much smaller than theirs, but well taken care of and beautiful from the outside. She could hear music and laughter as they approached. She looked up at him question-ingly. He gave her his usual blank expression and knocked on the door.

"Jorje and Lana wished to host our wedding dinner this evening," he informed her as the door opened.

"They live right next door to us?" Katie asked, surprised, just as the door swung open.

Lana beamed at Katie and drew her into a warm hug as if they'd been close friends for years instead of just a day. Katie hugged her back and allowed herself to be drawn into the warm, enchanting atmosphere. Who was she to turn down an authentic Mexican wedding feast? Especially when she was the guest of honour.

Katie had a genuinely good time getting to know Lana's large family and many of the people that now worked for Roman. Roman was never far from Katie's side and, though he let her chatter away to her heart's content with the women, he was quick to move her along whenever she happened to engage in conversation with a man. Such a chauvinist!

She stood at Roman's side, his arm tight around her waist. They had eaten and were listening to a band play lively music in the open air of a pretty patio while Katie attempted to a follow a conversation between Lana and two of her nieces. The girls worked in the neighbouring town and enjoyed the work because the pay was good. After that, Katie lost the thread of the conversation because the Spanish was too quick for her with a little too much local dialect thrown in.

Since her attention was drifting away from the women, she was all ears when Jorje approached Roman and said in a gruff voice, "I have news on Ramirez, boss."

Roman's dark eyes flicked down to Katie's face, taking in her curious attention. He gave her hip a squeeze and inclined his head to Jorje, indicating they would take their conversation elsewhere, away from the women. Katie understood. Cartel business. She crossed her arms to ward off the sudden chill when Roman moved away from her. She stayed with Lana and smiled indulgently when one of her nieces asked if she could touch Katie's hair.

"Don't be stupid, Ana," Lana snapped sharply throwing her hands up expressing her annoyance. "You act like you've never seen a blond before!"

Ana giggled, completely unperturbed and rolled her eyes at her auntie. "Well, never one so beautiful or freakishly tall or married to Roman Valdez. *Mierda*, he's so gorgeous!"

Lana gasped and slapped at Ana as she reached for Katie while Katie burst out laughing. Ana's sister grabbed her and hustled her away before her aunt could truly slap her silly for swearing and ogling the cartel boss.

"Wow, Lana," Katie said, reaching for her glass of wine and taking a hasty gulp. "I can see why you might not even want children if those are the sort of monsters your family are producing. And I am not freakishly tall, it's the heels!"

Lana laughed heartily and gulped her own wine with abandon, collapsing into a nearby chair. "*Si, niña*, and us Latina women are much shorter than you. Those nieces of mine can be very wicked."

"Amen to that!" Katie agreed, toasting Lana and taking the seat next to her. "Can I ask you something?"

"Of course," Lana said, her eyes scanning the room distractedly, making sure all of her guests were in order and having a good time.

"Who is Ramirez?" Katie asked in hushed tones, cutting straight to the heart of what she wanted to know.

Lana's eyes widened slightly and her entire focus landed on Katie. She glanced around anxiously for a second and then shrugged slightly. She kept her voice low as well when she replied, "I suppose it is no secret around these parts. The name is well known, although I would not go around speaking it to just anyone, child."

Katie nodded, having guessed that already. "So, who is he?" she persisted, taking another sip of her wine and glancing up. She could feel the heat of Roman's eyes on her. Sure enough, after a quick scan of the room, she discovered him standing just outside the patio doors alone with Jorje. The two men were deep in conversation, but Roman's gaze never strayed from his new wife.

"Ramirez is the name of the cartel that took out Roman's family and ran this area until recently," Lana said quickly, her voice dropping even more until she was whispering.

Katie glanced sharply back at Lana. She wanted to ask more questions. It had sounded like Jorje was referring to a specific Ramirez, not an entire group of people. But Katie could tell that Lana was uncomfortable and didn't want to push the other woman on the subject. Not in a room full of people loyal to Roman. She smiled and moved the conversation onto something more harmless, much to Lana's obvious relief. The two women drank and chatted together until Roman came to collect his rosy-cheeked bride.

"We're going?" she asked, turning bright blue eyes up to him. "But I'm having fun!"

He pulled her out of her chair, set her glass aside and guided her to the door. Leaning down, he spoke in her ear, "It is now time for *my* fun, *mi esposa.*"

His dark eyes met hers and he swept her out the door and into the cool night, picking her up when she couldn't keep up with his long, impatient strides. She gripped his shoulders and watched his clenched jaw as he strode through the black night with her toward their home. Though he had laughed and seemed to enjoy their evening together, the intensity of his emotions were now coming off him in waves. He seemed... enraged.

"Are you... angry with me, Roman?" she whispered hesitantly.

He stopped just before they reached the door and looked down at her. His dark brows were drawn down in a deep frown. His arms tightened around her and he didn't deny her question. She shivered against him. Was she going to be punished again for running from him? When would it end? When would he be done hating her for leaving?

Finally, he spoke, his voice quiet, despite the intensity she could feel vibrating through him. "You make me feel things, Katie... things I don't feel with anyone else. It's always been this way with you. I'm long past questioning this part of me. But..."

"But...?" she whispered, reaching up to touch his lips.

"I know you still want to leave me, even though I've tied you to me in marriage," he said bluntly, his eyes cutting to her fiercely, accusingly.

She gasped and dropped her hand. She lay stiffly in his arms, waiting for his next words.

"I know you so well, Katerina. Can see your thoughts

before you even have them. I know you'll keep trying to find ways to leave me and I will keep finding ways to tie you tighter to my side. Yes, I am angry," he snarled down at her, causing her to jump against him. "You bring out this savage in me that will do *anything* to keep you. I gave you your years of freedom and now you will pay for them."

She curled against him, blinking up at him. "What are you going to do to me tonight, Roman?" she whispered.

He chuckled darkly, his laughter reverberating against her body where she lay pressed against his chest. "I'm going to fuck my wife so hard that she won't forget she's mine. I'm going to exhaust her for one more night so she won't be able to walk away from me again."

He shoved the door open and strode into their home with Katie clasped so tight against him that she could barely breath. Her heart broke a little for her beast of a husband, because he wasn't wrong about her. The first chance she got, she was going to leave. She had no choice if she was going to secure their happy ever after.

# CHAPTER TWENTY-SEVEN

Roman didn't take Katie to her room. Instead, he took her to the master suite, a room on the floor below Katie's tower room, and set her gently on the huge bed. She sank into the smooth, plush bedding and leaned back. She watched him warily, heart beating with trepidation as he stepped away to remove his jacket and tie. As always, he stared back at her with a dark intensity that made her feel like both the only woman in the world and his hunted prey.

"Are you going to hurt me tonight, Roman?" she asked, a slight quaver in her voice. She pressed her knees together, aware of the ache still there from their earlier bouts of rough lovemaking. God, this man knew how to make an impression.

His gaze roamed over her body, lingering and warming over each part of her. That was what she loved about this man. He loved her wholeheartedly. Not just bits and pieces, but everything about her, from her face to her knees to her toes and everything in between. He'd never treated her like she was just tits and ass. That's how she knew if they made it to old age together, he would indeed love her to the end of her days just as fiercely as he did right now.

"Do you want me to hurt you, Katerina?" he asked, his hands going to the buttons on his shirt, the tattoos on his fingers flashing as he worked.

She thought about it for a moment. If she was honest with herself, though he did sometimes frighten her with his rippling power and intensity, the kind of sexual pain he dealt her was incredibly tempting. She met his eyes and shook her head slowly. "No Roman," she whispered. "I-I'm a little sore."

His lips curled into a wicked half grin. He reached for her with a suddenness that had her curling her legs up to protect herself. It was useless though, Roman would always have his way. He easily knocked her knees apart and held her open while he slid a big hand up the inside of her thigh and cupped her pussy through the silk of her panties. Katie gasped and squirmed against his possessive hold.

"Not too sore I hope, baby," he grunted, massaging her. She moaned, growing instantly wet for him, powerless against his masterful fingers and the slide of silk against her heated pussy. Still cupping her, he slid his fingers further down the back of her panties until they were pressed against her backside. "I can fuck you here instead. It's going to happen anyway, why not today? I fucked your pussy this morning. Should I take your ass, too, and make you mine completely?"

Katie's eyes dilated at his dark words, fear and adrenaline crashing together in a crazy symphony of need within her. She was helpless not to buck against him as sparks of pleasure shot through her core while he rubbed his fingers against her back passage, promising her the forbidden. She bit her lip and moved her hips restlessly, her knees falling open as he shoved her dress up her thighs.

He grunted and leaned on the bed, pushing her back until she was laying under him. He increased the pressure, sliding his thumb under the silk of her panties and pressing it against her clit. She tossed her head back restlessly into the bedding and thrust her hips up into his hand, cries of pleasure escaping her lips.

"Yeah, baby, tell me how you like it," he rumbled against her, nipping at the lacy edge of her dress, seeking access to her silken throat. "Never stop purring for me."

"I'll never stop," she moaned and reached for him, bringing his head down for a kiss. She told him with her tongue and her lips the things she hadn't been allowed to say during their brief wedding ceremony. She knew they were fucked up and they had a ways to go before they were ready for forever, but he belonged to her and she was ready to belong to him. At least for the one night, their wedding night. And this was the one thing they wouldn't screw up.

She pulled away from him for just a second, her hands tugging his shoulders down, and whispered against his mouth, "Make me feel so good, Roman."

"Fuck, baby," he groaned against her and kissed her so hard he arched her head back into the bedding and plundered her mouth with his tongue, fucking her in imitation of the way he would soon take her body with his cock. He shoved his knee between her legs and pushed them even wider. He pushed her panties impatiently to the side and plunged two fingers deep into her pussy.

Katie cried out sharply into his mouth, her hips bucking up to meet his fingers as pain from the sudden invasion of her still sore vaginal passage merged with pleasure as he began pumping his long, skilled fingers against her g-spot. She lifted her hips and moaned, thrashing underneath him while he slowly drove her insane, forcing her higher and higher toward the edge of mindlessness.

"Come for me, *hermosa*," he growled against her lips.

Katie did as he commanded and came with a scream and a rush of fluid across his still pumping fingers as he pressed them mercilessly against her. She bucked wildly under him, hanging onto his shoulders for dear life, her nails biting into the tanned skin over his tattoos. He forced her higher and higher, as more fluid soaked the back of her dress. She begged and cried for him to stop while urging him on with her hands and lips. He used his knees to force her legs impossibly wider.

"You are so good, Katerina, *mi esposa*," he praised her in deep, accented tones. "I have never seen such a beautiful sight. So abandoned, so full of life, and all mine. You have no idea what you do to me, baby."

"I can't take it Roman," she sobbed against his shoulder, rocking her hips into his lap while he continued to thrust his fingers in her soaked passage. "Please, you're killing me… it's too good…"

He chuckled and trailed burning kisses from behind her ear, down her throat to the edge of her dress. "Come for me one more time and I will take pity on you," he murmured against her ear.

"I d-don't know if I can!" she wailed, lifting her hips when he added a third finger and pressed them hard against her g-spot until she screamed and thrashed.

"You can and you will," he growled and placed a firm hand on her belly before dropping purposefully between her legs and pulling her clit into his mouth. He knew to be gentle with the tender flesh given the hard thrust of his fingers. It took only seconds for her to fly off the edge of another orgasm, much more intense than the last.

"Roman!" she screamed, reaching for his shoulders and digging her nails in. She needed something to ground her while her mind spun off in all directions as pleasure exploded from every pore.

Katie's body collapsed into the mattress, a boneless pile. She barely felt Roman shift her onto her stomach so he could unzip her dress and tug it off her limp body. He also took her bra and thoroughly soaked panties off. She stayed on her stomach and allowed her eyes to drift shut while Roman stood behind her and finished removing his pants and underwear.

"You tired now, baby?" he asked soothingly, running his big hands from her ass up her back in circular motions.

She moaned when his fingers pressed into the muscles and began to work incredible magic. She nodded slightly. "Mmhmm," she managed to murmur.

He nudged her legs apart, gently spreading them wide before settling his big body on the mattress between them. She didn't protest when he continued to work on her back, massaging her abused muscles. She didn't even care about the slight ache of his fingers drifting over the marks he'd given her the night before. It turned out he really hadn't whipped her very hard. Most of the marks were already fading into nothing. Katie turned her head so she could watch him work, enjoying the show of his magnificent pectoral muscles rippling in the dim lighting of the master bedroom. His dark hair and the facial hair he'd forgotten to shave, even on his wedding day, looked incredibly, mouthwateringly masculine on him.

He really was a gorgeous man. Despite the aura of deadly intensity surrounding him, Katie's heart couldn't help but skip that extra beat every time she took a good look at him. She still couldn't believe he'd chosen her. That eighteen years ago, this perfect man had staked his claim on a nerdy, gawky-looking teenager and then patiently waited for her to grow up. That even after all the shit she'd thrown at him over the years, he never stopped loving her. It made her want to be worthy of that love. To give them the future they deserved.

She groaned and arched her back a little when he pressed his thumbs into the indents at her lower back. "Ooooh

Roman, that's so good…," she moaned, wiggling under his hands.

"Fuck, Katie, if you don't lay still I'm not going to be able to finish working out the stiffness. Going to just fuck you raw, *mujer*," he growled, digging his fingers deep into her flesh.

She froze, not wanting him to stop. "I'll be good!" she promised.

He grunted and continued to work on her in silence. Katie relaxed under his skilled hands while he kneaded and pressed the flesh of her back, ass and thighs, gradually working any stiffness out of the muscles until she was a mass of contentment. As she began to drift off under his ministrations, she gradually began to notice a difference in the stroke of his hands. His long fingers began drifting closer and closer to her pussy, slowly stoking the embers of her orgasm.

Katie's lashes lifted from her cheeks and she glanced down the bed at Roman, watching him work. The muscles of his tattooed arms and shoulders flashed and rippled in the light while he stroked and touched her body, gradually working his way closer and closer to her core. As if testing him, Katie tried to close her legs. She couldn't. They were trapped wide on either side of his kneeling form.

Her breathing sped up as the long fingers of one of his hands began to dip between her legs. She was so primed from her previous orgasms that she jumped as soon as his fingers touched her labia. He brought his other hand down on her lower back, holding her still while he worked his fingers back inside her. Katie moaned and immediately began writhing, trained to his touch. He used two thick fingers to scoop her pussy juices and move them up to the puckered hole above.

Katie jumped and moaned, grabbing fistfuls of the bedding underneath her, preparing herself for the inevitable. She should have realized as soon as he mentioned taking her ass that he actually meant it. Roman always meant what he said. But she got so caught up in his touch and his mouth that she forgot. She thought he would fuck her pussy and then they would pass out in each other's arms and he would forget about his dark promise.

Oh god, she was scared! She had never done that before, not even by herself, and didn't know what to expect. But she was also exhilarated and excited by the thought of anal sex. She knew it would hurt in a wonderful way, especially at Roman's hands.

As always, Roman didn't wait for anyone's permission. He took care of Katie, but he also took what he wanted. Without warning, using the fluid he'd stolen from her pussy, he pressed one long, thick finger slowly and steadily into her ass the same as he had one year earlier. Katie cried out and tried to push back against him, but he held her down, whispering words of love and encouragement as he pushed steadily past the barrier of her anal ring.

"So beautiful, *mi amor*," he growled as he pressed his finger into her tight passage. "Never knew how good it would be. Only ever wanted you, baby, nobody else would do once I set eyes on my girl."

Once he bottomed out, he gave her a chance to just feel the incredible fullness within her body. It was a matter of seconds before the sizzling pleasure took hold, then she was lifting her hips for more. He gave her what she wanted, pulling his finger out and then pushing back in until she was mindlessly pushing her hips up to meet him thrust for thrust. When she was writhing and moaning, he scooped more fluid from her pussy and added another finger. Katie barely noticed the increased pressure as he steadily pushed both fingers into her and then pumped them in and out. She was moaning and begging for more as her body reach toward another orgasm, one that was different from any other she'd known before. It bit deeper than her usual orgasms, called to the masochist in her that loved that sting of pain with her pleasure.

"Roman!" she called blindly to him as she clawed at the bedding.

He yanked her hips back to him and lined his cock up against her pussy, steadily pushing himself deep into her wet, silken body. He went slow, mindful of any residual soreness she might still be feeling, though at this point Katie was more than willing to take whatever Roman would give her for more of his masterful touch. He blew her mind in every way when he set about playing with her body. They fit together in ways she thought only belonged in fairytales.

"I have you, baby," he growled from behind her, his voice strained but tender. "Just let go and feel."

Katie closed her eyes and let herself drift, safe in Roman's capable hands. She felt the near impossible fit of his cock glide through her vaginal passage, made even tighter from the bite of his fingers deep in her ass. She knew what would come next. Trusting Roman to take care of her, she just experienced the rhythm of his thrusts and the building orgasm.

Then he was pulling out of her pussy and replacing his fingers with his cock. He pulled her ass cheeks apart with his big hands and pressed her legs further up the bed with his knees. She moaned and arched her ass up to meet him, knowing it would hurt but trusting that Roman would make the pain worth a million hurts, because he knew her body better than even she did.

"Just breathe, *mi amor*," he urged and then pushed steadily into her.

Katie cried out and clutched the blankets underneath her, jerking them into her chest. She instinctively tried to drop her hips back into the bed to escape the pain, but he wrapped an arm around her waist and forced her back up into his body. She bit her lip and trembled in his hold as he continued to press steadily forward until he was seated completely within her. Katie was crushed beneath him, forced to bear his weight as he lay still on top of her, waiting for her to adjust to his invasion.

As with the press of his fingers in her ass, after a moment the feeling of his cock began to spark a deep visceral reaction within her. Her breathing changed and she began to wiggle against him, almost imperceptibly encouraging him to continue. A drop of sweat fell from his forehead, landing on the back of her shoulder, indicating the brutal hold he had on himself. Everything within him wanted to fuck his wife's ass with a savagery that would mark her, remind her who she belonged to. Instead, he waited patiently for her virgin ass to adjust to the feel of his cock before he began moving within her.

*"Oh my god!"* she yelled when he did start moving his hips over hers in shallow thrusts. Sparks of pleasure shot all through her. Nerve endings she didn't know existed suddenly came to life, throwing cascades of pleasure up and down her ass and all through her body. Unable to stop herself, Katie began pushing back into him, meeting him thrust for thrust until he was pulling out almost completely and slamming back into her.

The orgasm that built within her threatened to eclipse her previous two. She screamed and clawed her way toward it, unaware that Roman had to hold her down so she wouldn't climb up the bed in an attempt to escape the overwhelming pleasure he was forcing on her. Finally, as he neared his own orgasm and his cock flared wide within her tight passage, he reached underneath her and shoved his long fingers deep into her pussy, pressing them against her g-spot once more. Katie came with an ear-splitting scream. Her vaginal and anal passages clamped down on Roman so hard that he had no choice but to follow his woman over the edge.

*"Mierda!"* he snarled in her ear, unloading hot semen deep into her ass before collapsing on top of her.

Katie giggled at his bad language. Not very romantic. She

yawned widely and allowed herself to begin drifting toward sleep while he rolled off her and set about preparing them for bed. She was pretty sure he used a warm washcloth between her legs, but she was so far gone into sexual exhaustion that she wasn't betting money on her memories of anything that happened after he fucked her into the next century. Well, he certainly had accomplished his mission of exhausting his new bride to the point of making sure she couldn't run away.

# CHAPTER TWENTY-EIGHT

*"Mierda,"* Katie sighed, sitting up in bed and looking around. She was once more locked up in her tower room with her evil husband nowhere in sight.

*How the hell does he manage to do this to me without waking me up?* she wondered, climbing out of bed and twisting around in the full-length mirror to check out her ass. Yup, he really had gotten his name tattooed across her ass cheek and, nope, that really wasn't a crazy dream.

Katie had been at the hacienda for three full weeks now. Three blissfully wonderful (in a purely sexual way) weeks. But also, three extraordinarily frustrating weeks as her new husband treated her like a naughty puppy who would run away from home as soon as it was off its leash. Too bad he was right. Because the worse her crazy possessive husband treated her, the more determined she was to leave.

Every night except one, Roman took her to his bed and fucked her with vigour and imagination until she was too exhausted to keep her eyes open, let alone contemplate running away. Sometimes he was gentle and sometimes he was harsh, but he was always mindful of her pleasure before his. Then, each morning Katie would wake up in her own bed, alone and angry because he refused to spend the whole night next to his wife. She knew he wouldn't sleep with her because he didn't trust her until she was secure in the tower room. But it crushed her nonetheless.

Then, five days ago, he had a tattoo artist brought in. Together with Roman, they had designed a tattoo for Katie. No one asked her if she wanted a tattoo. No one asked her what kind of a tattoo she would choose if she were to get one. Certainly, no one asked her where on her body she would get a tattoo. When she did attempt to protest, Roman had simply informed her she could lay quietly through her tattoo or she could 'sleep' through it. Deciding an awake tattoo was better than a drugged tattoo, Katie had acquiesced with a glare, hiking up her skirt and laying down on the bed. God help her insane husband if she ever got her hands on that sleeping drug and a suicidal tattoo artist. He was so getting 'livin' la vida loca' tattooed across his forehead.

Roman had, of course, refused to leave. There was zero chance of him allowing another person to touch her body, let alone the flesh of her ass cheek, without him in the room the entire time. Never mind that he was paying the other person to do this for them. As Katie studied the pink rose with Roman's name scrawled through it, she had to admit that she actually kind of loved it.

Then her fingers strayed lower to the flesh of her thigh and the slight bump there. Now this little baby made her want to punch Roman Valdez in the throat like nothing else. The bastard. Immediately after her tattoo, he'd ushered the artist out of the room. But before Katie could get up and straighten her skirt, he'd ushered someone else in. A doctor, apparently. Without bothering to explain a damn thing, Roman had held her down while the doctor had swabbed her thigh and injected something into the area.

Katie had howled and smacked at Roman. He'd held onto her until the doctor put a bandage over the injection site and then discreetly left the room. As soon as Roman let her up, Katie jumped away from him, her hand flying to her thigh. She winced, but explored the reddened spot after peeling the bandage back. Her eyes widened as she felt the tiny device, as small as a grain of rice, under her skin. Then she turned narrowed eyes on her captor.

"You implanted me with a fucking tracker?" she hissed angrily.

He raised a dark eyebrow at her language. Katie was raised with a mom that didn't allow her children to use bad language. It hadn't stuck with her brothers, but Katie rarely swore unless she was really pissed off.

"Can't have you running on me, baby," he said matter of factly. "Got too many enemies out there now. You'd be a prime target."

She growled at him and shoved herself back on the bed, scooting away from him. She curled into the far corner turning her back on him and tugging her skirt down over her bent knees as if to protect herself. Tears gathered in her eyes. She knew he was crazy possessive of her and the past weeks had shown that he wasn't willing to give even an inch of leeway, but she had thought maybe eventually she would convince him to work with her. Now… after this, she knew he wouldn't change his mind about her. All these mafia guys were the same. Misogynistic assholes.

"Don't bother coming for me tonight," she said against the wall. "You can go fuck yourself for all I care."

She could feel the heat of his anger from behind her and knew he was controlling himself so he wouldn't reach out and grab her. Probably didn't want to hurt her too much more since she was already in pain from the tattoo and microchip. She glanced over her shoulder and saw that he was indeed standing next to the bed, his fists clenched. She shuddered almost wishing she hadn't issued such a challenge to him. He was not a man to take her lip lightly.

He must have sensed her regret because, instead of callously insisting she come to his bed, he said only, "You can have this night only to recover. Tomorrow you come to me." Then he turned and left the room.

That had been the night Katie had planned her escape from casa Valdez. The only night Roman hadn't exhausted her to breaking point. Tonight, she would execute her plan. She had everything she needed. She would pretend she had her period and couldn't perform her wifely duties. In reality, Katie's period was irregular and came pretty much whenever it pleased within a four to seven-week window. She had no way of knowing if Roman would respect her wishes anyway, but she was hoping. She was going to send Lana with the message later and beg for some Advil so it would look like she was feeling achy as well.

Though he was a demanding husband with a possessive streak a mile wide, Roman wasn't entirely cruel. If he thought Katie wasn't feeling well, he would want her well taken care of. She doubted he would drag her off to his bedroom to suffer just so he could get his rocks off. In fact, she was banking on him rushing to her bedside to see how she was doing and seeing with his own eyes that it was indeed just cramping and back pain that was causing her illness.

Katie wasn't wrong in her assumption. She had barely informed Lana that she wasn't feeling well and Roman was at her bedside, literally minutes later. Katie was sitting up in bed a pillow hugged to her chest. She watched in real awe as the door was shoved open with unnecessary force and her dark husband was stalking toward her. Katie had to stiffen her back to stop herself from scrambling across the bed to get away from him. She stared, open-mouthed as he strode directly to her bedside, his unreadable expression slipping for just a second to reveal true concern in the form of an angry scowl. Her heart pounded in response as a flash of remorse for her duplicity shuddered through her.

"Lana informs me that you're sick?" he demanded, reaching out to cup her chin and tilt her face up so he could study her. After a moment of frowning scrutiny, he said, "You seem fine to me."

So, Lana hadn't even had time to explain what was wrong with the lady of the house before Roman had come tearing up to her tower room. Wow. Aside from the whole locking her ass up every chance he got, Roman made an extremely attentive husband. Well, time to pull out the acting abilities since, apparently, Lana hadn't been very helpful and Roman hadn't given her time to slip under the covers and start moaning pathetically.

She dropped her eyes and curled her legs up into the pillow. "It's n-not a big deal, Roman," she said, clutching the pillow hard against her middle and blushing furiously. "I'll be fine… but do you think I can spend the next few nights in my room. A-alone." Her voice had dropped off to a whisper by the last word.

He growled and took her by the shoulders. "Damn it, Katie, just tell me what's wrong. Are you hurt?" he demanded, reaching down to yank the pillow out of her hands. He began running his hands over her arms, checking for an injury.

Katie was so surprised she let the pillow go without a fight. Knowing the depth of Roman's feelings for her, she had expected concern from him, but she hadn't expected this level of upset. Now that she thought about it, it made sense. Roman was all about control, especially when it came to her. He wouldn't be able to handle the thought of her being injured unless he was applying the pain himself and in complete control of every aspect of her torture.

She caught his hand as he started pulling her leg out so he could examine it. "Roman!" she gasped and then giggled because he pressed his thumb into the arch of her foot. "Calm down, I'm not hurt, *mi amor.*"

He froze, his dark eyes colliding with hers. She saw relief and something like smug happiness there as well. She rarely used any kind of endearment with him, let alone Spanish. She gripped his face between her hands and brought it down for a light kiss against his lips. She may have anticipated his concern, but she hadn't taken into account the stab of guilt she felt over giving him anxiety.

"It's my lady times… come to visit," Katie told him. She dropped her eyes, finding that she couldn't meet his eyes, though she didn't release his face. "I'm just not very comfortable right now. My back hurts and my belly feels heavy and swollen."

She felt some of the tension leave his shoulders as she explained what was wrong with her. She knew he had little to no experience with women's reproductive issues. Not that it would bother him. Roman was a good man, he would most likely educate himself on this new aspect of his wife now that the thought occurred to him. In the meantime, she was going to use his lack of knowledge against him.

"I just don't think I can have s-sex right now…," she trailed off as if too embarrassed to keep talking.

He nodded and sat on the edge of the bed, his hand stroked over her arm. "Of course. I'm not a monster, Katerina," he said, his deep voice almost hurt. His sharp gaze took in her flushed features. "You're not lying to me?"

Katie shook her head and clutched his hand while rubbing her other hand almost absently over her lower belly. Her legs were curled protectively underneath her. She was wearing a pair of royal blue satin pyjama pants and a light blue sleeveless lace-edged sleep shirt. "I do genuinely feel pretty crappy, Roman. I could use an Advil, actually. They usually calm the cramps enough so I can get some sleep. I'm exhausted," she said, smothering a yawn for emphasis, "but I won't be able to sleep with the aching."

He took her hand and rubbed his thumb over the back of it. "Of course, you will have what you need." His serious eyes continued to search her and then he seemed to come to a conclusion. "You have been here for just over three weeks. It makes sense that you would menstruate eventually unless you became pregnant. It was my hope, since I have withheld your pills, but… ah… well, maybe next month."

*Note to self*, Katie thought, gritting her teeth mentally, *the second you're free go get the damn birth control shot until this man learns how joint decision making works.*

Without warning, Roman stood, lifting Katie high in his arms, and striding toward the door. He then proceeded to have one of the most embarrassing conversations with Miguel that Katie could remember having to endure as he ordered the giant guard to have anything Katie might need sent to the master suite. At one point a matter of clarification came up and both men turned curious eyes down toward Katie's tomato red face.

"Tampons… regular," she gritted out before hiding her face in Roman's shoulder and deciding next time she created a brilliant escape plan she was going with *anything* else besides a pretend period ploy. Apparently, men had no shame anymore when it came to women's delicate times. The only person that seemed to be embarrassed by the direction of their conversation was Katie. She wondered if it would be common knowledge around the compound by morning that Katie had her period.

After securing Katie's needs, Roman strode down to the stairs with her held securely in his arms. Luckily, she had anticipated his wanting her in his room for the night so he could watch over her. Though it made her plan a little more difficult, she had to admit to a warm glow of happiness over his possessive care of her. He was so good to her when he wasn't being a barbaric pig and locking her behind doors. Not to mention curtailing her best skill. Her stunning ability to lift priceless artwork undetected. Except for that one time she got caught and forcibly married. But she didn't think that should count since Roman had been one step ahead of her since she was thirteen years old.

It was Katie's turn now.

# CHAPTER TWENTY-NINE

He felt her loss before he opened his eyes. It was like a missing piece of his soul. He'd felt it the day his mother died. He felt it each time Katerina did her dark little dance out of his life. He felt it now. She may still be close, but he'd been steadily losing her over the last few days. It was why he'd implanted her with a tracking chip. Because he knew his little escape artist. Knew that she plotted and planned. Yet he'd fallen for her cheap trick because his concern for her welfare combined with his desperate need to believe he could trust her had caused him to make a mistake. One that he was going to bitterly regret.

Flinging the blankets off his naked chest, he rolled from the empty bed and searched the darkness, a hunter attempting to track his prey. The master bedroom door that he had locked securely before bed was now standing open. Roman pulled on a pair of worn jeans and rushed into the hallway bellowing, "Katie!"

He knew she wouldn't respond. She had either found a way out of his fortified compound or she was hiding from his wrath. But his shout did bring Miguel and one other guard running to his side. He instructed them to wake everyone and search the property. Roman went immediately to check on Woman with Folded Arms. Katie was unlikely to leave without her precious painting unless she had no other choice. He was relieved to find the gallery room and painting untouched.

His next stop was the laptop in his office. He wasted no time in activating the signal in her implant. His heart leapt in relief and some of his panic eased when he realized she was still in the house. From what he could tell, she was on the top floor, in the tower. No… she was on the roof.

He texted Miguel to meet him on the roof, but not to approach her unless she was easy to reach. He knew Katie, knew her penchant for high places. He didn't want her feeling trapped. She might do something stupid.

Roman took the steps two and three at a time until he was at the top. Miguel was standing by the door that led to the roof. "Jorje is keeping an eye on her," he muttered, nodding toward the ledge just before a steep drop off, more than thirty feet off the ground.

Roman tensed as he headed out onto the ledge. Jorje took his arm and helped him ease past. Katie stood on a ledge, at the corner of the house where the South and West walls came together. It was pretty much the worst place for her to stand. There were too many trees and fences on the ground for his security to get a good view. Plus, she had chosen a spot with at least two obstacles – a balcony and a window hanging – on the way down. He shuddered as he cataloged the possible injuries she could sustain if she fell.

"Stop thinking that way, Roman," her quiet voice reached him, sweet and clear in the night. "You'll drive yourself crazy, *mi amor*."

She turned her pale face toward him. She looked completely otherworldly standing there in the dark night in nothing but her blue satin sleep pants and sleeveless cotton shirt. Her blond wavy hair, which had grown past her shoulder blades now, was blowing slightly in the breeze. Strands were floating across her face, obscuring her beautiful eyes where they watched his every move.

"You call me love, Katerina, yet you stab me in the heart by putting yourself at risk," he growled, prowling closer.

She laughed sharply, bitterly, and shook her head. "*I'm* stabbing *you* in the heart? You've locked me up and threatened my freedom at every conceivable turn. You haven't even considered discussing the easement of my restrictions. You've taken my career away from me and you dare to talk to me about what I'm doing to your heart?" She glared at him and turned swiftly, ripping a growl of warning from his throat. "Stop moving or I will jump, Roman."

Roman rubbed a frustrated hand over his head and unshaven jaw, wanting with every fibre of his being to stalk over to his woman and yank her off the ledge before tearing her flimsy pants from her body and fucking her raw right there on that roof for daring to play games with him. Instead, he was forced to stand still and listen to her. Give credence to her words so she wouldn't jump and end both of their lives in one reckless move. It made his blood boil that he couldn't control this situation, control his woman.

"Please, just come to me, Katie love," Roman said in as even a voice as he could manage. "We'll talk about it when you're safe, baby. Can't talk like this when I'm worried about you falling."

She laughed, her beautiful voice like a sad, husky chime in the wind. "As soon as you get your hands on me, you'd lock me up so tight we both know I'd never see the light of day again. Not unless I was chained to your side, barefoot and pregnant with even fewer choices than I have now."

They stared at each other, his dark eyes clashing with her blue ones. Every muscle in his body strained with the effort it took not to lunge across the several feet separating them and drag her back from her ledge. He read something in her eyes that shook him deeply. She was dead serious. She wasn't playing a game with him. Katie meant every word.

"Deny it, why don't you!" she yelled at him, her body shaking with anger as she balled her hands into elegant fists. He growled, hating the way she swayed with emotion, both toward and away from the ledge, heedless of the precariousness of her position.

Fury coursed through him, prickling the back of his neck. He gripped the ledge next to him to hold himself back and answered her truthfully. She knew anyway. "I'd imprison you in my fucking basement. Build a cage that puts your current bedroom to shame and hold you in it until the end of time or until I was sure," he snarled, stabbing a finger at her, "you had nowhere left to run. I would hunt down and kill everything you loved until there was nothing but ashes for you to run to. Is that what you want to hear, Katie?"

"At least it's the truth!" she yelled back at him, azure blues blazing fury. She'd never looked more beautiful or crazy to him than in that moment.

Unable to hold himself back from reclaiming his wife, Roman took a lunging step toward her reaching out to snatch her from the ledge. Katie danced backward with breathtaking swiftness, tearing a shout of anger from Roman. A similar shout of warning echoed from Jorje who stood behind Roman watching the strange marital tableau playing out on their rooftop.

Katie teetered precariously on the ledge as though she were about to go over the side. Roman watched in horror as she easily righted herself with a careless laugh and then brought her leg up with knee bent then straightened it out to the side with toe pointed. Then, just as quickly, she dipped into a ballerina pose with her leg curved gracefully over her back and her body low to the ledge. She grabbed the ledge with both hands, but kept her eyes on him the entire time to make sure he wouldn't try to grab her again.

"Oh, is this another thing you didn't know about me, Roman?" she asked innocently, batting her long lashes deviously.

He wanted to wrap his hands around her long, graceful neck more than he wanted his next breath. "Knew you fucking danced when you were a kid," he snapped impatiently.

She laughed and straightened. Then she stretched completely backward, bending her body in half and gripping the ledge behind her head. He began sweating and paced backward then forward again, knowing exactly what she was about to do and knowing there wasn't a goddamned thing he could do to stop her unless he wanted to either knock her off the ledge himself or give her a reason to jump. She kicked her legs up in the air, nearly giving him a heart attack, and brought them gracefully down onto the ledge of the South wall behind her, standing up as though she didn't have a care in the world.

"I continued with dance and also gymnastics," she said with a teasing grin, twirling easily on the ledge before coming to a stop on one foot with the other one curved up next to her inner thigh.

If he didn't want to spank her ass into the next century, he would have admired her skill and grace as well as her insane bravery. Now he knew where she was getting her adrenaline fixes in between jobs. She was dancing on rooftops. She stretched her long leg behind her and reached back to grasp it in one hand, tilting forward. She teetered a tiny bit before finding the correct balance.

"I was very good at ballet, you know," she said almost absently as he took another shuffling step forward when her eyes flicked off him for a split second. "Only I'm too tall, so I couldn't dance professionally. Can you imagine, Roman? A few inches shorter and my entire life would have gone in a completely different direction. I could have been a dancer instead of an art thief."

She laughed wildly and he couldn't help but crack a tiny smile at her audacious humour while taking her life into her hands on the edge of an almost four-storey drop. Fuck, she held *his* life in her small hands, too. If she fell, so did he.

"It doesn't matter what direction your life had gone, *mi esposa*, you are still a little psycho," Roman said affectionately, despite the rage and fear still pumping through his veins.

She laughed and nodded in agreement, dropping her leg and stretching into some kind of bowing finish with her arms held high over her head. Her blazing blue eyes locked on his. His heart sped up, knowing she was headed toward some kind of grand finale. And not the kind that ended with him handcuffed to a hospital bed and her gone from his life. Fuck, he thought she'd ripped his heart out of his chest a year ago when she'd done that to him. Now, he realized, at least he knew she was safe and sound wherever she had gone. Faced with this situation, he would a thousand times prefer to have her run from him than put herself in danger.

"There is something else I studied over the years besides ballet and gymnastics. Something that fed the dark adrenaline junkie in me. Something you never could have found out about. I didn't practice this past year, because I knew you had me followed all over the world, you stalker. I hope I'm not too out of practice or this is going to hurt."

"I don't care, Katie," he growled and then softened his tone until he was pleading, sensing that she was getting closer and closer to her point. He desperately wanted to stall. "Just please, come down. I'll give you anything you want. We'll negotiate if that's what you want. Please, don't do this, please don't do whatever you're thinking of doing, *mi mujer, mi esposa*."

"You won't," she said sadly, straightening and dropping her

arms, all pretence at play gone. She stood on the ledge, looking down at him like she was his queen, her eyes cutting straight through him as she spoke. "You'll take me and lock me back up. Just like you said. We're caught in a broken love story, Roman. You want me desperately and you're terrified I'll disappear from your life. For my part, I've messed up by pushing you away because I never thought I was good enough for you. And now that I know I am good enough to be your equal, you don't think I'm strong enough to stand by your side."

"What do you want from me, Katerina?" he asked, his voice rough with anguish. He dropped to his knees and slapped a hand over her name on his bare chest, knowing that there was nothing more he could do. He'd begged, he'd threatened. Nothing moved her.

Finally, he saw it. A flicker of truth in her eyes, something other than the perpetual guarded pain that was her entire existence. It was the blazing love she felt only for him. The love she so rarely let free. She smiled slightly.

"Now that is the question I've been waiting eighteen years for you to ask, *mi amor*," she whispered on the wind. "Come find me and I will tell you."

She looked away from him and jumped off the roof.

# CHAPTER THIRTY

Domingo Ramirez smelled yucky.

Well, his place smelled like shit anyway. Literally. Like there were no functioning toilets in the cesspool that Domingo was passing off as a home these days. Given his penchant toward ickiness, Katie was willing to bet the man himself smelled equally bad.

"This is *so* far beneath me," Katie lamented, wrinkling her nose in disgust.

With a sigh of disgust, she pulled on her leather gloves, more to protect her delicate hands than out of worry for leaving fingerprints, and set about finding her prize. She allowed herself the occasional grumbling complaint as she sorted through the dirty clothes, broken furniture and gag-worthy amounts of empty booze bottles that littered the entire hovel. She reminded herself repeatedly as she searched that if everything went according to plan she could go back to breaking into gorgeous penthouses, castles and chateaus while leaving this disgusting little shanty a one-time deal.

While she was crouched, sorting through a plastic bag full of empty liquor bottles, a book shifted and slid off a table to her left, causing Katie to shriek and fall on her ass. Wide eyed, she watched in horror as some kind of rodent scurried out and ran into a trash pile. She tried to determine if she was more surprised by what she suspected was a rat or the fact that Domingo had actual reading material in his home.

"Oh my god, Domingo, you've really come down in the world," she announced, thinking of the dark but gorgeous accommodations at the hacienda. She didn't know if he'd actually lived right in the house, but rumour had it his family had.

Finally, after searching the entire place top to bottom, she was forced to face up to the fact that her prize was not there. He'd either sold it, for copious amounts of booze and porn magazines, or had it on his person. Either possibility meant that she would need to do the unpalatable and talk to the guy. She found the cleanest patch of hovel, a forgotten chair in the corner of what she thought might be a kitchen, and sat.

She went over several scenarios in her head, trying to decide which one to go with when Domingo finally stumbled in, slamming his front door against the wall so hard the entire cottage shook. Katie jumped in surprise. As she heard him stumbling around the entrance, swearing and falling into walls, she realized none of her usual scenarios were going to work. Which was really a shame, because she was looking forward to using the 'lost gringa tourist that accidentally wandered into Domingo's place and hit him over the head with a frying pan after manipulating information about Filipe's knife' scenario.

Oh well, now she was going to plan B: ask drunk Domingo where the knife is, hit him in the head with a frying pan anyway for being a dick to Donna Marie and then get out. Domingo came stumbling into the kitchen, nearly falling over a pile of bottles on his way to the kitchen sink, which was full of nasty, unwashed dishes. He shoved his head under and turned the tap on.

Was he trying to end it all by drowning himself? Because that was not a good way to do it in Katie's opinion. She was pretty sure he could still breath around the water that was slowly going up his nose. It was beginning to look like the drunken Domingo was falling asleep with his head in the sink, water pouring into his ear, over his face and onto the floor.

With a sigh of disgust, Katie stood with her hands on her hips. "Hey, Domingo, you got a minute?"

Domingo jerked so hard his head hit the cupboard above the sink. Katie snorted, but calmed quickly. She didn't think he would appreciate humour at his expense. Her eyes fell to his belt as he spun around, surprisingly agile for a majorly drunk guy. The dagger she'd come for was sheathed at his waist. Well damn. If she'd known that, she never in a million years would have pawed through his dirty underwear, sheets, socks, porn collection... seriously no amount of bleach was going to erase her time in this place.

"The fuck you doin' here, *puta*?" he demanded.

*Well that was a rude assumption to make*, Katie thought grumpily. *How did he know she was a whore?*

He eyed her up and down, making her skin crawl in a way that made cuddling with the rat look like a great idea. She really wished she didn't need to approach him for the dagger. She wondered if she could get him to just slide it across the kitchen floor toward her, like people did in movies. Oh wait, did she need some kind of leverage to get him to do that?

"Did the boys send you over?" he asked drunkenly, lurching away from the counter and stumbling toward her. "Dey know I like me some blondies."

"Oh... no," Katie gagged. "Oh my god... ew. So gross!"

He reached for her just as she planted her heavy, reinforced leather boot in his crotch. He went straight over backwards into a pile of empties. Cockroaches scattered across the kitchen. Katie screamed and jumped around in terror as the cockroaches ran while Domingo clutched his aching balls and howled in pain. She forced herself to reach down and snatch the dagger from its sheath.

Holding it up to the light, she ensured that it was the one she'd come for. A perfect match to the one Roman carried with him, only instead of a wolf etched into the handle, this one had a scorpion. According to Lana, this knife had belonged to Felipe, Roman's uncle. A man that was more of a father to Roman than the man that had sired him.

When the Valdez cartel had fallen, Felipe had helped Roman escape at the expense of his own life. When Domingo had caught up to Felipe, he had tortured Roman's uncle brutally for the boy's location. Felipe had died never giving his nephew up to the Ramirez cartel. According to Lana, he'd been gutted, then had his throat slit by this very knife, a knife given to him by his own father, Roman's grandfather. The story and the knife had become legend, which is why Katie refused to allow the treasure to remain with this scum.

Katie turned to leave, the dagger tucked safely away into a sheath she'd brought with her. She turned back, glaring down at the disgusting pig of a man. "This is for Donna Marie," she snapped, drew back her foot and kicked him in the ribs. He howled in pain, but with a swiftness that took Katie by surprise, Domingo grabbed her booted ankle and yanked her right off her feet.

Katie's legs went flying out from under her and she landed sprawled out on top of Domingo. Before she had time to process whatever nasty thing was crusted onto his shirt, he had his hands wrapped around her throat and was rolling her underneath him. He squeezed her neck with enough strength to choke the breath out of her. Katie gagged and choked as black dots danced in her eyes. She clawed at his hands trying to pry them off of her throat.

He rocked his hips against her, shoving what was unmistakably an erection into her. Katie felt vomit rushing up her throat and had to swallow it. She tried punching every part of him she could reach, but he didn't feel a thing, probably numb from the amount of booze in his system. Finally, she managed to punch him in the nose and he loosened his hold on her neck. He swung his head, shaking it while she scrambled, trying to get out from underneath him.

"Going to kill you, bitch, then fuck your scrawny ass until you beg to die," he snarled grabbing her neck again and reaching for her shirt, clearly intent on tearing it. His aim was clumsy and he only managed to tug the sleeve down a little.

"Oh god, your breath is so… bad!" Katie gagged hoarsely, looking around frantically. The rat, or possibly a new one, scurried past, running over the ends of Katie's hair and then over an empty tequila bottle. Katie's eyes widened and she grasped the neck of the bottle. She swung it into his head with all her strength, catching him in the temple.

Domingo's eyes rolled back and he slumped sideways. Katie wasted no time scrambling out from underneath him and back onto her feet. As grateful as she was to her rat buddy for showing her the way to get Domingo off, she wasn't interested in getting her hair stepped on again. She quickly checked to make sure Domingo was alive. Killing him wasn't part of her plan. Not yet, anyway. Then she backed up a little and kicked him in the foot. She'd learned her lesson about kicking boys in the ribs, they could grab her foot when she was least expecting it.

"You wanted to fuck my ass and *then* kill it, you total and complete idiot," Katie told his unconscious form with disgust dripping from every syllable. "Otherwise you'd be fucking a dead woman. Word order matters, moron. God, Donna Marie is so much better off."

Shaking her head in annoyance, Katie whirled away from

him and stomped toward the front door, more than ready to leave Domingo Ramirez's less-than-friendly abode. Roman could have him, gift wrapped with a bow on top, for all she cared. She didn't like the asshole one little bit. Hmm. Could she arrange a gift-wrapping?

# CHAPTER THIRTY-ONE

He'd found her.

She felt the prickling heat of his gaze as it landed on her and scorched every bit of her bikini clad form where it was stretched out on the lounger. She knew he would find her eventually. It wasn't like she'd done a great job of hiding this time. She loved the Mayan Riviera and had chosen a particularly gorgeous location to escape to while she waited for her irate husband to catch up with her. Using his credit card to purchase clothes in Cancun and then paying for a two-week stay at an exclusive five-star resort was like begging him to come find her sooner rather than later. And her gorgeous, dark man hadn't disappointed.

She *had* slowed him down a bit though by digging the vile locator chip out of her thigh. It was the first thing she'd done after crawling out of bed the night she'd left him. She'd grabbed a knife and hurried up to the roof, certain he would activate the chip as soon as he realized she wasn't in bed with him. Gritting her teeth, she had cut into her thigh (not very far, because the chip wasn't deep) and pulled it out with the tip of the knife. She had dabbed antiseptic on the wound, but left it open since it was still bleeding. It had hurt to dance and jump with a wound in her thigh, blood dripping slowly down her leg as she twisted and turned. But the pain had not been nearly as bad as watching Roman suffer at her hands, terrified that she was about to kill herself. As long as she lived she would never forget the look in his eyes.

She wondered what he'd thought or said when he'd discovered the little chip in a water glass along with a bottle of antiseptic and a few bloodied cotton balls up on the rooftop. Katie winced a little. On second thought, she really didn't want to know what he thought when he saw that stuff, it probably wasn't complimentary.

She could see Roman out of her peripheral vision as he approached on the beach. Oh, yummy! He certainly didn't fit in with his dark blue jeans, tight black T-shirt, leather vest and boots, but he was always the star in her fantasies. A smile drifted across her lips as she felt his eyes drinking her in, from the top of her head, covered in a wide-brimmed sunhat to protect her pale skin from the sun, down her long, lithe body, clad in a hot pink bikini, to her toes, painted coral with delicate crystals set in the big toenails. She'd stopped into a salon in Cancun and paid for it courtesy of her generous *esposo*. She knew he enjoyed her new curves, some of them regained after he'd removed the stress of Colin from her life and some of them from the enforced satisfaction of marriage at the hacienda.

Roman sat heavily in the lounge chair beside hers. He faced her, his knees spread, his arms loose but tense between his legs. She didn't look at him, but she glanced down at his boots, dug deep in the white sand. Such a strange juxta-position.

Before he could say anything, a waiter appeared with a tray. "Your drinks, Señor and Señora Valdez."

Roman didn't take his eyes off of Katie as the server set their drinks on the small table between their two chairs. Two shots of tequila and a margarita. Katie smiled and thanked the man, handing him a generous tip. She waited for him to leave before reaching beneath her towel on the other side of her chair. She took the dagger she had stolen from Domingo and stabbed it into the wooden table between their two shot glasses, causing the liquid to jump. Roman's eyes went to the knife, recognition burning immediately within their dark depths.

"How?" he demanded, his eyes on the dagger still quivering in the cheerful lime coloured wood of the table in between their two chairs. "I've been searching for this man for a year. We both know I'm a born hunter, baby. I could find you anywhere in the world. How did you find Domingo Ramirez in my country when I have failed?"

She smiled and took a sip of her drink. "Oh baby," she purred, "don't take it personally! You're a damn good hunter, everyone knows that. You can find anyone and, given enough time, I have no doubt you would have found Domingo as well."

A delicate shudder rippled through Katie's frame as she remembered Domingo and the state of his home. She hastily took another long sip of her drink, enjoying the warmth that spread through her belly and chased away the awful scene in Domingo's cottage. That was something she would never tell her husband. He didn't need to know how close to rape and death she had actually come in her insane quest to prove to her husband that she was equal to him. Not for herself, because, yes, he would undoubtedly rage at her and spank the life out of her. No, she didn't want him to feel guilt. He would twist the scenario around and eventually blame himself for driving her into a corner.

"Domingo left a girlfriend behind, did you know?" Katie asked, looking at her husband from beneath her lashes. He still looked good enough to eat, but their weeks of separation had clearly weighed on him as much as it had on her. No more of that. She was done running.

Roman's lip curled in disgust. After meeting the man in person, Katie tended to agree. She nodded. "Donna Marie," she told him, sipping nonchalantly at her drink. "A cute little thing that he absolutely didn't deserve and I was quick to tell her so when she brought in the freshly washed laundry each week."

"Son of a bitch!" Roman exploded quietly in the seat next to her. "How did I miss such a thing?"

Katie giggled wickedly. "It turns out even though dude is a disgusting cockroach of a douche, he kept in touch. Mostly to keep an eye on your situation because he knew Donna Marie was working at the big house. I can't believe," she stopped to make a gagging sound, "that *man* – and I use the word lightly – actually thought a woman of that calibre would wait around for the likes of him. She never told him shit, by the way, so don't even think about unleashing any kind of hell on her for blabbing. She mostly just lamented that she was almost thirty-five and unmarried. I told her she needs to get some self-esteem, get a better job and boyfriend worthy of her gorgeous ass. Because, girl please…"

"Katerina!" Roman cut her off sharply. "I don't want to hear about Anna-Marie's…"

"Donna Marie," Katie corrected him.

"Whoever!" he growled impatiently, pulling the empty glass from her fingers and slamming it on the table. "You mean you managed to get all of this information from my staff when I did not, and then you sat on it? You did not come to me?"

Katie sighed and looked away from the accusation in his eyes. "No, Roman, I didn't."

"Why?" he demanded, his voice taking on a savage edge. "You know it is my right to avenge my family. My uncle. The man Domingo sliced open from ear to ear because he would not give away my location."

Katie sat up and swung her feet off the lounger. She reached for the dagger and pried it out of the wooden table so she could make her next point. It wasn't easy, dammit! This is why she didn't mess around with knives. Roman's dark eyes tracked her every move. Finally, she worked the blade free and held it loosely between her thighs.

"Vengeance is still yours, Roman. I never intended to take that from you when I went after him." Yeah, she was definitely never going to tell him how close she came to filleting Domingo like a fish when he was laying helpless on the floor and she was standing over him with the knife. For *so* many reasons.

"Then why did you do it?" he demanded, pain evident in his voice now. His voice dropped to a low growl as the words tore from his throat. "I wanted to die when you went off the roof, woman. Jorje had to hold me back or I would have leapt with you. But you fucking climbed down like you were born a monkey."

Katie's breath left her in a rush. She had been counting on Jorje holding him back from doing something rash. She'd known he would rush after her. Known how great his panic would be until he saw her safe on the ground. It had been the one part of her plan that had been hardest to execute. Roman didn't deserve that kind of pain. But it was the only way she could think of to make him really listen to her for a few minutes, then make a quick escape without falling back into his hands.

*It was worth it*, she reminded herself. He was here with her now and if he was willing to actually listen with open ears and an open mind, perhaps they could move on to their version of happily ever after.

"Parkour," Katie murmured.

"Yeah," Roman said gruffly. "I figured that out once my

heart started beating again and I remembered what you said about learning a new skill. But fuck, you could've told me before you jumped. Think I aged a good thirty years over that stunt."

Katie laughed and shrugged. "If I'd told you, you would've realized what I meant to do and tried to grab me before I was ready to jump."

"Still, fucking dangerous, Katerina. People die doing that shit," he grumbled.

"Says the cartel boss," she laughed, rolling her eyes.

He stared at her as though seeing her for the first time. Her heart pounded as she waited for his verdict. Was he thinking of extra evil ways to lock her up now that she'd revealed all of her cards, or was he looking at his wife and seeing the potential powerhouse he could have at his side? Was he looking at her with the respect she craved from him since their first meeting eighteen years ago? God, she hoped so!

"What do we do about Ramirez?" Roman asked gruffly.

Katie's heart took flight, soaring into the clear blue Riviera sky. He said *we*, not I! She turned her face up to him and flipped the blade in her hand. She held it out to him, offering the gleaming bone handle to her husband. His hand closed over it, brushing against her fingers and sending sparks sizzling through her.

"He's all yours, *mi esposo*," she said with a quick grin. "Consider him the wedding gift I never gave you."

Roman's eyes glowed with a new kind of warmth she wasn't used to seeing. A combination of love and respect. It stole what was left of a heart she thought he'd taken completely long ago. Flipping the knife easily in his hand, he looked down into her face. He looked like he wanted to swoop at her like a huge, dark and dangerous bandit about to steal her away. Katie really, really hoped so.

He stared back at her, studying her with steely resolve,

clearly trying to decide if he was going to pick up her challenge or throw her on his shoulder, carry her back to the hacienda and lock her ass back up. Finally, he picked up the shot glass still sitting on the table. He handed her the other and said in his deep serious voice, "Equals, *mi esposa*," before tossing the drink back.

# CHAPTER THIRTY-TWO

Katie grinned and gulped hers back as well before whooping with joy and hurling herself across the lounger and into his lap. Roman was quick to toss the blade aside before his reckless woman accidentally stabbed herself. He knocked her ridiculous hat off and kissed her thoroughly before demanding, "Now tell me where the fuck that *culero* lives?"

"I have a map to his place in my room," she said huskily, kissing along his jaw. She rocked back on his lap with a grin and earned a tortured groan from him.

"It's a damn good thing that's exactly where I want to be right now," he growled and bent down to toss her over his shoulder using one arm. Katie laughed and clung onto him with one hand while gripping her hat with the other. She was glad she'd left her sandals in her room or she was pretty sure they wouldn't make it.

He reached for the dagger and demanded, "Now point the way to our room. I have apparently paid a lot for our stay here and intend to fuck my wife until she is too weak to leap off high buildings and break into the houses of my enemies."

Katie giggled and pointed toward a set of condos. "Well,

when you put it that way, it sounds like I might have done something wrong, Roman."

"We can discuss your punishment when we get to the room."

"Roman," she warned, her voice taking on a pleading note as she remembered the whipping.

"Katerina, *mujer*," he returned, his own voice unsympathetic as he strode in the direction she'd indicated. "Do not even pretend you don't love what I do to you."

She dug the key card out of her bikini top and handed it to him when they arrived at the room. She thought he would immediately demand the map, but instead he kicked the door closed, locked it and tossed her on the bed. She landed with a gasp and a bounce. He looked like some kind of crazy Mexican villain, straight out of the movies, standing over her with a wicked looking dagger. The breath caught in her throat and she instinctively tried to back away from him up the bed as he stepped slowly toward her, his expression dark and hungry.

Though he seemed to understand that their marriage had to be a partnership if it was going to work, it didn't mean he wasn't going to punish her for running away from him. Again. And probably a little for jumping off the hacienda roof. And damn, she really hoped he didn't find out she actually met Domingo Ramirez, because she suspected he wouldn't enjoy that little tidbit.

Her breath came out in a panicked rush when he pressed his knee into the mattress and began stalking her across the bed. Her back hit the wall of pillows. She had nowhere to go and her dark predator of a husband was closing in on her with that frighteningly unreadable expression in his eyes. He gripped her ankle in one large hand and yanked her back down the bed. Katie cried out in protest until she was lying completely prone underneath him.

She stared up at Roman, her breasts heaving in excitement

and fear. She pressed her hands flat against the mattress at her sides and waited for his next move. Roman was never predictable, but the one thing she could count on was a wild ride.

"You're going to want to stay very still, baby," he said, his voice deep and amused as he straddled her hips. He slid the flat of the blade up her arm until it was under her bikini strap. "I don't know how often Ramirez sharpened the blade."

"I don't know either," she whispered as he slid the knife through the fabric with ease, "but I had it sharpened for you in Cancun. It wouldn't have made much of a statement if it hadn't stuck in the table when we were talking."

He chuckled and continued to cut away at her clothes, careful to keep the blade away from her skin. Knowing how much she enjoyed the feel of metal against her flesh, he did run the dull side over her breasts and nipples once he bared them. She arched into the sensation and moaned for him, loving the feel of his cock hard against her belly.

"Do you regret getting it sharpened for me, now that I have you under my hands? Are you worried I might cut you?" he growled, working his way down her body. He slid down her long, athletic legs so he could slice through the sides of her bikini bottoms. She moaned, knowing the crotch was soaked through already.

"Never. You would never hurt me, *esposo*," she breathed, arching her back so he could tug the bottoms away from her. She blushed when they stuck a little to her pussy and he had to give them an extra tug to peel them away from her dripping wetness.

"You know me better than anyone, my beautiful wife," he growled flipping the knife off the side of the bed. He reached for her legs and hauled them over his arms, dragging her core closer. "Now you will pay for denying me what is mine for these past several days. I am a starving man, Katerina."

She shrieked and arched her back as he swooped down to claim her pussy with his mouth. She'd been expecting the intimate kiss, knowing how much he loved to taste her, but she hadn't imagined the intensity, the frantic need he would have for her. No matter how much she begged or pleaded, he continued to eat her like a man dying of starvation. When she tried to push his head away so she could gain a reprieve, he captured her wrists in one hand and held them tight against her belly.

"Roman, it's too much," she squealed, squirming in his too tight hold, knowing there would probably be bruises on her wrists.

"Should have thought of that before you jumped off a roof," he growled against her slippery flesh before pushing his broad shoulder further into her thigh so he could free the hand that was holding her leg high. He plunged two fingers deep into her slick passage and began massaging her g-spot with short, brutal strokes.

Katie's screams grew louder until she was sure everyone in the resort would think someone was getting murdered in her room. Her hips rocked against him, meeting him thrust for thrust despite her cries for mercy until her world exploded in a psychedelic rainbow of colour. Her neck arched back as she rode the waves of pleasure while he lapped up the juices that flowed from her overheated cunt.

Instead of leaving her to bask in the happy afterglow of her orgasm, Roman continued to drive her toward another unwanted peak. It took Katie a moment to realize what he was doing when her overstimulated body refused to come down from its perfect high. She woke up to the fact that he was still wedged between her thighs, his tongue stroking her with purpose, his fingers pressing even deeper into her snug channel.

"Roman, oh my god… Roman… too much… hurts so good…" she garbled as he coaxed her body higher and higher while she thrashed under his skilled hands. He completely ignored all of her pleas as she begged him to give her a break.

"I won't make it! Can't... can't come again!" she shrieked.

"You can and you will," he growled pressing his fingers so hard against her g-spot that she saw stars. He swooped back down and, instead of licking her, he bit down on her sensitive clitoris, taking it into his mouth and using his teeth against the flesh, claiming it.

Katie screamed, falling apart in his arms again as another orgasm, more intense than the last, crashed over her. This time the waves were black velvet instead of colourful. She barely held on to consciousness as she felt Roman set her back down on the mattress. Through the rushing sound of her own orgasm and the crash of waves against the beach, she heard the unmistakable sound of his zipper dropping.

She managed to open her eyes in time to see him lean over her limp body. His lips hovered over hers. She turned her face to his and saw an expression in his eyes that she'd never seen before. It looked like... peace. She smiled up at him. She'd given him that by giving him herself. She reached for him, wrapping her arms as far as she could around his broad shoulders. He accommodated her by dropping his big body onto hers until every part of them were touching. He was still wearing all of his clothes, too impatient to undress.

With one thrust he was inside her, filling her up completely. Katie gasped as pleasure and the incredible sensation of being completely full sparked throughout her. She lifted her knees along his denim-clad thighs and clasped him close to her. He pulled her up into the heat of his body, hugging her to him, and began rocking his hips into the cradle of her thighs. After the intense explosion of the orgasms he'd forced on her, this sweet tenderness was in complete opposition to his usual style of lovemaking. But Katie sensed he needed to just hold her now.

She pressed her face against his neck and breathed in his

scent, loving the male smell of him. Like sun, sweat and man. He was all hers and now she was all his. Forever. He reached underneath her, took a handful of her hair and tugged her head sharply until her throat was bared to him. He bit down on the exposed column, marking her. She moaned at the exquisite pain and rocked her hips into his. He began thrusting faster and harder until she felt him flare thicker within her, filling her completely with his cock. Her heart swelled and she clung to him while he filled her with hot jets of semen.

Roman was careful to collapse slightly to the side of Katie so he wouldn't crush her completely. She still struggled a little since he was so much bigger than her and his broad shoulders were pressing against most of her upper body, with his legs and hips pushing against hers. She wasn't going to say a word though. The discomfort was so worth having Roman with her again.

He must have realized anyway, because he shifted onto his side, pulling her over with him. His eyes traced her features as though he couldn't believe he finally had her and she was willing to be his forever. He hooked his fingers around hers and brought her hand up to kiss the back.

"I'm sorry, *mi amor*, for all the years of pain I have caused," he said quietly. "I chased you for selfish reasons without understanding how strong you were."

Tears glittered in her eyes and she shook her head. "No, you watched over me and you chased me because you never stopped loving me. I think I would have found a way to kill myself years ago if you hadn't been around to love me. You saved me, Roman. Never be sorry for that."

His entire body tensed at her words and she wondered if she'd made a mistake in disclosing how close she'd come on multiple occasions to just jumping and ending it all. Roman was the only thing holding her back. Thinking about him had kept her from taking that final leap. Finally, he relaxed and nodded. He saw her strength and knew that she was no longer in danger.

"*Te amo*, Katerina," Roman murmured. He pulled his fingers from hers and brushed the hair off her face. "I couldn't love another person more than you. When it is your time it will be mine also, because I refuse to live on this Earth without you."

She looked steadily back at him, tears escaping from her lashes to drip over her cheeks. She pressed her hand against his heart before moving it to cover the tattoo of her name. She leaned over to press her lips against his, knowing nothing she could say would come close to what her wonderful, possessive husband had just declared. So, she sealed his words with a kiss.

# CHAPTER THIRTY-THREE

Katie crossed her legs impatiently and then uncrossed them again, tapping her shoe against the floor. She glanced down and wondered if she should run up to the master suite and change her shoes. She'd chosen the black and red Louboutins with the metal silver heel that finished in a tiny snake slithering along the side of the shoe. Maybe they were too much? She wore them in honour of Roman's revenge. Today was the day he'd hunted down the last Ramirez.

She'd paired the shoes with a sexy little black dress with spaghetti straps. It landed mid-thigh and, though it hugged her body like a sheath made specially for her, it was also loose enough to be easily removable. Katie was learning quickly that if her clothes weren't accessible, then her barbaric husband would either tear or cut them away depending on his level of patience that day.

Occasionally, his caveman attitude toward her wardrobe was panty-wetting exciting… until he'd destroyed her $900 Oscar de la Renta blouse. Not that Katie was big time into name brands, but now that she was settling down she'd decided to discover what styles she liked best and spend some of the copious amounts of money she'd saved up over the years in the process. It turned out her tastes were expensive.

She was sitting in his office trying to concentrate on the blueprints in front of her. True to his word, Roman was treating her like a partner. He'd given her access to every part of his home and his life. Though she didn't invade his office when he was occupying it, recognizing that they had their separate interests. Plus, she suspected she didn't want to get that close to the ins and outs of cartel just yet. She did enjoy his office space when he wasn't in it. She loved feeling his heavy, masculine presence surrounding her when she couldn't have the real thing. She sat in his big leather chair and imagined it was him holding her close. She looked at the spot on the wall next to his big, black bookshelf and imagined the exact painting she wanted in that spot. Then she forced herself to focus on the blueprints in front of her.

Two hours later, the door to the office opened. Katie slowly opened her eyes. She had given up concentrating well over an hour ago, curled her legs up in the big chair and drifted off the sleep, knowing her husband would come find her as soon as he finished his business. He always came to find her first when they were forced to be apart for any reason.

"Is it done?" she asked as he approached the desk.

He nodded, his dark eyes gleaming, though his expression gave nothing else away. He watched her in the warm glow of his office, taking in every beautiful line of his wife curled up in his chair, behind his desk. Though he refused to acknowledge it, the best thing that had happened to him had been when Katie jumped off the roof, because every day after he'd found her at the resort had been the best day of his life. She opened up to him like a flower, accepting their life together wholeheartedly and without reservation.

That didn't stop him from welding the door to the roof shut. For her own protection. Which in return didn't stop

Katie from sneaking out a window and climbing up anyway to practice her dance and parkour skills when he was out working. Just to stay limber. Hey, what husband didn't know wouldn't hurt him.

"Do you realize what you have done today, my love?" Roman asked, his dark eyes roving over her face.

"I helped you bring down the last Ramirez?" she asked, turning in the seat and placing her feet delicately on the floor. She crossed her long legs.

He nodded and tapped a thick, blunt finger against his lip, his dark eyes roving over her bare legs. "Yes, you did that, but you did so much more. You helped secure the Valdez cartel. *Mi mujer* helped to bring down the last of the enemy cartel and placed herself firmly as an equal at my side in the eyes of my men."

Her gorgeous blue eyes shimmered up at him as he let the words sink in. She smiled, brilliantly, beautifully. "You trust me, Roman?" she asked, her lips quivering.

"*Si, hermosa*," he agreed seriously. Then his eyes crinkled as he thought about it. "Well, I trust you to protect my back and the Valdez cartel anyway. But I definitely don't trust you not to jump off the top of the damn house. Or not to break into a fucking art gallery or something. Come, baby, you must admit, you like the rush, no?"

She grinned at him. "Oh *si*, Roman, I love the rush! Not much you can do about that."

He chuckled darkly. "I think there are some things I can do about that."

She crossed her arms over her breasts and raised an eyebrow. "You think so? You think you can keep me satisfied?"

"*Si, mi esposa*. As a matter of fact, there is something Ramirez told me," Roman began walking around the side of the desk, slowly and deliberately, giving Katie enough time to realize she was in trouble, but not enough to get away from him, "that makes me want to work on your little adrenaline addiction problem. Right. Fucking. Now."

His last few words were said with enough deliberation and just a hint of anger that Katie knew Ramirez had spilled the beans on their meeting. Well crap, she'd really been hoping Roman would cut out the guy's tongue before he could tell on her. Wasn't that how these evil cartel dudes worked? Cut the tongue out then beat the guy to death. Damn it, had she gotten the whole torture thing backwards?

"Umm… about that," Katie stammered then quickly swung the chair around so it was facing away from Roman and bolted.

Roman shoved the chair aside and easily caught her before she even made it two steps. Katie lamented her lack of appropriate footwear. She should've paired the dress with running shoes. Not that she would have made it far, given Roman's longer stride and angry determination to intercept his devious wife, but she could have made it further than the desk. Now he had a surface to work with.

"Can we talk about this?" she asked as his hands tightened around her arms and he hauled her into his rock-hard chest. Her heels brought her to six feet so she was only four inches shorter than him. She tilted her head back and gave him a tremulous smile.

"You took the fucking knife off the man himself, correct? Then you kicked him in the balls, screamed like a banshee, kicked the man while he was down so he could grab you again and drag you to the floor. Nearly got yourself fucking raped and killed in his stinking shack. Tell me if any part of this story is wrong? Woman, you are fucking insane!" Roman growled at her, his voice rising with each sentence.

Katie's eyes widened. Freaking Domingo had *really* talked. Next time she'd cut out the guy's tongue herself before she left Roman a wedding present that could potentially talk. "Uhhh… umm… well, technically…" Katie stalled while he glared down at her, "he was already rolling around on the floor when I took the knife off of him because I'd already kicked him in the balls at that point. Really, the big problem was when I went in for an extra kick. I underestimated how hurt he was. I didn't think he'd be able to grab me and drag me down let alone strangle me a bit… and, oh… you didn't know that part, did you?"

Roman's snarl of fury was answer enough. Domingo had not told him about the partial strangulation. But Katie had. Well, confession complete. Her big, towering, angry husband now knew exactly how close she'd come to death in that disgusting, smelly cabin. Oops. The domestic bliss of the past several days had really helped her forget what a scary bastard Roman Valdez could be. Never underestimate the devil you know.

"Why the fuck didn't you just leave when you couldn't find the dagger?" he asked from between gritted teeth, his hands tightening on her arms to the point of pain. "He could have killed you."

"I'd already come that far. And besides, I needed the dagger so I could show you I was your equal," she whispered, begging him with her eyes to understand.

"You were always my equal, Katie. Fuck, woman, you were better than me in every way. Why do you think I followed you around like a dog on a leash?" he groaned. "I locked you up because you are breakable. Couldn't take the thought of anything happening to you."

A smile tilted the edge of her lip. "Unless you're the one doing something to me."

He spun her around so she was facing the desk. His hands went to the top of her dress. He didn't give her a chance to protest before her dress was in shreds on the floor. He rocked his hips into her ass while jerking her shoulders into his chest.

He breathed in her ear, "Fuck woman, you deserve everything I give you."

She reached over her head to pull him into her, loving the way he knew exactly how to sink his teeth into her flesh until she was shivering in his hands and creaming her panties. "I want it all, Roman."

He took her by the neck and shoved her over the desk, pushing papers, pens and her laptop to the side. She moaned when he brushed his broad thumb across her delicate pulse point before moving to spread his hand across her upper back. She had deliberately worn a tiny white lace thong, knowing he would likely tear it from her body when he came home. She wasn't wrong. The panties came away with a stinging snap, leaving Katie gasping and her pussy flooding in anticipation. She knew Roman would be amped up, savage and in need of blowing off some steam after his morning… activities. Even if Domingo hadn't told him the particulars of Katie's little escapade.

Roman kicked her legs further apart until she was completely exposed to him. She tried to relax so it would hurt less, but she knew what was coming and it was impossible not to tense in both anticipation and fear. Though Roman was undoubtedly turned on, he was also angry that she'd taken her prank with Domingo a few dozen steps too far. She could have easily proven her point with Roman and not put her life at risk.

His hand fell full force on her ass, rocking her body into the hardness of the desk. *Motherfucker that hurt!* Yes, he was definitely pissed about the Domingo thing and not holding back. This was no erotic spanking meant to amp up her desire. Husband dearest was proving a point for the next time Katie intended to put herself at risk to prove her own point. He might not lock her up again, but he was definitely willing to find other ways to punish his headstrong, manipulative wife.

Katie held her cries in for as long as she could while he spanked her ass, alternating cheeks until she was sure her posterior was going to catch fire. Finally, she gave him what he wanted and let the screams loose. She begged him to stop and tried to reach behind her and slap at his arm. He took her wrist and held it against her lower back while he continued to work her ass over. His final strike landed right between her legs. Her cheeks flared red at the wet sound his hand made. To make matters worse, he brought his fingers, wet with her juices, up to her face.

"Suck," he ordered, his voice hoarse with restrained excitement.

Katie opened her mouth and licked his fingers. They were hot from slapping so violently against her ass and they tasted both sweet and tart, like her. She moaned and sucked them deep into her mouth, giving him just the edge of her teeth to show him a little violence of her own. She opened her eyes to meet his and seeing the barely leashed heat, smiled wickedly up at him.

"You like to suck, baby," he growled.

"Mmhmm…" she moaned around his fingers.

He pulled his fingers out of her mouth, ignoring her grumble of disappointment. Dragging her off the desk, he gripped her arm and pushed down until she was kneeling on the floor. She stared up at him, loving his sexy black jeans. They looked so damn good on his long, muscular legs. She reached up his thighs and rubbed like a cat while he unbuckled his thick leather belt and unzipped the pants. He pulled his vest off and then yanked his black T-shirt off impatiently.

"You okay for this, *hermosa*?" he asked, pulling his engorged, veined cock from the denim.

Katie nodded eagerly and reached for him, her smaller hand covering his. Her lashes fluttered shut as she licked him, realizing that this was the first time she'd had the pleasure of taking Roman into her mouth. He was a generous, but impatient man. He always wanted his tongue somewhere on or in her. He rarely had the patience to allow Katie free reign with his body. As she flicked her tongue against the broad purple tip of his penis, taking his precum into her mouth and savouring his flavour, she determined there would be a whole lot more tasting of Roman in her future. Damn, he tasted good!

He let her set the pace while she explored him with unhurried movements. She could tell from the constant tensing and releasing of his muscles that he was having difficulty controlling himself. The small… okay, large… sadistic streak in her was enjoying the fair turnabout on her playtime. She continued to suck and lick at her leisure, exploring every inch of him until she was ready to move down and explore the heavy sac underneath with her lips and tongue.

His hands landed on her head and pulled her off with a forcible tug. Katie would have gone sprawling if he hadn't had a good grip on her hair. She gasped when he hauled her to her feet with a growl. She cried out in pain when her ass met the hard wood of the desk as he picked her up and dropped her on the hard surface. He pulled her legs up over his arms and, without giving her time to adjust, slammed into her in one thrust. Katie arched back on the desk and reached over her head to grip something, anything to relieve the pressure of his brutal entry. Now she knew what happened when she teased the beast with her tongue, and it was exquisite!

Roman gripped her by the waist and slammed into her over and over, grunting with each thrust. He drove them both higher and higher with each savage thrust of his hips into Katie's tight body. She thought she would die from the pleasure and pain as it merged and stole her breath. She could hear the whimpers escaping from her throat and wanted to snatch them back so she could make a sound that was sexier, but it was the best she could manage. Roman was wild and untamed. He demanded the same from her.

"Going to come!" she managed to yell as he continued to jerk her body into his.

He grunted something at her, but she didn't know what. She heard something crash to the floor and shatter, she spared a brief second to hope it wasn't her laptop before she was soaring over the edge of a towering orgasm. She felt the silken glide of fluid as it slid from her body and stroked Roman's cock while he continued to slam into her, harder and faster than before. He flared wider, his grip on her waist clenching until she knew there would be bruises. Untamed. He came with a roar, filling her with hot semen.

She was a little disappointed she hadn't gotten to taste it. Maybe next time she would convince him to come in her mouth instead. She could imagine how that conversation would end. It would probably take a few conversations before she would convince him. Roman stood, looked down at her for a moment, his expression unreadable and then staggered backward to collapse in the leather chair. Katie pushed herself up on the desk and watched unabashedly as her gorgeous husband tucked himself back into his jeans and zipped up. When he finished, he beckoned her over.

She eagerly climbed off the desk and into his arms, cuddling close against his warm chest. She lazily traced the tattoo of her name with a fingertip, enjoying the way he watched her from beneath hooded eyes. His expression rarely gave anything away, but Katie always knew what he was thinking.

She stretched one long leg out and asked innocently, "You like my shoes? I wasn't sure if I was going to wear them today, but they seemed fitting since you were going to catch a snake."

He chuckled and tucked her leg back so it was curled in his lap again. "I like them. They suit you. Definitely like fucking you in them."

She giggled. "I noticed that."

He trailed a hand over his hip, drifting it over her reddened ass cheek. He frowned when she flinched. "You'll be okay?" She wasn't sure if he was asking her or telling her.

She shrugged and said mischievously, "Until the next time I do something to piss you off."

He stiffened and reaching for her chin, tilted her face up to his. Growling, he demanded, "You plan on doing something stupid, *esposa*?"

"Well…" Katie said, biting her lip and lowering her eyes so he couldn't see them. And then, in honour of their partnership, she sighed and decided to give him the truth. She rolled her eyes toward the far corner of his office. "You see that empty section of wall over there by that bookshelf. I think I can get my hands on a Carlo Cignani's Madonna and Child. Your fault, really, for lying about having a seventeenth century Virgin Mary. Now I'm obsessed with getting my hands on one and I know exactly who doesn't deserve to keep his locked up in a lonely vault in New Zealand… and why are you looking at me like that?"

**THE END**

# A NOTE FROM NIKITA

*Dear readers,*

*Thank you for reading Thieving Hearts! I hope you enjoyed reading Katie and Roman's eighteen-year journey into love as much as I enjoyed writing it. Anyone that has read any of my books knows by now that I enjoy exploring dark erotic romance themes, which are pure fun and fantasy.*

*In this particular book, I touched on a few more serious themes such as depression, poor self-esteem and image, and self-harm. These are subjects I have come across in my work and among people I care deeply about. I believe that the subject of mental health is something that needs more mainstream attention and discussion. In Thieving Hearts, I have attempted to handle these subjects with the care and respect that they deserve.*

*Thank you again for reading,*
*Nikita*

# NIKITA'S NEWSLETTER!

Sign up today for Nikita's newsletter and receive a FREE copy of Nikita's bestselling dark romance novella, Stalked! CLICK HERE to sign up today!

"Lovely."

The deep voice echoed through the darkness, penetrating the warmth of her dungeon. She turned, heart beating erratically, knowing it was finally time for her to meet her captor face-to-face.

It had been two days since she'd been taken. She had no idea where she'd been brought. The men had stormed into her tiny, underground place in Portugal and put a bag over her head. They'd hustled her into a car, sped her through the rainy streets and then onto a private aircraft. When she tried to fight and wrestle the bag off her head, a man had wrenched her arms back and ruthlessly zip-tied them. When she'd screamed curses and begged her captors to let her go, the same man had pressed a gun against the side of her head and told her to stop speaking or die. She had chosen silence.

Though she had no idea where she was, she knew who had taken her and why. Katie Pullman's last call had held a chilling warning. Her voice had screamed out for Source to run. There was only one man connected to Katie with the resources to hunt someone as invisible as XSource. Source had done her best to heed the blond cat burglar's warning, erasing sensitive files and throwing necessities into a bag at hyper speed.

She hadn't thought there was any chance Ivan's people could be so close. He must have a truly stunning amount of resources all over the world to be able to grab her in such a small and insignificant place. There was a reason she'd chosen the small seaside town in Portugal to hang out. It wasn't for the seafood. The place was gloomy as fuck.

She thought when she arrived at wherever she was that Ivan would confront her and demand she work for him again. At least that's what she hoped the plan was. Knowing what a cold-blooded bastard Ivan Vogel was, he might have just brought her here to torture and kill her for turning down his incredibly kind offer of employment. Instead, she'd been left alone for two days, imprisoned in some kind of old-fashioned dungeon with stone walls and barred windows while she awaited his arrival. Granted, it was a comfortable dungeon, warm with a large comfortable bed, reading materials and plenty of food. But still…

Now it would seem her captor had arrived. And he was in the mood to inspect his newest acquisition.

"You are a pleasant surprise," he drawled in flawless English, stepping through the shadows toward her. "I was led to believe you were a man."

He stopped so close to her she could feel the heat from his body. She had stood up to greet him, not wanting such a predatory man to have any kind of physical advantage. Not that it mattered. He was still almost a foot taller than her. She shuddered as his dark eyes roved hungrily over her, taking in every part of her, despite the shadows. Instinct screamed at her to back away, but pride held her still.

"Of course, had you been a man, you would be dead," he said easily, as if he'd been informing her of the time.

She bit her lip to stifle the whimper that threatened to break free. "And why is that?" she asked, attempting to infuse strength into her husky voice. She didn't speak often, preferring her own company.

His lip lifted in a cold smirk. He was in his early forties with a face that looked like it was sculpted from granite, hard and masculine, with barely any inflection except what he allowed. His body was built out of the same rock as his face, all sharp planes and hard muscles with long, masculine limbs. She'd thought he was a handsome man when she'd seen him at the Athens ball. And now? Now that he held her fragile life in his ruthless hands, she didn't think so.

"You refused to work for me," he said simply, his eyes never leaving her face.

"And no one has ever refused you before?" she asked sharply. "I somehow doubt that."

His brow lifted in surprise, as though reminding her of her precarious position. A small shudder rippled down her back. She needed to remember who she was dealing with and somehow rein in her impulsive tongue. There was a reason she was a hacker. She preferred not to develop the social skills necessary in dealing with the masses. She didn't like interacting with people or giving them the required responses to their inane conversation.

"No one refuses me for long, little Miss Source," he drawled her nickname out as though teasing her with it.

"And you withheld services from me repeatedly. Refusing my advances, despite my ever more lucrative offers."

He stepped closer to her as he spoke, purposefully using provocative language. He lifted a finger and ran it over her cheek, testing the softness of her skin. Her eyes flared wide and the breath strangled in her throat. She stumbled back a step, but her legs hit the edge of the bed. He stepped closer, trapping her against the high bed she'd been sleeping on for the last two days.

"P-please," she whispered, terrified of the giant man. She'd heard so many horrific stories of the international arms dealer over the years. He worked in and out of the shadows. The one story she should have listened to when he first started pursuing her a year ago was that Ivan always got what he wanted. "I'm sorry."

He looked down at her, lifting his hand again and touching it to her cheek before drifting it down her throat and then her arm. He lifted her hand and brought it to his face, caressing the back with his lips. Her skin was only a few shades darker than his. Her hand looked so small and delicate in his much larger hand. His tongue darted out to touch the back of her fingers.

"You are sorry you didn't come to work for me?" he asked against her hand, pressing the soft skin against his hard jaw and then rubbing his rough cheek against her. "A little late for apologies, don't you think?" His sardonic gaze flickered around her prison before settling back on her face.

She could barely breathe, let alone keep her thoughts straight when he touched her like that, yet she knew she had to force her brain to bwork. This man was brutal, intelligent and deadly. She was way out of her depth and completely alone in the world. There was no one that would miss her if she disappeared forever. Except, perhaps, for her friend that was now in the clutches of the Mexican cartel. She needed to use her head and get out of this with her principles intact.

She raised her chin and said in as clear a voice as she could manage, "No. I don't work for organizations, only for myself. What I'm sorry about is that you're the kind of guy that won't take no for an answer."

His fingers tightened painfully around hers. She tried to jerk her hand away, but he refused to let her go. His eyes blazed down into hers for a moment and she feared he would just give into the fury and get rid of her. She knew Ivan wasn't used to denial of any kind. He could buy, bully and steal anything he wanted. He was one of the most powerful men in the world.

Well, he couldn't have her.

He reached for her so quickly, she thought a blow was coming and cried out. Instead, he sank his hand into her sable hair and jerked her head back until her face tipped up toward his. She gritted her teeth against the pain. His eyes flashed in cruel approval. Her chest lifted and dropped as she breathed rapidly, standing stiffly against her kidnapper.

"What is your name?" he demanded, his cold, dark eyes searching her face as though he could pull the answer from her.

She wouldn't to give him anything. She would lie to him, give him one of her aliases. She hadn't said her real name in years, preferring to bury herself under layers of false identities. When the last of her family had died, so had her real identity along with any sense of belonging. She opened her mouth to give him one of her most used names, Pari, but she must have hesitated too long. Or maybe he saw the flash of dishonesty in her eyes.

Suddenly, he seized her by the throat, lifted her off the floor and slammed her down on the bed. The fluffy quilts softened the blow to her back, but he came down heavy on top of her, straddling her flailing limbs. She would have screamed, except he was choking the breath right from her body. His actions were so swift and precise she didn't stand a chance. He had her arms and legs completely pinned and her throat in a tight grip that she knew would leave bruises later.

Tears rushed to her eyes as she stared up at her cruel captor. He didn't even look angry that she had been about to lie to him, just slightly irritated, as though he expected it and was put out at having to mete out discipline.

"You don't want to lie to me," he said, his deep voice glacial.

A tear escaped from her eye and ran into her hairline. She nodded. She could feel his erection pressing into her belly where he was straddling her. He wasn't completely unaffected by their little struggle, but he didn't seem to notice or care. Neither his actions nor his expression indicated he was about to ravish her. Or maybe that was wishful thinking?

He eased his grip on her throat and gave her an expectant look.

She licked her lips and whispered the name she hadn't spoken in six years, "Jaya."

Genuine satisfaction suffused his features, giving his angular looks a softer cast. "Victory," he said.

He didn't mean that he was victorious over her. Her name meant victory in Hindi. And somehow, he knew that. Though she hated him with every fibre of her being, a small part of her couldn't help but be impressed.

"Yes," she whispered.

His eyes cut to hers. "You think you will be victorious, little hacker?"

She glared up at him, hating the way he played with her. She was ill-equipped to deal with a man like him. He was sophisticated, a world traveller. An international criminal and an arms dealer. She might be international in her own way, but she lived in basements and cellars in tiny towns, in places no one ever heard of so she could stay off the radar, hiding from people like this psychotic villain.

"You tell me," she snapped, arching her back in an

attempt to dislodge him. He was so much bigger, all she managed to do was buck her body up into his and show him the curve of her full breasts against her T-shirt. "You're keeping me in this dungeon for no good reason. Either let me the fuck go or let's get on with whatever this is! Because I'm telling you right now, I won't be working for a criminal like you."

He raised an eyebrow and chuckled at her audacity. She got the feeling it was a gamble with him. Either he would laugh at a person's hastily spoken words or he would take offence and murder them swiftly and without remorse. He rolled swiftly off the bed, leaving her where she lay. He watched her as he adjusted his clothing, the amusement fading from his face.

A muscle twitched in his jaw as his eyes darkened with something she couldn't define. "And I'm telling you, little Jaya. I will be keeping you… until I get what I want."

As his eyes roved over her prone body, she suddenly didn't think Ivan wanted her hacking services at all anymore. She rolled onto her side and pulled a pillow against her stomach, giving him her back. He clearly didn't intend to let her go and she didn't have anything else to discuss with him.

She waited until he walked away and closed the door to her dungeon before she allowed the tears to fall.

---

*Now available for purchase!*

"Fuck," Riley grumbled, twisting to make sure she was correct. Nope, she didn't have the right tool.

It was late at night and all the guys had gone home so she couldn't call out to one of the other mechanics and ask them to hand it to her. Damn. With an aggrieved sigh, she pushed herself out from under the car. Shoving her long ponytail out of the way, she crawled toward the toolbox and rifled through until she found what she was looking for. Loud, thumping music filled the garage from where her iPhone was plugged into its port on top of one of the tool benches.

Turning back toward the '69 Camaro, Riley adjusted her lamp and prepared to slide back under. This baby was a thing of beauty. It called to her from the moment it entered her shop, which is why she was still working on it at 2:00am. If she did it up right she'd be able to turn a pretty profit on this little sweetheart and take Cilia on vacation. They desperately needed some bonding time.

The music switched off and a deep voice reverberated through the darkness of the garage. "I'm looking for Mr. Bancroft."

Riley froze for a few precious seconds before her head snapped up, judging the distance between a shadowed man and the gun in her toolbox. He stepped forward into the circle of her light, closing the distance between them. Riley's heart slammed against her ribs as his face became visible and she recognized the most ruthless man in the city. Soloman Hart, mafia kingpin, was standing in her garage, staring down at her with cold intent. He now stood directly between her and her gun. Not that she thought it would do any good against a man like him.

Riley felt incredibly small and grimy next to his large, well-dressed frame. She sat crouched on the concrete beneath him, wearing her usual tank top and grimy, oil-stained over-alls with the top left to hang down. Her shiny, dark brown hair was pulled back in a messy ponytail and she wore no make-up.

He seemed to be looking her over, taking in every inch of her with interest. Her eyes narrowed in return. She was used to guys staring. She was a thirty-year-old female mechanic, working in a garage full of men. She looked younger than she was and knew she was attractive. Definitely fantasy material for some guys. Which is why she tended to work in the office and on cars in the back, well away from the clients. Very few people knew who actually owned the garage.

"How did you get in here?" she demanded, pushing herself up and standing to her full height, which was still several inches shorter than him. She crossed her arms in front of her chest and glared at him. She had a damn good security system or she wouldn't have been alone in the shop blaring music in the middle of the night.

He ignored her question and raised a dark, thick brow. "Mr. Bancroft?" The single question sent a chill down her spine, letting her know that the next words out of her mouth better be an answer, because Soloman Hart was not a man known for patience.

Riley pressed her lips together for a moment and wondered how best to answer him. The truth of 'Mr. Bancroft' was complicated. And Riley was starting to suspect she may be in some danger. The likelihood of a man of this caliber showing up in her garage for any reason was slim. Which meant something not good was going down. Soloman had men to deal with his car issues, he didn't deal with things like this himself.

She moistened her lips and then stopped when his sharp eyes followed the movement. Taking a breath, she said, "Mr. Bancroft is dead. He died two years ago."

His brows drew together in a frown that made Riley shiver from head to toe. Yeah, he didn't want to play games with her. His next words confirmed this thought.

"Don't fuck with me, little girl," he growled. "Everyone knows Alan Bancroft is dead. I'm looking for the owner of this garage. Alan's son, Riley Bancroft."

"Okay," she whispered. "Why are you looking for Riley?"

Holy shit, she was going to die! The look on his face suggested that the last person that questioned him instead of instantly giving him the answers he was searching for had died a really extra terrible death.

Surprisingly, he answered, his deep voice clipped as he spoke. "Someone stole one of my vehicles yesterday. It was my favourite and I want it back. Thought it might show up here."

Shock flickered across her face. Who would be stupid enough to steal one of Soloman Hart's cars? Well, that explained why he would show up on her doorstep himself at 2:00am looking for answers. She ran the biggest chop shop in the city. Only very few people knew she ran the garage. She had a very good team of mechanics, mostly inherited from her father, that helped keep her safe behind the scenes. Few people even knew the name Riley Bancroft. Except, somehow Soloman did.

"Wh-what kind of car?" She asked hesitantly, hoping like hell it hadn't gone through her shop. She usually did her homework and found out where the vehicles came from so this kind of shitstorm didn't come down on her head, but that didn't mean things didn't get under her radar once in a while.

"Koenigsegg Regera." His voice held no inflection as he named one of the most expensive vehicles in the world. A car that would be one of a kind in the United States.

Riley took a few seconds out from her terror to be impressed. Damn. Soloman must like him some nice luxury racing automobiles. Too bad the man was such a cold-hearted, ruthless bastard. Under different circumstances she wouldn't mind getting under the hoods of his fleet, see what he had going on up in there.

She breathed a sigh of relief. "Nope, I definitely would've noticed one of those. Never even seen one in person, let alone had one in here."

He nodded, still studying her carefully as though taking in every minuscule expression that crossed her face. Finally, he said, "I'd still like to have a conversation with Mr. Bancroft."

Fuck. That was going to be a problem since there was no Mr. Bancroft. Instead, she nodded her head.

"Sure, no problem. I'll have him call you tomorrow." She'd get one of the other mechanics to call and reassure him that his car was never there and if it showed up he would be the first person they called.

He reached out and took her hand before she realized what he was about to do. He held her fingers in a grip that told her she shouldn't pull away from him. He had tattoos over his hand and knuckles. He looked down at the black, chipped nail polish and rubbed his broad thumb over the tops of her much smaller nails. She shivered at his touch. Based on his reputation and the few glimpses she'd had of him she'd always considered Soloman Hart cold, but his hand was surprisingly warm.

"What's your name?" he demanded, his voice deep and compelling.

Riley tried to pull her hand away, but he continued to hold her. She turned her body away and said in a haughty voice, "None of your business."

He stiffened next to her and she bit her lip, worried that she was about to find out what made this powerful man so feared among their underworld set. He chuckled lightly, running his thumb over her knuckles. "I think you'll find I can make it my business."

She shivered and dropped her eyes, still refusing to answer. She did not want this man finding out who she was. For more reasons that the obvious. When he was alive, Alan Bancroft had taught Riley everything he knew, but he'd kept her existence on the down low in case they ever needed to pack up shop and run. There was also the complication of her mother. Cilia Bancroft, shady accountant to the super rich, was a handful and best kept out of the notice of men like Soloman Hart.

"You can fly, little bird," he said quietly. He looked down at her, capturing her brown eyes with his bottomless dark eyes. "I will let you go for now."

"F-for now?" Riley asked hesitantly.

He released her hand and stepped closer, towering over her, his chest nearly brushing hers. Riley gasped at his unexpected movement and tried to move back. Her leg bumped against the car she'd been working on and she was forced to stand still next to him. Her head swam as his subtle, masculine scent enveloped her. It made alarm bells go off in her head. He didn't immediately move away from her.

"For now," he confirmed. "I think the day will come that we will see... a lot more of each other."

Her mouth opened and she stared at him. Was that a threat? He was looking down at her with something she couldn't entirely define. Speculation? Possessiveness? But how was that possible? He didn't even know her. Though she'd seen him before, they were just meeting officially for the first time.

His eyes brushed over her one last time and she had a keen awareness that she was being granted some kind of reprieve. But it came with a time limit. One that would eventually run out. Her heart slammed against her ribs.

"Do you know who I am?" he asked.

She blinked and then nodded slowly.

"Say my name," he demanded.

Riley gaped up at him for a moment and then, desperately wanting the dark man to leave, she gave him what he wanted. She licked her lips and whispered, "Soloman."

He turned and strode away from her, resetting the alarm before leaving the garage.

---

Soloman slid into the passenger side of his second favourite vehicle. Turning to his friend and bodyguard, he said, "Did you catch that?"

Roman nodded. He had been standing in the shadows

near the door where he'd disabled the alarm and unbolted the lock to allow his boss entry to the garage. Though Soloman didn't need back up, the two rarely worked separately, especially since Soloman's climb to the top had earned many enemies. Both knew it was better to have a loyal man guarding each other's backs than to go it alone.

"I want her," Soloman said quietly, not taking his eyes off the passing street lights.

Roman grunted, but didn't say anything. He already knew. The boss rarely pursued women, beyond having them brought in for a quick fuck. That he even asked for this one's name was surprising. "I'll find out who she is."

Soloman nodded. "I want to know everything. There's something about her… I think I might keep her for a while."

Roman grunted. He'd get their information guy out of bed and working on the problem of the chick immediately. Find out who she was so the boss could get laid. Soloman Hart wasn't used to being denied. No one needed to be around the man when he wasn't happy. Much better to just bring him the woman's information and then the woman herself all wrapped up and tied in a bow. Fewer people would die that way.

"And find out where the fuck Riley Bancroft is," he snapped, drumming his fingers restlessly on his leg. "I want my goddamned car back."

---

*Now available for purchase!*

Ignacio Hernandez had never before brought a woman to a meet. Then, they'd never met at a club before. The entire scene was unprecedented. Reyes didn't do unprecedented, but he was willing to make an exception because he was curious. He could sever the Miami connection if he had to. It would cause some shockwaves, but it wasn't out of the question. Ignacio was beginning to annoy him anyway. His poor decisions were beginning to affect the Bolivian. Such as bringing a woman like *her* to a meet with a man like *him*.

Something that was meant to show off Ignacio's power and wealth would become a big mistake.

His gaze flickered over the woman, calmly drinking her champagne and orange juice as though she weren't sitting at a table with four of the most dangerous men on the continental East coast. Two kingpins and their right hands. Only Reyes didn't think she was as calm as she appeared. Her wrist trembled slightly, giving her away. She had enough presence to make sure that tiny shake ceased by the time it got to her slim fingers where they clenched the crystal of her glass. It wasn't the fingers or her ability to remain coolly poised while the men around her talked business that captured his curiosity. It was the mark on the back of her delicate hand, permanent slash lines, viciously marring her porcelain skin.

Anger burned deep in his gut, surprising him. Reyes rarely felt anything. Ever. Certainly not for a woman. This was how he made effective decisions. How he moved trade across borders with ease and cool logic. Emotion had been removed from him. First by a ruthless father, then by a vicious military stint in his home country and finally by an unrelenting, merciless prison sentence that had systematically broken him before he had, in turn, broken down the prison itself and owned it from the inside out. By the time he was released it was into a world of his own making; a world shaped by him on the inside and ruled by him on the outside.

Yet the sight of this cool, blond beauty, so broken yet utterly resilient was doing something to him, forcing him to *feel*. He shifted in his seat, sliding his arm across the back of the leather, his eyes never leaving her while he listened to the other men speak. Negotiate terms. He didn't need to add his voice. Alejandro, his right hand, knew the terms. Knew not to fuck up while in pursuit of new deals for the boss.

Reyes wanted her. The electrifying anger he felt when his eyes caressed that mark assured him he would take the woman and make her his. Not because it infuriated him that she had been abused. No, he was not a good enough man to care about that. He was under no illusions he would treat her any better than Ignacio. Hell, he'd probably treat her much worse. Because Ignacio undoubtedly set her up like a trophy in his great mausoleum of a house and then ignored the unapproachable beauty.

Reyes had no intention of ignoring her. He was going to take her and fuck every inch of her, just the way he wanted. Hard, brutal, mean. Exactly how he was. Exactly how this world had shaped him. Because he could. She was about to become spoils of war.

No, he wasn't angry about the mark on her hand at all. He was pissed that the mark was twisted into the shape of an "H" and not an "R." He wanted her to belong to him, to the King. When he got his hands on the woman, that would be the first thing he changed.

Finally, after nearly an hour of sitting in the booth together, his eyes rarely leaving her face, she lifted hers to meet his uncompromising gaze. And for the first time in his life, he felt his heart stop in his chest. He was unprepared for the impact. Her eyes – one startling green and the other amber brown – were vivid, stunning and unrelenting. Though her expression didn't flicker once from the blank mask of icy beauty, he saw the burning disdain, the heated fury buried deep within those fiery orbs for the men that surrounded her. She despised all of them.

His lip lifted in an answering sneer. She refused to drop her eyes from his challenge, despite her husband sitting at the same table. He wanted nothing more, in that moment, than to take this scarred Queen from her throne and tame her. He vowed, then and there, that he would eventually have her.

---

**Now available for purchase!**

# ALSO BY NIKITA SLATER

If you enjoyed this book, check out some other works by #1 International Bestselling Author, Nikita Slater. More titles are always in progress, so check back often to see what's new!

## SINNER'S EMPIRE

Book 1 - Sin of Silence - Preorder

Book 2 - A Silent Reckoning - Coming Soon!

Book 3 - Goodnight, Sinners - Coming Soon!

## THE QUEENS SERIES

Book One – Scarred Queen

Book Two - Queen's Move

Book Three - Born a Queen

Book Four - The Red Queen (Coming 2021)

Alejandro's Prey (a novella)

The Queens 4 Book Box Set

## FIRE & VICE SERIES

Book One – Prisoner of Fortune

Book Two – Fight or Flight

Book Three – King's Command

Book Four – Savage Vendetta

Savage Boss (a novella)

Book Five – Fear in Her Eyes

Book Six – Bound by Blood

Book Seven – In His Sights

Book Eight - Burning Beauty

Book Nine - Chasing Ecstasy (Coming soon!)

Fire & Vice 6 Book Box Set


## THE DRIVEN HEARTS SERIES

Book One - Driven by Desire

Book Two - Thieving Hearts

Book Three - Capturing Victory

Novella - The Princess and Her Mercenary

Driven Hearts 4 Book Box Set


## THE SANCTUARY SERIES

Book One - Sanctuary's Warlord

Book Two - Sanctuary on Fire

Book Three - The Last Sanctuary

Book Four - The Road to Wolfe

Book Five - Skye's Sanctuary (Coming soon!)

The Sanctuary Series 3 Book Box Set


## LOVING THE BAD BOY SERIES

Loving Vincent

Loving Jared

Loving Rico (Coming Soon!)

## STANDALONE BOOKS

The Assassin's Wife

Because You're Mine

Mine to Keep (a novella)

Luna & Andres

Kiss of the Cartel

Stalked

## AFTER DARK

*In collaboration with Jasmin Quinn*

Collared: A Dark Captive Romance

Safeword: A Dark Romance

Chained: A Mafia Marriage Romance

Good Girl: A Captive BDSM Romance

Hostile Takeover: An Enemies to Lovers Romance

The After Dark Box Set

Visit *nikitaslater.com* for more information
and the latest updates!

# STAY CONNECTED WITH NIKITA!

Don't miss one dark and sexy moment. Keep in touch with Nikita for her latest news and updates about all of your favourite characters!

- Get more info and updates on Nikita's **Website**
- Like and follow me on **Facebook**
- Follow me on **Twitter (@NikSlaterWrites)**
- Check out my **Instagram**
- Connect with me on **Goodreads**

**Sign up** for the newsletter today at receive exclusive updates and access to *bonus content and chapters* not available anywhere else!

https://www.authornikitaslater.com/

Nikita Slater is the International Bestselling dark romance author of the Fire & Vice series, Angels & Assassins series, The Queens series and several standalone novels. Her favourite genre is mafia romance, the bloodier the better, though she loves to write about every subject under the sun. She lives on the beautiful Canadian prairies with her son and crazy awesome dog. She has an unholy affinity for books (especially erotic romance), wine, pets and anything chocolate. Despite some of the darker themes in her books (which are pure fun and fantasy), Nikita is a staunch feminist and advocate of equal rights for all races, genders and non-gender specific persons. When she isn't writing, dreaming about writing or talking about writing, she helps others discover a love of reading and writing through literacy and social work.

9 781990 355035